KU-523-598

The Dressmaker

The Dressmaker

Elizabeth Birkelund Oberbeck

W F HOWES LTD

BOURNEMOUTH
2006
LIBRARIES

This large print edition published in 2006 by
W F Howes Ltd
Unit 4, Rearsby Business Park, Gaddesby Lane,
Rearsby, Leicester LE7 4YH

1 3 5 7 9 10 8 6 4 2

First published in the United Kingdom in 2006
by Hutchinson

Copyright © Elizabeth Birkelund Oberbeck, 2006

The right of Elizabeth Birkelund Oberbeck
to be identified as the author of this work has been
asserted by her in accordance with the
Copyright, Designs and
Patents Act, 1988.

All rights reserved

A CIP catalogue record for this book is available
from the British Library

ISBN 1 84632 847 0

Typeset by Palimpsest Book Production Limited,
Grangemouth, Stirlingshire
Printed and bound in Great Britain
by Antony Rowe Ltd, Chippenham, Wilts.

For my mother and father

A Note to the Reader

For storytelling purposes, the dates of some of the couture collections have been changed. The Paris shows for spring are typically held in the beginning of October; New York collections usually take place in September.

PART I

CHAPTER 1

Blossoms fluttered everywhere that morning outside the dressmaker's studio. They cascaded from above, settling at the base of the century-old apple tree like a pool of white satin at the hem of a wedding gown. Wedding gowns. Claude Reynaud had designed and sewn hundreds of them, but still, he thought, as he stitched on a lacy trim, they made him uneasy: the symbolism of the white dress, the secrecy of the veil, the surprise of the bride's sudden appearance before the slow, irrevocable procession down the aisle . . .

A fresh breeze from the wide-open window interrupted his thoughts. Drawing in the scent of apple blossoms, Claude studied the gnarly trunked tree that his great-grandfather had planted a century ago. The sap ran through this tree's branches as surely as blood pulsed through his own body and those of the generations of gentle Reynauds before him, traditional dressmakers all.

But times were changing, as was Claude's clientele. Thanks to a favorable article in a widely read French national newspaper and several devoted clients, Monsieur Reynaud's talent had begun to attract sophisticated Parisiennes willing to drive forty minutes out of Paris to be 'fitted.' They broke the speed limit as they entered the humble town of Senlis, situated twenty-nine miles north of Paris as the crow flies, on the rue Vieille de Paris, an ancient thoroughfare for textile merchants traveling from Paris to Flanders.

Claude Reynaud and his assistant, Antoine Boudin, often called Vite Boudin – fast Boudin – by Parisians who preferred speed over all else, produced a dress, suit, or gown every three to four days. Now that it was early spring, wedding-dress season was in full swing.

As he sipped his *café crème* and broke the brioche that his sister had dropped off that morning on her way to work, Claude reviewed his appointments for the day.

'Pédant,' he said, peering into the blinking green eyes of his tall, full-feathered blue-and-golden-fronted parrot, 'we have a new client today. A Mademoiselle de Verlay. Referred by Madame de Champy. A July wedding.'

He reread the note scrawled next to Mademoiselle de Verlay's name. The bride-to-be had given her dressmaker total freedom over the gown's design. Claude had never been awarded such trust for a bridal dress. Most affianced young women arrived at his studio clutching wrinkled magazine photographs of brides, convinced their childhood dreams of a fairy-tale wedding would be fulfilled to the last detail.

A bird, he could not tell what kind, suddenly crashed into the closed upper portion of the window. When Claude looked up, he noticed that the wind had died down momentarily and the apple tree's white gown of blossoms was complete.

Eleven A.M: a barely audible knock at the door. Despite the gentleness of the intrusion, Claude jumped. A woman entered, the wind urging her in from behind.

'Bonjour?' the voice called, out of the dark vestibule into the sunlit room.

Claude extended his hand. Long tapered fingers outstretched, a small face emerging out of a dark scarf, large smiling eyes, a pointed chin – these were Claude's first impressions of his new client.

'Bonjour. I'm Valentine de Verlay. Pleased to meet you.' The words caught her breath in them; hers was a lovely, rich, windy voice.

Claude took her lightweight camel coat to the closet, noting as he did the dark brown sheath of hair resting just below her shoulders, the almond-shaped eyes, the smile on the corners of her lips. She strode into his studio with composed confidence, her head high. He scrutinized her attire: navy wool pants, wide-ribbed cappuccino cotton cardigan with sleeves that skimmed the knuckles of her hands, and another dark beige sweater, this one cashmere, tied around her neck. Simply elegant.

'Thank you for agreeing to design my wedding dress,' she said. She looked directly at him; then, as if the gaze were too intense, she lowered her eyes, her face suddenly veiled under a blanket of shyness. 'Charlotte says you are very busy, but she insisted I ask for you.'

'*Bonjour! Bonjour!*' Pédant's words caught her attention.

'How delightful,' she said, now at the parrot's side and smiling. 'I love birds, but I'm not familiar with ones that speak. *Bonjour* to you!' She gently touched a blue feathered wing.

The front door slammed loudly and Antoine barged into the room. 'Whom do we have here this morning? Antoine Boudin at your service,' he said, taking the mademoiselle's hand in his own and bending in half to kiss it. 'Shall I start pinning up?'

Claude had not prepared himself for Antoine. He wanted to experience his new client without interruption, to grasp her coloring, skin texture, shape, and personality.

Antoine Boudin had worked for him for two years, but Claude still felt the occasional urge to defend himself against the onslaught of Antoine's full-throttled chest, wide domed forehead, and penetrating brown eyes. In his assistant's presence, Claude felt small, like a shell-less escargot ready for eating. Claude imagined Antoine relishing the briny taste as he whipped the morsel around in his mouth.

As Antoine entreated the new client to accept a

glass of water after the 'arduous journey from Paris,' Claude's eye lingered on the tilt in the long arc of her neck, her half smile.

'My notes indicate that you have no ideas, no preferences for this dress, mademoiselle. Is that correct?' asked Claude. Pédant made scratching sounds. Claude wished he had placed the distracting bird in the other room.

'*Mon Dieu*, Claude,' said Antoine, 'why do you ask? Isn't it obvious? Can't you see her in a champagne satin gown with a robust bustle at the back? The bustle should have a long train, which would trail like a river down the church aisle.' Antoine stretched out his arms and waved them to create the effect of a flowing river.

'Did you have *any* dress in mind?' Claude redirected the question to the woman.

Mademoiselle de Verlay paused before turning to face Claude. 'I was told that *you*, Monsieur Reynaud, would choose a design that would suit me.'

The spurned Antoine frowned and headed to his small sewing room.

Claude asked Mademoiselle de Verlay to step onto the platform that his grandfather had built a century ago, now a warped dark wood. She unwrapped the sweater she wore around her neck and took off her cardigan to reveal a white T-shirt: an unraveling. Within moments, Claude had memorized her measurements: square shoulders, small bust, wider curve at the hip, very long neck.

Delicately, Claude eased his worn yellow measuring tape along her neck, waist, arm length, leg, and torso. Unlike his father, who recorded every detail of a person's size, Claude kept no client files. He never forgot a body. His photographic mind easily memorized the distances between wrist and collarbone, hip and hip, ankle and waist. He used the measuring tape as a distraction while he absorbed skin, hair texture, color, and the way his client moved.

His greatest talent – and what he was becoming renowned for beyond the small town of Senlis – was his ability to match a client's natural colors with enhancing hues and textures. He obsessed over color classifications and names. Inadequate descriptions frustrated him to the point of fury. He would yell across his studio to Pédant, 'That is not the color pink! *Non!* That is the color of dawn reflected on the yellowing marble steps of the Trevi Fountain.'

A beam of sunlight caught his client now – and the edge of his black work coat, upon which he noticed white dust. He thought of brushing it off but was afraid she would notice. She was squinting.

'There's too much glare in here,' he said. 'Shall I close a shutter?'

'No, please! Never too bright. I could sit in the sun all day.'

'Mademoiselle may be fascinated to know that our dressmaker is the sole surviving practitioner of the ancient art of the measuring tape,' yelled Antoine from the kitchen, where he was refilling his coffee cup. 'In Paris, major design companies are using computers to record measurements in a matter of a few minutes. But our Claude, here, he swears by the "touch" you get with a measuring tape.'

Claude heard his assistant but refused to listen to him. He sensed the growing warmth of his client in the direct sunlight and noticed that his fingertips were moist with perspiration.

'I think I have it.' He caught a glimpse of her smiling in the mirror at him. He stood up and rewound the tape into a tight circle. 'I envision you in a white sleeveless tunic. A column of white to the floor, but not touching it, to accentuate your height, and white silk tulle, fluffy white tulle coming off the waist, flowing to the back of the dress, loosely floating into a pool of white at the back. No cream! *Blanche,* only the whitest of white. No thick veil, only a chignon, with a thin layer of tulle falling from a pearl comb and joining the pool on the floor. I must think more about the neckline.' He paused, looking out the window at the apple tree for answers, then back at Mademoiselle de Verlay. 'It should be a *bateau* neckline, straight across the shoulders: no curves.'

'The veil! You must let me do the veil, Claude. I know the veil!' insisted Antoine, who now stood alarmingly close to their client. 'The veil should be thin, as I said before, not tulle – *non, non,* too froufrou – but silk!'

Mademoiselle de Verlay's calm face changed

color. Was it Antoine's proximity? Perhaps she was dismayed by the suggestion of a silk veil. Claude felt his own face redden. He tried to place the color of her eyes. Cornflower blue? No, the blue of the seaside in Brittany, when a cloud obscures the sun, but brighter still. No, blueberries, a bowl of summertime's dark blues in a white porcelain bowl.

Was it the mademoiselle's quietness that unsettled him? It wasn't that she was shy: some secret, some joke, a memory of something amusing lurked behind her smile. He studied her face as she gazed out the window: the eyelashes that turned up at the corners; the dark-brown straight hair curving around the shining pale face, its pointed chin like the period at the bottom of an exclamation mark. Most of all, he was taken by her eyes; they asked him to speak to her. Claude scolded himself back to the task at hand.

'Antoine,' he said, 'please entertain our client while I work up a preliminary sketch. Only a few minutes, mademoiselle.'

'*Mais bien sûr!*' exclaimed Antoine. 'But you see, Claude, a computer would have produced the prelims for you.' He offered Mademoiselle de Verlay a chair as he perched on the stool near her. 'Claude.' He sighed. 'One day, he'll wake up to realize he's living in another century! I don't think I'm willing to wait for the alarm to go off!'

Only a short distance away, seated at the kitchen table with pencil and paper in hand, Claude listened attentively to Antoine's small talk.

'Where do you get that glow, mademoiselle? Surely not out of a bottle? You could light a dark seabed with a face as pearly white as yours. No, pearls do not do it justice. Only the moon . . .' Antoine moved in closer, his talk dimming to a whisper. 'A waist like this! It is rare to witness a waist like this, so much curve . . .'

Antoine was an accomplished flirt. He fine-tuned his smooth talk at every opportunity. Claude never gave Antoine's patter much thought; it had never seemed to offend his clients. Indeed, some confided to him, giggling, that they drove the forty minutes expressly to hear his assistant's sweet nothings.

But this morning, as the sun polished the tip of Mademoiselle de Verlay's earlobe, Claude felt oddly protective of her. She did not react, smiling or rejecting. Her face was quiet and composed. Had the edge of her lip lifted slightly?

'*Monsieur Boudin, laisse-la tranquille!* Enough, please.' Claude glared at Antoine before offering Mademoiselle de Verlay a cup of coffee and the extra brioche from his sister.

'*Non, merci,* but I would love to see the drawing.' She was standing close to Claude's shoulder.

'Mademoiselle, this is a rough sketch,' he said firmly, trying to conceal his nervousness. 'I will fax you the final sketches on Friday for your approval.'

'*Merci,*' she said, walking toward the door.

Antoine blocked her passage. He held her coat aloft. 'Mademoiselle, allow me to escort you to your car.'

11

'No, thank you,' she said quickly, dipping her arms into the sleeves. 'I can find my own way.'

As if she had forgotten something, she turned and darted back into the room past Antoine and held her slender hand out to Claude.

'*Enchantée, monsieur.* Such a pleasure to meet you.' She smiled and flung up her scarf in one motion. As she left, Claude envisioned a train of white silk tulle in her wake.

That afternoon the sky was so gray and low, Claude felt he could reach up and pull it down like a shade. Sketching Valentine de Verlay's tunic wedding dress only accentuated his sense of melancholy. Bouts of despondency were not unfamiliar to him. Sometimes, the dip lasted an hour, sometimes two days, occasionally several months. He usually managed to escape by focusing on his work. But today, designing yet another bridal gown prompted Claude to reflect on his own wedding: a mistake.

His marriage to Rose-Marie had not begun so well and had not ended so well. What was in the middle was also not so well. The beginning was his car accident en route to the church, when he had lurched into reverse instead of first gear and bumped the car behind him. The incident, with its usual fanfare of police and information gathering and one bent fender, delayed the ceremony by an hour. When he caught sight of her face between the white marble columns lining the interior of

Notre-Dame de Senlis, Rose-Marie wore a red-lipped pout. Her brown eyes burned. '*Comment?* How could you have?'

The words stained even the earliest days of his marriage. He saw in her a cozy future of loving domesticity. She saw in him talent and escape from small-town life. It took only a few months to realize that the disappointment was mutual. On their first anniversary, Claude rejected an offer to work at a major couturier in Paris despite Rose-Marie's pleas to take the job.

'But this is the chance of your life! You have *no choice!*' The words were to become Rose-Marie's familiar refrain.

She had left him eight years ago. In their five years of marriage, they had had no children. She told him she was grateful for his talent and the clothes he had made for her, but she had grown tired of his ways and wanted to see the world. Her farewell complete, she squeezed through the narrow front vestibule, her two bulging brown suitcases banging at her heels. In all that time, he had not received so much as a word from her – not even legal documents asking for a divorce, which puzzled him, still.

With the next cool spring breeze through his window, Claude dropped the memory. Like a connoisseur, he sifted through the endless variations of apple-blossom scents delivered by the everchanging breezes. Claude depended and thrived on the predictable rhythms of daily life.

With a scientist's keen eye for detail, he observed the sun's daily patterns on the white-duck-clothed mannequin at the center of his studio. Every afternoon at four-thirty, he looked forward to the clanging of bells from the lycée across the street, signaling the end of the school day and the burst of children's voices on the worn white marble school steps.

He glanced at his watch after the second knell. Any moment now, his nephews would pour unannounced into his quiet abode and bombard him with hugs and demands for pastries and a puppet show. As if on cue, he heard them clamoring at the door.

Pell-mell, in the four boys thronged, romping around the few small rooms, throwing pillows from the bed in a domesticated form of rugby, fiddling with the hands of the grandfather clock, gobbling down *éclairs au chocolat* and spinning the mannequin at the center of the studio, sending pins flying. The older boys, Henri and Jean-Hugues, professed themselves too grown-up for the show performed by their uncle Reynaud's hand-sewn puppets, but they watched anyway, glued to the action, until it was homework time and home-going time and they once again crammed out the old oak door, four at once, one on top of the other, schoolbags bursting out last.

Claude returned the puppets to their silk satchel behind the closet door, brewed a fresh cup of coffee, and tightened the belt on his work coat.

This was the daily prelude to his evening work, when he found himself most productive. In the evening quiet after the bustle of morning sittings, appointments, and phone calls, the mannequin drew him to it like a magnet. Armored with thimbles, a pale green pincushion attached to his belt, his faded yellow tape measure around his neck, he pinned and unpinned the dark blue velvet, spinning the mannequin with each touch. He squinted to catch the overall effect as the mannequin whirled in a pinwheel of midnight blue. Pédant shook his feathers and squawked. Claude smoothed the mannequin's shapely sides and paused, carefully scrutinizing his velvet creation. As the grandfather clock chimed 9 P.M., Claude declared his work finished. Stealing one last look at the mannequin in the mirror, he caught his own reflection. What a long nose he had, his mother's; intense dark eyes, his father's; wide cheekbones, whose? Smallish round lips, like his sister Juliette's. He touched the dark hair at his forehead, which had begun to thin and recede evenly on either side. He grabbed a handful of it at the back, still a good thick crop.

He returned his attention to the mannequin. As he touched the fabric, his gaze softened. Pédant twitched, fluffing feathered wings before nestling his beak once again into cushioned plumage. The dressmaker paused in the velvety richness of the darkening, noiseless moment. Then, he switched on the overhead light and reached into the pantry closet for a handful of potatoes for dinner.

CHAPTER 2

Who would have believed that two years before the new millennium, with the Internet revolution in full force, a dressmaker cut from the pattern of the last century could conjure the presence of cell-phone-bearing Parisian society women? They flocked and descended, appointment by appointment, into the three-room atelier on the narrow cobbled rue du Châtel.

Claude observed the time: 10:04 A.M. The doorbell. Another ring. *Et voilà!* Before he had arrived at the door, she had opened it.

'*Bonjour,* Madame Gilotte.'

'I've been up all night thinking of a dress!' She entered the room in a blur, throwing her bright orange-plaid trench coat on the nearby armchair.

'I'd like it to be peach-colored. What do you think? A long deep cut down the back. It's for a party I'm giving in May, a spring garden party. Oh, you might have some of my friends calling on you, because, you see, the party has a theme. It's the fruits of spring. So of course I thought of peaches . . . well, who knows when they ripen, but who cares about details! Yes, Claude, a marvelously silky long peach-colored gown. You do the rest!'

With her lithe body, her armful of gold bangles, her black eyelashes and rosy lips, her sweet-smelling perfume (was it lavender?) swirling around her, Madame Gilotte's presence transformed the spartan studio into a female salon. Claude enjoyed her heady nonstop banter and barrage of playful abuse. She was known as a hostess with largesse in Paris, and she beamed for photographers. Rooms brightened with her smile.

'A peach-colored dress would suit you perfectly,' Claude told her, absorbing the palette of her almond-colored hair and creamy skin. Only the wrinkles bordering her eyes betrayed her age; her coloring had the vibrancy of a twenty-year-old's. 'Please stand for me.' Claude motioned to the raised wooden platform. 'You have excellent timing,' he continued, his fingers now pinning muslin around her figure. 'Just yesterday, I discovered a peach-colored silk at Monsieur Farouche's. I wanted to buy the available eight bolts, but I didn't have an excuse. Why don't we add some darker peach in taffeta at the sleeves? I see your hair cascading onto your collarbones, a pale peach taffeta ribbon at your neck.'

'May I have it in two weeks?' she asked. 'Must I stand any longer? With the traffic in Paris, it took me an hour and a half to get here, and I have a lunch at twelve-thirty, dead center of the city. Why can't we computerize your business? I have a wonderful tutor, who comes once a week to help my boy, Jean. Perhaps—'

'Could a computer image ever capture your true coloring?'

'Yes, yes, you need the exact colors.' She removed a gold lipstick case from her purse and applied the pink color with her eyes closed. 'But that's just the point. My face could appear on your screen, and you would have all of me – right at your fingertips. I guess not *all* of me! Ah, but you're such an old fuddy-duddy. Hurry, Claude. Such a penance you exact. Yes, you do only need a few fittings, which is incredible compared with some. I just hope you save your best ideas for me.'

'It is easy to create for you, madame.'

'Call me Madeleine! Why must you continue with this *madame* act? Are you so formal with all your clients? And, by the way, where is your parrot?' (Pédant had accompanied Didier, one of Claude's younger nephews, to a show-and-tell session at school.) 'Such a relief not to have that fowl's beady eyes staring down at me. I always leave wondering what piece of my gibberish he's stuck on and you have to abide by. Makes one choose one's words more carefully, that's certain. Please do send him away every time I come. But really, must I stand this long while you push and pin me? Don't you know my shape by now? I know, you need to remeasure; well, I *have* added a little weight around the middle, but peaches, are – well, you know, round.'

Madame Gilotte had departed, her lavender fragrance trailing behind her. As his tailor father had trained him, Claude laid his tools – thimble, pincushion, tape measure – one by one on his side table, much like a surgeon would arrange his instruments in preparation for his next patient.

Papa Claude. Claude had learned everything he knew from his father. By six years of age he was spending his afternoons at the studio, closely observing the mannequin's changing attire. One of his daily childhood rituals involved running around the spinning headless figure as if it were a maypole, delighting in the colors and smells of the pinned fabric it wore that day, his fingers tracing the different weaves and textures.

Papa Claude had approached his work as a mathematician, priding himself on his exactitude. The measurements – little scraps of paper covered with miniature numbers in blue ink – were treated with reverence, neatly bundled with yellow rubber bands, layered in labeled folders in the age-old oak desk in the entry hall. Grandpapa Claude, also a tailor, had handcarved the sign still hanging outside the studio, which read REYNAUD, TAILLEUR. He had hammered together the now-creaking weather-stained wooden bench where the townspeople of Senlis sat and chatted while Grandpapa hemmed a skirt or sewed a button. Most of the present Claude Reynaud's designs were stitched on Great-grandfather's well-oiled black treadle sewing machine.

While Papa Claude and Claude stitched side by side, Claude's mother's domain had been house, family, and accounts – or rather, in the correct order, accounts, house, and family. Her refrain, 'The accounts *must* be done!' signaled quiet to Claude and his two younger sisters. The modest jubilations his father shared with his son over this periwinkle-blue bonnet or that brilliant purple-blue fringe ('Look how the color shimmers when it moves!') were banished to the studio.

'Claude, come!' Papa Claude would beckon his son in his hoarse excited voice. 'Watch the way this cotton falls to the ground in exactly three folds all the time, never ever four, never five! Imagine that! Only three, from now until eternity! You must appreciate each fabric's natural *tombée*. Never fight the fabric, son. Feel the fabric. The fabric will show you its way.'

His mother lived number-bound in the stuffy windowless back room, which contained only an ancient brown file cabinet, a scratched and stained oak desk, and a rolling wooden chair. His two sisters, younger by four and six years, played in the garden, occupying a seemingly mysterious realm that Claude felt too old and too serious to enter. In any case, there was no doubt as to which part of the family their brother belonged: the son would inherit his father's craft.

Fortunately for young Claude, he found it and everything about his father irresistible. Like Papa Claude's reverence for time. His father relied on time as one of the few trustworthy things in life: like fabric, it could be measured and counted on. Papa Claude attended church, but his son had concluded at an early age that his father worshiped time more faithfully than God. He prefaced every sentence with it.

'It's ten o'clock. Ten minutes for a coffee.'

Claude would glance at the scratched face of his father's antique Bréguet watch, a gift from his father for his sixteenth birthday.

'Ten-ten, son, back to work.'

While Claude's wife, Rose-Marie, had found her father-in-law's obsession annoying (she would dangle her watch in front of Claude, whispering 'Ticktock, ticktock'), Claude found comfort in his father's hourly interruptions to check the time, relying on the hours to fit life into a meaningful plan. Every announcement of time confirmed that all was well and 'meant to be' in this perfectly calibrated father-son world.

He recalled the last time he gauged the time with his father: 4:46 P.M. on Sunday, January 13, a rain-drenching day. Claude had bent low to catch his father's faltering, barely audible voice. 'If my calculations are correct,' Papa Claude struggled to say, 'this is the day I will not finish.'

'Turn the light on. It's too dark in here,' his mother reproached him from the doorway. And, a few minutes later, 'Claude, leave your father be.'

Undeterred, Claude continued to press the withered old hand. He leaned over the heavy head tilted back on the pillow, the draped half-shut eyes, which cried waterlessly, the mouth yawning open, as if bored with life. In every cell of his body, Claude felt it happen: the end, his father's final leave-taking.

He remembered, seconds later, catching his mother's face in his peripheral vision. Her quick fierce eyes accused her son of robbery. Out of filial duty, Claude observed the time on his father's watch. 4:46:11. He held his breath and watched the second hand take one full rotation.

CHAPTER 3

The door opened to the sounds of swishing cars on the cobblestone street outside, then slammed shut. From the cupboard, Claude unhooked a pale blue cup, its inside slightly stained brown, and poured his boisterous assistant black coffee.

'*Bonjour*, Claude!' Antoine trumpeted into the room. '*Mais c'est fou, ce temps!*' Without taking off his raincoat, he pulled out a chair so it scraped the wood floor and sat down, dripping with rain, next to Claude.

'Claude' – he leaned over the table, his wet sleeves blurring Claude's blue-marked design pages – 'I'm in love! I'm erupting with happiness! The rain can soak me, but it cannot extinguish my overflowing passion!' Antoine often spoke to Claude of his most recent attachments.

'And who is your newest true love?' Claude asked.

Antoine could not contain himself. His large almond-brown eyes, his heavy brow, his forehead that looked like a wall – every particle of him appeared enlarged and out of control.

'I know it's crazy and I know you will not

approve, but she's none other than the most lovely Mademoiselle de Verlay, who graced us with her presence yesterday. I have left a message on her answering machine inviting her to a party with me this weekend.'

Claude swallowed involuntarily. With more emotion than the statement required, he pointed out the obvious. 'She's getting married in three months!'

'Ah, but she's not married *yet*,' countered Antoine with a sly smile.

'But Antoine' – the words shot out of him – 'this is not acceptable. You may not do this.' His voice shook. 'For you to prey on women who come to my studio with references from important clients? *Non,* this is not acceptable. Plus you have chosen a woman who is soon to be married!'

'You are concerned, I see. Do I detect . . . can the impenetrable Claude Reynaud be jealous? No! I didn't think it possible!' Antoine sat back in the chair and laughed.

'This is ridiculous,' Claude said irritably, looking at his watch. 'Madame Rigaux will be here any minute. Have you finished the lining on her linen suit?'

Antoine sighed dramatically and strode into the side room, from which, immediately, the buzzing of the sewing machine severed the silence. Claude returned his attention to Mademoiselle de Verlay's design.

Where was Madame Rigaux when he needed her

to distract him? Presumably, late as usual. Claude labeled all excessive excuses *Rigaux excuses*: 'The car was parked in the wrong direction, and it took an hour to turn it around . . . I couldn't get my dog's leash untangled when he chased after a lawn mower! Imagine my dog all cut up by that horrible machine!' Was there truth in any word she uttered? Today, he found himself hoping the angular madame would skip the deluge of excuses and get straight to demanding the price of hemming the atrocious pink linen pants she would invariably bring. He could respond with a number, something concrete to distract him from this blurred feeling of anger and – yes, he admitted it to himself – jealousy.

Abruptly, the door banged open.

'You won't believe what happened to me!' the breathless woman panted as she entered, along with a tale of the garbage truck that chased her out of town to the racetrack at Chantilly. 'I was so distracted by the obscenities the driver was yelling out the window, I was careening around the periphery of the track before I knew it. There we were, the horses racing beside my Renault and a cursing driver's reeking garbage truck.'

Claude's sister Juliette lived in a two-story stone house with glossy black shutters just outside Senlis, a ten-minute walk from Claude's studio. While Claude had been raised under the heavy hand of his father's exactitude, Juliette had escaped all forms of discipline. After rereading every book in the house (their grandfather had been an avid reader and prided himself on his small collection of leather-bound books), she had devoured the limited supply in the Senlis library. She found her hunger for books satisfied after university when she was employed for the lowest salary as a reader for Éditions Garouche, one of the largest publishing houses in Paris. Seventeen devoted years later, she had risen in the ranks to become one of four fiction editors. She commuted every working day to and from Paris by train, head bent as she scoured manuscript pages, never managing to finish reading all she carried.

Juliette had a calm dreamy character, but after her fourth child was born, *dreamy* dissolved into *disorganized.* The dark oak floors in the house were barely visible for the multicolored, mud-splattered clothing scattered on top of them. After a time, the children weren't surprised by the taste and color of mold on bread and fruit. Weren't long sprouts supposed to erupt out of potatoes and onions?

Juliette's husband, Bernard, worked as a lawyer locally, but even he, who rarely complained, had realized that inviting his widowed and fastidious mother-in-law, who was living in a small apartment in town, to stay in their house would be worth the loss of family privacy. Three months after their fourth son, Arthur, was born, and the highly acidic smell of urine pervaded the house, Bernard made the call. Between diapers and manuscript pages, Juliette was grateful for the new arrangement. Her maternity leave would end in two days.

Claude's mother had adjusted to the move immediately, resolved to 'whip this house' – said with arrogant disdain – 'into shape.' Only hours after she had unpacked her bags and cleaning utensils, the house gleamed. When Juliette and Bernard entered their home the following evening, they found floors polished, laundry in drawers, dinner cooked, vegetables eaten, and four boys clean-faced, hands washed, and slippers on both feet, wearing pajama pants and tops that matched.

With his mother happily ensconced in her new role and home, Claude began to visit his sister's house more frequently. Before long, he was dining with the family every Sunday evening, bringing with him dessert and his repertoire of puppets. Tonight was no exception. After the boys inhaled the *tarte tâtin*, he delighted them with a performance in which Mui-Mui, the baker, reprimanded Isabelle, the poodle puppet, for stealing the last croissant. Jo-Jo, the elephant whose trunk was very loose, predictably interrupted the action and complained of the impending doom of a trunkless elephant. The button-eyed owl Hilbert provided the moral at the end.

Pédant perched on Claude's shoulder as he acted out the parts, screeching '*Bonjour,* madame!' repeatedly throughout the performance.

'You're not leaving without that filthy bird!'

Claude's mother called from the kitchen as the children clapped their hands. Pédant had trespassed one too many times in her domain.

'Yes, yes,' Claude said. 'The bird returns with me today.'

Claude found Juliette alone in the kitchen, a rare occurrence in her busy, peopled life. He pulled a stool up to the counter and, in the most casual voice he could muster, asked if she knew of a Valentine de Verlay. Juliette had a wide circle of friends from her Sorbonne days and her publishing job in Paris.

'The name is familiar. What does she do?'

'I don't know. She's come to me for a wedding dress. Antoine embarrassed her and me by flirting aggressively with her.' Claude could feel his face growing hot.

'I can't place the name. But anyway, she's come to the right place. You'll turn her out exquisitely.'

For a moment in the quiet room, as Juliette wiped off the counter, he wanted to tell his sister, Juliette, this woman has embedded herself in my mind as a sparkling jewel in a pronged gemless ring. Is this what happens after a certain age, that your weakened heart falls for a pretty woman in less than half an hour? That the only image you see afterward is her face, the only sound you hear is her voice? You even remember her breath, which, like a butterfly that passes gently by, you wish you had cupped and caught in your hands. How do I sever this clinging, unsettled feeling? I immerse myself in work to push away all distracting thoughts of her, but my work is *her* dress! What, wise sister, should I do?

In the years following Rose-Marie's departure, Juliette and friends had arranged many dates for Claude. Before long, Claude could not walk down a street in Senlis without passing a dinner partner from the past. He would dip his chest, nod an embarrassed *bonjour,* and feel a lingering guilt that the rendezvous had not worked according to everyone's wishes. And yet the sequence of women appeared to him now as beads on a necklace, with Valentine holding the center, a resplendent sapphire among glass. Never had he imagined that he would encounter such a precious stone.

Arthur, the youngest of Claude's nephews, hurtled into the kitchen. Tears streaked his face. 'Jean-Hugues hit me! They say I stink at riding!' Juliette's second son, thirteen-year-old Jean-Hugues, skidded into the kitchen to defend himself.

'Come, *mon chéri.*' Juliette lifted the eight-year-old into her arms. Jean-Hugues scuttled out to avoid punishment. Arthur's crying subsided. 'What kind of wedding dress are you making for this Valentine?'

'The moment I saw her, I knew the dress, as if it were waiting for her in my mind, as if it were the most crucial work of my career. But, it's so simple, so obvious: a straight tunic of a gown with tulle at the back and for the veil.' He took a deep breath.

'You like her!' His sister's placid green-blue eyes became animated. 'But, Claude, she's come to you for her *wedding* dress!'

He looked down.

'When is the next fitting?' she asked quickly.

'Next week.'

Was it possible to become somebody else at his age? Where was the boy of five who had secretly wept when his father left the house for a day? The man of thirty-three who married a woman he barely knew? Was it possible, at the age of forty-six, to fall in love for the first time? In this kitchen in which countless dinners had been prepared, with patient Juliette on the wood floor stroking her son in her lap, he wanted to finally read his heart aloud.

'Juliette!' In walked Bernard, in ran a few children, and out of the oven came dinner.

CHAPTER 4

In the next morning's brightness, Claude arrived at a rational explanation for his agitation: unlike other affianced women, who cheerfully volunteered their wedding plans, Valentine seemed unusually reserved about the big event.

'I found out more about your client last night, Claude. Such a small world!' Antoine declared loudly, as he entered the studio and unhooked a coffee cup from the open cupboard in the kitchen off the main room.

Claude held his breath. If Valentine were bound heart and soul to her fiancé, why would Antoine feel free to make advances?

'My friend Patrice Ricard knows the man she's marrying. He's the *commissaire-priseur,* the top dog, at Hôtel Drouot, the auction house in Paris. He's held the position for two years and has spent his career working his way up. She works there too. They're going to the Mauritius Islands for their honeymoon.'

Ignore him, Claude ordered himself. 'Fine,' he said aloud. 'How nice for them.'

'I'm still going to invite her for a drink,' Antoine

said, too loudly. 'She was attracted to me, I could tell! Thank God for long engagements.' He closed his eyes. 'Her face is a moon that is always full; her smile, a wingèd entrance to a thousand heavens . . . I must get this down.' Antoine dabbled in poetry. He hurried into the adjacent sewing room to record his epiphany.

Feigning nonchalance, Claude concentrated on the designs on the pale blue graph paper on his desk. He frowned, crumpled the paper, and threw it in the garbage container under his desk. After a moment's thought, he deposited several hours' worth of sewing work onto Antoine's table. We'll see if he has time to go out with anyone! he said to himself.

Despite a busy schedule of sittings, fittings, cuttings, and trips to Farouche's, his fabric supplier in Montmartre, the week dragged. Claude could think only of Tuesday, his next appointment with Valentine. In that precious hour, he would use every God-given instinct and insight to determine if his feelings were warranted. He considered sending the boisterous Antoine on an all-day errand, but the action felt too calculated. Would he ask Antoine to leave the premises if she were any other client?

Finally the day arrived and Valentine glided, swanlike, into his studio for the second time. A thin fuchsia cotton scarf swaddled her neck. Her heart-shaped face looked different this time; what had seemed soft was now sharply defined. The kohl-rimmed dark-blue eyes surprised him again, sparkling out of the milky face. Her hair was pulled back in a ponytail; she wore black Capri pants, a pastel pink cotton shirt with three-quarter sleeves, and black heelless narrow-toed leather slippers. Again, understated elegance. And that smile, always that slight smile. His rehearsed speech failed him; he hadn't noticed the little bump in her delicate nose, the tip of which rose not too far from her pale lips. He scrutinized her like a bolt of material he was considering buying at Farouche's.

Still, it was her eyes that dazzled. Were they happy or sad?

'How have you been, Monsieur Reynaud?' She looked for a place to drop her light camel overcoat, then placed it over the back of the chair near his desk.

'*Très bien, merci;* very well, thank you. Please, let me take your coat. Call me Claude.'

She walked over to Pédant's stand. '*Et toi, Monsieur Pédant, comment ça va?*'

'*Bonjour,* madame!' the parrot squawked in refrain.

She laughed and returned to Claude. Her slender white-fingered hand touched her ponytail. The shape of her hair fit like a remaining puzzle piece into her palm.

'Monsieur Reynaud – I mean Claude – I wanted to ask you about dresses for my two nieces and an outfit for my nephew, all of whom will be in the wedding. And by the way,' she added in her hushed voice, tipping her head and looking him directly in the eyes, '*how* did you intuit the dress that was exactly what I wanted – no fuss?'

Why no fuss? he thought excitedly. Surely this was a clue. And yet she talked of the wedding as if it were the most perfect logical progression in her life.

'*Avec plaisir,*' he replied. Everything about him, in him, pulsed. Could she hear his heart beating? 'Mademoiselle, it is the finest day we've had this April. Before we get to work, won't you join me for a stroll in the garden?' He watched himself from afar, mortified, but continued. 'The apple blossoms are in full fragrance.'

He opened the back door and motioned her into the little garden surrounded by the crooked wood fence, in which the very old gnarled apple tree, loaded top to bottom with delicate white blossoms, gave off a scent as ambrosial as he had promised.

'How delightful!' she said, moving to the door. They laid footprints side by side on the patch of earth where vegetables would be thriving in three months, walking past two rainstained wooden chairs and a matching table just big enough for two cups of coffee, the small section of long grass, a hint of a country field. He broke off a long thin branch from the tree, replete with blossoms. Petals fell like snowflakes as he handed it to her.

'This smell takes me back to my childhood home

in Normandy,' she said pensively. 'Our next-door neighbors owned an apple farm. My sisters and I helped pick apples in the autumn. We'd climb the ladders. How we stretched and reached into the leafy sky! In springtime as the blossoms fell, we ran up and down the rows, pretending we were heroes, home from huge adventures with throngs of admiring crowds throwing confetti. In the late fall, after the good apples were picked and the ground was covered with the overlooked and bruised ones, we would slip and slide to our hearts' content. We were apple slush when we got home. How funny.' She stopped walking and pointed at the tree. 'That branch looks like it's waiting for someone to sit on it.'

'Room for two people, actually,' he said, on the brink of suggesting they perch there like two kids and swing their legs, but their attention was diverted by the sound of a door slamming inside the studio.

Antoine, thought Claude.

'Where will the wedding be held?' he asked, aware even as he uttered the words how abrupt and out of context they sounded. He watched her expression change gears slowly.

'Mont-Saint-Michel, in the little chapel,' she said. 'My father and mother were married there, as were my two sisters.' He waited for a hint. She seemed unswervingly calm. 'When we visited the chapel as children, we were told that a dragon lived under the stone floor. We really thought we saw smoke rising out of the cracks. We used to put our ears to the floor, straining to hear a muffled roar. One time, we were completely convinced we heard a burst of flame!'

'Has the dragon chased you to the wedding altar?' he asked, cursing himself the moment the words were out of his mouth.

She laughed, shaking her head, as if shaking off his question. 'I can no longer resist.'

They had walked full circle, and his hand reluctantly cupped the knob of the back door.

'Thank you for the stroll, mademoiselle. Now I will get you back to Paris as quickly as possible. If you would kindly try on the gown as it is, so we know it's a good fit—'

Antoine sat sipping his coffee, khaki pant legs and brown loafers resting on the table. He jumped up.

'Well, if it isn't Claude the tailor, entertaining a future bride in the garden!' He swept the chair back from the table. 'Mademoiselle, please join me for a cup of coffee.'

'Mademoiselle de Verlay should not be required to entertain us all day long. I've promised to keep this short, Antoine. The fitting room is in the corner there.' He nodded in its direction. 'You will find the dress on a hanger inside. Please be careful of the pins.'

Valentine headed toward the room, but Antoine stopped her midway. 'I would like to have a word with you,' he said quietly, but loud enough for Claude to hear.

Claude's chest constricted with anger. He

watched Valentine maneuver past Antoine and enter the small room where her dress awaited her.

Antoine rapped his knuckles on the louvered door of the small room. Claude's eyes widened in disbelief. 'What do you think you're doing?' he whispered, as he hurried over to Antoine.

'I forgot to tell her something important. Valen-teen,' Antoine called out. Valentine's head and long neck emerged gracefully, her head cocked in question.

'Antoine,' Claude said, 'I cannot have you disturbing my client. Please. Leave this room.'

'Valen-teen.' Antoine continued to approach the dressing room.

'Enough! You will leave this studio now!' Claude's voice shook.

Antoine turned around and forced a laugh. '*Ce n'est pas possible!* Claude Reynaud is asking me to leave his studio over a woman. Over a woman!' he repeated. 'I didn't think you had it in you.'

'Please leave.'

Antoine glowered at Claude. 'If that's what we've come to, I've been looking for a good reason to escape this backwater excuse of a small-town tailor shop. Why should I waste another minute of my time?' He grabbed his jacket off the back of the chair, almost causing it to topple, and stormed out of the studio.

Moments later, he popped his head back into the room and addressed Valentine, still in the changing room doorway, her long gown held up under her slender white arms. 'Mademoiselle, please excuse your tailor, Monsieur Reynaud. He is petrified that you will agree to go out with me. I will call you tonight.' Blowing her a kiss, he slammed the heavy oak door.

'Mademoiselle Valentine,' said Claude, gesturing toward the wooden platform, 'you may safely come out now. Please forgive me; I could not let him enter while you were changing. Talk about dragons breathing fire! To subject you to this, this . . . I will finish as quickly as possible with the pinning.'

She laughed as she walked barefoot to the platform. Relief spread across him like a warm blanket on a cold night.

'Please, step up here. Did you bring the shoes you will be wearing?'

'I forgot,' she said, looking down at her feet.

'Not a problem. Do you think your heels will be three inches or more?'

'Two inches should do the trick.'

'If you'll just stand tiptoe.' He placed two-inch wooden wedges under her heels. Such close proximity to her sent the blood rushing to his head. What an effort to touch and, at the same time, not to touch!

'There, two or three more pins.' He stood up slowly, breathing in her scent.

Pédant scratched and fluttered on his stand. Claude shut his eyes. She had forgotten her shoes. She was not planning for the event to transpire after all.

'One more moment, please. I need to determine the length of the veil.' He gently placed a pearl comb, found on a recent trip to Paris, on her head. Holding his breath, he disturbed only two or three strands of hair, which he replaced with care like a professional burglar returning stolen jewels to their velvet case. The stiff white tulle veil trailed down voluminously from the pearl comb. When he glanced for an instant at the mirror opposite her, Claude knew he had achieved the desired effect. The lustrous white gown mirrored the light that shone from within.

'It's perfect,' she said.

'*You* are,' he said.

The words, now delivered, rippled in the stillness of the room.

'*Non, non, alors,*' she said and smiled her broad smile at him. She waited for him to speak again.

'I will deliver the dress within the next two weeks and we can have the fittings for your nephew and nieces the week after.' He tried to sound as professional as possible.

'So soon?'

'I'm not known as the two-fittings dressmaker for nothing,' he said, but he immediately regretted his words.

Perhaps she was secretly hoping for another trip to visit him or Senlis? Why had he rushed the process? Should he say that, on second thought, with this kind of tailored tunic dress a third fitting would be appropriate, even imperative?

She laughed. The moment was lost.

'Mademoiselle de Verlay.' He abandoned his composure, again wondering who was speaking. 'Before you leave, may I confess something?' He resisted waiting for her response. 'I do not know who you are, but I have the strange feeling of being deeply connected to you. *C'est bizarre.*'

'That's funny,' she said naturally, unabashedly. 'I feel I have known you from before also, as if I had spent my whole life in this room looking at that snowing apple tree, observing it changing its garments according to the season, talking to it, talking to you.' She paused, looking sad.

Please don't stop, he thought.

'I'm sorry about your assistant,' she said finally.

'No! Please, forgive me!' He caught her eyes. Did they steal a quick glance at the door? 'I've kept you too long. Feel free to change in the fitting room. This time, you can be assured, no one will disturb you.' He bowed his head. 'I will be in the garden.'

When he returned to the studio, he found a note on the kitchen table. Her script was round and delicate.

I think there are two dragons in Senlis! Thank you for the dress and the apple blossoms.
Valentine.

He felt a draft from the entrance hall. The door had been left slightly ajar.

★　　★　　★

The following week, filled with administrative details, appointments, and endless sewing with no outside help, proved draining. Claude's eyes grew blurry at night and Pédant screeched, begging for more attention from his master. Claude placed an advertisement for a tailor's assistant in the daily paper.

For the first time in his career, he questioned the use of the word *tailleur*. 'Perhaps,' he said to Pédant, 'I am not a tailor. Perhaps I am a couturier?'

His restlessness increased daily. At last, the wedding dress was ready for sewing, the last ribbon pinned carefully and gently into the veil. It took only two feverish days to sew his masterpiece together. He worked ferociously, knowing each stitch by heart. He delayed sending off the gown in his signature long white box by overnight post as he delivered dresses to other Parisian clients. Once the dress was out of his hands, Valentine could disappear. No, he would hand-deliver this one.

His tactic was rewarded. By week's end, an invitation had arrived, the envelope addressed in dark blue ink, the handwriting immediately recognizable.

Madame and Monsieur Eric de Verlay
Request the pleasure of your company
for a celebration

In honor of
Valentine and Victor
Saturday, the Eighteenth of April,
7:30 p.m.,
Cave du Roi, 21 rue du Roi,
Paris.
RSVP 01 14 65 72 37.

The return address was 2 rue des Haudriettes, Paris 75003. He ran his fingers over the embossed letters and numbers on the large linen card. He read the words aloud to Pédant. He did not know which to do first: jump three feet in the air, kiss the fluttering parrot, or laugh at his own foolishness. Why would this woman ask him to a party? He quickly chased away his skepticism. What mattered most was that he would see Valentine again.

Claude tore to his desk like one of his nephews scrambling to play soccer. Perhaps he should write his response on a weighty card. He would have to buy one. But no! The event was next week. A last-minute invitation. He would call her. Why not now? He dialed the number, sighed with relief when the answering machine picked up, and left a message. 'This is Claude Reynaud. I would be delighted to attend on the night of the eighteenth. I will bring your dress at that time.' He consciously avoided the word 'wedding.'

Workdays came and went. Few fitting appointments passed during which the conversation did not turn to Valentine de Verlay's wedding. Claude marveled at how small Paris and his circle of clientele was, that one woman's wedding was the talk among them all, even thirty miles from the capital.

'The best thing that ever happened to her fiancé. Isn't Victor lucky?' 'After all these years, she's finally said yes.' 'One can only suppose she is getting older and wants a family.'

Claude adopted as casual a tone as he could muster. 'And how old do you call *getting older*?'

'Oh, she must be thirty-five by now.'

It was also confirmed that Victor, the *commissaire-priseur* of l'Hôtel Drouot, the biggest *maison des ventes* in Paris, was handsome and from a well-respected 'good' family. They owned several Parisian residences and a seventeenth-century château and estate in Normandy. Victor traveled the world for his auction house, talking to owners of renowned masterpieces who wished to buy or sell. Apparently, Valentine and Victor had been considered a match from an early age. His surname – Claude found it hard to believe, but it was true – was Couturier. Victor Couturier.

CHAPTER 5

The last time Claude had driven into the capital to visit his favorite ribbon shop in Montmartre on the rue des Abbesses, he had found the narrow, winding cobblestone streets claustrophobic, the pace hysterical, the traffic frustrating. But now, on his way to Valentine's party, Paris opened herself up to him. He parked his orange Peugeot on the side alley of the rue du Chemin Vert and took in his surroundings. The trunks of the sycamore trees, still undressed by winter, wore hints of verdant green. The townhouses on the left side of the street reflected the last rose-dappled glow of evening. Pedestrians sauntered; some smiled as he passed. He noticed the rounded cobblestones, resembling an elderly person's yellowing teeth. He wondered what tales of footsteps, carriages, and galloping horses each stone could tell.

Eight P.M. Too early. On the other side of the street, a woman in high heels clattered to the Cave du Roi's entrance. A man joined her. Together, they pushed the large wooden door open. Another couple rounded the corner. Awkwardly carrying the large rectangular white box that contained Valentine's wedding gown, Claude propelled himself forward.

Without warning, the evening breezes stilled and the spring night turned warm. Perspiration gathered on Claude's forehead. He shifted the box in front of him, delicately, as if it were a candle-lit birthday cake.

Claude delighted in the workmanship of the intricately carved motifs above the Cave du Roi's door, the shields, the crests, the powerful images of eagles, lions, and lilies. Lilies? He entered. A mustached butler officiously crossed his name off a list and asked monsieur if he would prefer to check his unwieldy package. Claude declined, clutching the large box tighter.

The inscriptions on the copper plaque at the top of the staircase spiraling downward described this former king's dungeon, now converted into a world-renowned wine cellar. For two centuries, political outcasts, traitors, murderers, petty thieves, and vagabonds had been tortured, shackled, and then cast down these steps. Claude imagined the moans and shrieks of pain that must have echoed up the steep stairwell.

Another plaque on the wall near the bottom step told the story of the dungeon's use during the French Revolution. The torture chamber had been transformed into a hiding place and living quarters for the royal families escaping the guillotine-hungry revolutionaries. Behind a secret wall, a maze of tunnels, used as escape routes, snaked in different directions. One extended all the way to Brittany. Before its newest incarnation as a wine cellar, the 'cave' had been the site of a rarely visited museum of torture.

As he descended to the rumbling sounds of the party, Claude began to feel uneasy. Why had he come? He realized immediately that the jackets to his left and right were a good two inches shorter in hem length than his own and cursed himself for living in a small provincial town and not reading up on the latest men's designs. The long jacket gave him away.

He observed women in top-of-the-line designer cocktail dresses or suits, some pantsuits. He recognized the same Chanel suit on two women (what a shame), a faultlessly tailored Givenchy jacket (the delight of the lines!), Ungaro flounces on a mossy green crêpe-de-chine skirt (the swish of fabric was unmistakable): fashionable women with slim figures, immaculately groomed. The men wore conservative suits or navy double-breasted jackets with gold or silver buttons over solid blue or white or striped shirts, Bright, colorful silk squares – *'pochettes'* – enlivened their suit pockets. Waiters circled the guests, filling champagne glasses, proffering caviar, salmon on celery, goat cheese canapés, skewered lamb brochette.

Where was Valentine? He recognized Dorothée de Talance from a sitting a year ago. The lavender linen dress and jacket with narrow lapels he had designed for her then would have suited her better than the maroon silk dress she now wore, which clung too closely to her hips. He wished he could send her home to change. The straight black hair that hung below her shoulders elongated her long oval face. A chignon would do wonders.

Valentine's smile released him at last. Her rosy cheeks erased the world of his worries. As she brushed her softness against his sharp stubble, he caught the scent of lilac blossoms – or was it lilies of the valley? – spring in the making. She looked down at the long white box under his warm underarm and opened her arms to receive it, like a child with eyes closed, expecting a gift.

'How can I thank you enough?' she said. Her eyes reflected the candlelight in the chandelier just above her head.

What sounded like the flapping wings of wild geese prevented an answer.

'Valentine!' Guests landed beside them. 'Where have you been?'

The group surrounded her in their colors, their sandstone silks, pink chiffons, their pale pastels and long jackets, their embroidered pointed shoes with delicate stiletto heels. Claude recognized one of his creations, a cocoa-colored taffeta off-the-shoulder dress with fitted bodice and knee-skimming pleated skirt.

Valentine handed the white box over to a waiter and whispered some instructions before addressing the flock. 'Meet the man who designed my dress!'

As Claude's eyes followed the box's departure, he heard the voice of Madame de Vigny. *'Oh, mon cher Monsieur Reynaud!'* She hugged him so tightly that feathers from her dress floated up to his eyes and nose.

'This darling man,' she announced to her companions, 'is the most talented designer in France! Remember the black evening gown that cosseted every inch of me? I don't think anyone will ever forget it, the transparent sleeves and the transparent back . . . Monsieur Reynaud, that was art. We're so glad you're here for our Valentine. She's not the type to have found you on her own, *la pauvre,* not a big shopper, but she will be. Oh, you'll need monsieur, Valentine! The events you'll have to attend. Your little black dress will do no longer! But tell us, monsieur—'

'Call me Claude,' he interrupted.

'Mais bien sûr! But of course. Claude, why don't you buy a little studio in Paris, come winter. Then we won't have to traipse so far from town. Of course, we don't want you to become too popular, monsieur – I mean, Claude – or you'd never have time for us.'

'Let's give Claude some breathing room,' said Valentine softly. She placed a chilled champagne glass in his hand.

He sipped to soothe his hammering heart.

'Come, let me introduce you to Victor.' She took Claude's hand and, looking downward, avoided the attention of others as she parted the way. 'Oh, and my mother wants to meet you too. We'll find her after Victor.'

She interrupted a circle of laughter. A tall distinguished dark-haired man in a well-cut black linen double-breasted jacket stood at the group's center. Wax dripping from the candle chandelier just above formed a white crust on his collar. How could he not notice?

The man smiled brightly when he saw Valentine. Valentine introduced Claude to the group as 'the designer of my wedding gown. Claude, I'd like you to meet Victor Couturier.'

Claude felt shorter than his five feet ten inches as he stood in front of the towering Victor.

'Welcome, Claude,' Victor said quickly. 'Please join us. I was just telling a story . . .' Claude admired Victor's carefree attire. He wore a Mediterranean-blue silk and cotton shirt with a blue-and-black zigzag-patterned tie that accentuated the jacket's slight wing shoulders.

Claude felt a pang. This attractive man of genteel breeding, cultivated diction, and a deep voice like the underbelly of the ocean had spent his childhood with Valentine and now anticipated a lifetime of her companionship. His magnetism was riveting. Those around him seemed more interested in the teller than the tale.

'The funny thing was that Marcel didn't notice that his wife was watching!'

Claude had missed the first part of the joke, something about the husband going to town to fetch some medicine for his wife. It appeared the wife did not have the advantage. The group guffawed. Victor seemed serious about his fun. He glanced occasionally at Claude and smiled at him once. Perhaps Valentine had described their walk in the garden, told her fiancé about the sweet little tailor in the quaint countryside.

'Now, monsieur: the dressmaker of my beloved's wedding gown.' Victor addressed Claude with renewed energy. 'Won't you please ease our suspense and give us an idea—'

Valentine stepped inside the circle. 'Only if you, Victor, will tell our guests something about our honeymoon. I, for one, would love to know more. He insists on keeping it a secret!'

In that moment, somehow, everything in the room stopped, all sound and bluster. The world grew quiet as Victor looked down at Valentine. He covered her hands with his.

'Darling,' Victor said, not shifting his gaze from her face, 'our honeymoon is our life together. Shall I tell our guests about my every Valentine-graced day from now until eternity?'

Claude watched Valentine's eyes warm as they locked on to her fiancé's and, offering a softly muttered 'Excusez-moi,' he drifted uneasily from the group.

The conversations around which he moved, as if in a trance, ranged from summer vacations to Valentine's wedding plans to the most recent sale at Drouot. Claude thought of his sister Juliette and her love of words, the time she spent undressing and dressing them, making them stand up and behave themselves. Written sentences could be dissected and excavated for meaning. Spoken ones flew out of the hatch unedited, unattended to, often disintegrating into nothingness.

'Claude.' Valentine was at his right shoulder, her head so close to his he could feel her breath at his neck. 'You must be so bored with all this talk. Please, I want to show you something. The cave below this room contains some of the oldest wine in France. Come. The owner took me on a tour before the party.'

With her left hand, she played with her hair. Her dress, a gray-blue cotton-rayon blend, made her skin look pale but accentuated the deep blue of her eyes. He disliked the waistline, which dropped too low for her figure and flattened her chest.

They withdrew quickly and, it felt to him, secretly, into a very small cavelike room. She took a key from a pocket in her dress. How had he missed such a pocket? It seemed a small miracle, so perfectly placed on the A-line, just big enough for a key and a slender hand. His next dress design would include many such pockets! Valentine hastily turned the key in the lock and opened a small, arched, heavy stone door.

'Watch your head,' she whispered.

They ducked into a still smaller room, cool and cedar-lined, lit by a single chandelier that grazed his head when Claude straightened up. The damp mustiness was overpowering. He smelled dulled vinegar, the scent of empty oak wine casks. The wall to his right was darker in color, from moisture. They heard dripping somewhere overhead.

Why me? Claude thought. How had the lowly tailor snatched his elegant hostess's attentions from her debonair fiancé?

She pulled another door open, this one of heavy glass, and they entered a refrigerated, dimly lit tunnel lined on both sides by wine bottles. After a few steps on the uneven stone floor, she stopped in front of a deep sapphire-blue bottle with an extremely wide base. Removing the bottle from the rack, she blew the dust off the label.

'Read,' she whispered, pointing to the label: *1764, La Cave du Palais-Royal*. Amazingly intact gold crowns and blue stars distinguished the top and bottom of the label. The script was barely visible.

'Imagine! 1764!' She fell serious. 'Let's see: the revolution was brewing. A restless disquiet had begun in the countryside . . . Touching this makes me feel so strange – ghostly, even. Imagine the people who held this bottle, now long dead! We too, one day . . .' She paused. 'Let's smash it right now! On this stone floor! Let's be the last hands to touch it! Come, Claude, let's!'

She waited.

'No, I know! Even better. Let's open it and drink it! Now!'

She dipped her head to examine the cork, her

hair falling on either side of her face. 'Claude, help me open it!'

Claude's first instinct was horror. '*Non, non!* That's all the more reason to keep it. It's been here for so long . . . it's so valuable . . .'

Who was this Valentine, the tender and lovely woman, who now wanted to dash a treasure of history? He slowly took the bottle from her and carefully replaced it on its side. He watched her surrender, disappointment in her eyes. The silence around them was punctuated by an occasional drip. He took her empty hands in his and peered into her dark blue eyes. In this slightly claustro-phobic place, weren't the two of them also corked in a centuries-old airtight bottle of sorts? Inside, there lingered no thought of the looming future, no concept of hands wishing to destroy precious vintages. Courageously, he kissed Valentine's upturned, inviting, rose-colored lips.

A closed, cool meeting of lips. There was more here, though: he sensed desire, a flood of welcoming beyond the gates. She broke away and looked down, shivering.

'I'm sorry you came to me for a wedding dress,' he whispered.

'I am too,' Valentine said quietly. It seemed they both held their breath. Then, quickly, she added, moving back and out and into who she must be, 'You know, I should go in. It's cold in here and – Victor . . .'

She moved quickly now, five steps ahead of

Claude when they reentered the clamorous party room. Victor caught sight of them immediately.

'But my darling.' He was at her side. 'I've searched seven tunnels for you. I have my entourage looking in the other hundred.'

She laughed. 'I was giving Claude a little tour. I wanted to taste a wine from the eighteenth century, but Claude would have nothing of it.'

Victor's eyes registered confusion. 'Oh. Well, come, come, mademoiselle the wine docent!' He took his fiancée by the waist. 'My father arrived half an hour ago and would like to be greeted by the hostess herself. *Viens!*'

As she glided out of his view into the kaleidoscope of color and movement, Claude caught a sliver of the face that turned back to look at him: torn and apologetic.

He glanced at his watch: 9:38 P.M. Valentine had forgotten to introduce him to her mother. Or had she decided against it? He was tempted to stay, to meet Madame and Monsieur de Verlay, but instead he headed for the exit and flew up the stairs, two at a time, out of the cave of centuries of pain to his orange Peugeot. With no notice of the Paris whose every delicious detail had left him entranced just two hours earlier, he drove blindly to the autoroute, out of La Grande Ville.

CHAPTER 6

On the drive home in the rain, one thought filled and stretched the seams of Claude's mind: Mademoiselle de Verlay must not love her fiancé. If she did, wouldn't she have lingered starry-eyed by her betrothed's side instead of leading a stranger into a remote cave and allowing him to kiss her?

'Squawk yourself!' Claude scolded Pédant as he hung up his raincoat. He sat down to study the next day's schedule. The calendar scribbles blurred as he reflected on Valentine's party.

Who were those faces? The red lips and flawless complexions, the unmovable, stylized hair. Were they masks under which real beings lived, or machinery wound up to speak and move? Did they care for Valentine de Verlay? How was one to tell who anyone was? Between the outward face and the inner being loomed a vast and mysterious terrain.

There were those whose appearances lit the way to their souls, like his sister Juliette and his friend the pastor Anatole. Instead of revealing herself, Valentine seemed to illuminate those around her.

Who knew what really lay behind the neverending blue of her eyes?

Surely, Valentine was captivated by Victor's strong presence, his compelling voice, his warm green eyes. Even Claude had felt the tug of the man's dynamism. Against his will, Claude imagined how stunning their children would be.

Sleepless and restless during the night and the early hours of morning, Claude began to design something more compelling than dresses: he drafted ways to win over Valentine. His ponderings continued during church the next day. I will write her a note, he thought, during the priest's homily about John the Baptist. I will ask if she would like me to design her a fall wardrobe, he resolved during prayers.

Back home, he decided to call her. 'Pédant, quiet! She'll be out, I know she will. Simply thank her for the party and mention that I'll be in Paris on Tuesday. Could she meet me for a bite at midday? We have yet to discuss the wedding party's attire. Yes, yes, that's good.

'Valentine, *tu es là?*' She was there. He continued. 'Le Saint-Louis for lunch, just over the bridge on Île Saint-Louis? Tuesday? *Très bien.* I will see you there.' Finished, the receiver replaced.

Tuesday came, undeserved and more quickly than Claude could have imagined. The day drizzled gray. Claude shortened two of his jackets and tried one on in front of the mirror. He looked better than he remembered, healthier, stronger. He leaned out his back door and nodded at the age-old apple tree, as if for approval.

Claude's sister Juliette had once told him that Île Saint-Louis and Île de la Cité, the petite boat-shaped islands on the Seine River, were the geographical heart of France: all French distances measured from point zero, just outside Notre-Dame. How fitting that he had situated his rendezvous with Valentine there, in the very heart of France!

Le Saint-Louis, the intimate wood-lined café on the little square off the bridge, was renowned for its *tarte aux pommes,* one of which rested in the corner window of the restaurant, winter and summer alike. Claude was familiar with the café from his days as a young tailor, when he bought muslin from a Turkish shop in the nearby Latin Quarter. (In those days, Claude draped muslin on his mannequin before cutting into expensive fabric.) After several trips to his car with the heavy portage, Claude would often reward himself with a café au lait and a slice of the apple tart at Le Saint-Louis and watch the swallows on a summer's midday swoop in and out of the window as if they were part of the pie's filling.

Punctual as usual, Claude took a seat at the best table, just inside the door, under the tart-laden windowsill. A light rain blew fresh moist air into the room. Before he knew it, Valentine's slender figure blocked the dim light from the doorway. Her dark brown hair was swept back from her face in a chignon. Her arched brows echoed the shape of her almond eyes as they squinted in the darkness to find him.

When their eyes met, a smile escaped. He stood to greet her; their heads danced in cheek kisses, the scent of her soft lilac perfume escaping him.

'Excuse me for taking you away from work. You must be so busy,' he said, as he waited for her to sit down.

She wore a white and yellow wisp of a dress in crêpe de chine with a softly ruffled neckline. The yellow was too pale for her skin. Why was everything she wore not quite good enough?

'Ah, but it's the other way around, Claude.' Her eyes smiled. 'All the women in Paris say Claude Reynaud is too busy to design a dress for them! They anguish over this and that gathering and who will be wearing which of your dresses. You were the most talked-about guest at my party!'

'Monsieur, madame.' The white-aproned waiter curtly interrupted them. 'What may I bring you to drink?' he asked, unsheathing two menus from his side pocket as if they were swords.

Claude looked quickly at the wine list and ordered the house Bordeaux from Saint-Émilion. As a child, he had visited Saint-Émilion's vineyards. He remembered looking out a tall castle window, transfixed by the sun-doused red-tiled roofs.

As he closed the menu, Claude noticed that the sky outside had darkened. They heard thunder in the distance. Intermittent raindrops pattered on the outer edge of the windowsill; random drops fell on their table. An older full-figured woman in a white apron that fell to her wide calves bustled over to them.

'*Oh-la-la, la pluie! Excusez-moi!*' She reached awkwardly over their table, her heavy upper torso nearly overturning their wineglasses as she retrieved the tart from the now-drenched sill. Both hands on the sill, the patroness lost her footing for a moment and, with a shriek, overturned the café's famous *tarte aux pommes* into Valentine's lap.

'Oh, madame!' Valentine cried, a hint of annoyance in her voice. With cupped hands, she unloaded the pie in pieces from her dress onto the empty pie plate on the table. Raindrops landed on her face and hair. Claude quickly closed the creaky wooden windows.

'What a mess!' Valentine said. As she looked at him, she surprised him with a laugh, the giddy giggle of a playful child.

Claude leaned over the table and tried to wipe the stain with his napkin. '*Comme c'est fou!*' he said, looking around for another napkin.

'*Venez!* Come with me and we'll wash you up,' the proprietor of the restaurant ordered Valentine, as if she were at fault for the rain and the fallen tart. When she returned, Claude could not help but notice that Valentine's bikini underwear was clearly visible through the dress. 'I know a fairly good shop nearby,' he said, as the waiter poured the wine into their glasses. 'Please allow me to treat you to a new dress before you return to work.'

The sound of rain near their window table drowned out much of the lunchtime noise. After they had ordered their entrées and main courses, Claude asked, in the most natural voice he could muster, how she had met Victor.

'I was ten years old. He was twelve. His father was a childhood friend of my father's and convinced my parents to buy a neighboring property in Normandy. For two summers, we stayed in their house until ours was renovated. We played together from that summer until we went to university. We rode his horses and picnicked on every field in Normandy. We told each other our deepest secrets and made hundreds of promises that we sealed with kisses. We felt as if we owned everything we saw, even the cows, to which we gave our future children's names, starting with the letter A. I remember one very ugly-looking Hubert . . .'

Claude watched jealously as her face glowed in happy reflection. He fidgeted with his knife and fork.

'I rode Sugar,' she continued, 'a perfectly white pony, and Victor rode Spice, black as black. The ponies would not leave the stable without each other; they would stomp their hooves, shake their manes, and buck and kick if separated and trot stubbornly back to the other's side. That's how we behaved. We made a pact that nothing would separate us. And it was true; we've been apart only for a short time, when I studied art history at the Sorbonne and Victor was working in England, and then later, when I was at the École du Louvre and he was working at the Uffizi.'

Claude gulped. His head felt heavy, as if his neck might snap. While they were at the Sorbonne, the École du Louvre, the Uffizi, he had been at the Fashion Institute in Grenoble or home in Senlis.

'But now' – she looked down into the just-served onion soup; her brow tightened – 'now, I'm so confused. You . . . Victor . . . the approaching marriage. A life's decision. My parents, Victor's father, all helping with the wedding plans . . . to the smallest detail, like the color of the ink on the table place cards.' She stirred her soup and raised the cheese coating, then curled it around her spoon. He held his breath, leaving his *foie gras de canard* untouched.

'Oh! Enough of me!' She broke the moment of soup-involved consternation. 'You, my talented dressmaker, tell me about you! How did you develop such a gift? Look at those fingers . . .'

She left her spoon in the soup and took Claude's hand into hers. He wanted to pull it away; it was sun-stained with freckles and dark spots, coarse and calloused on the underside.

'They're so long, but what a practical palm. It's huge!' She measured it against her own. 'It's three

61

times mine! These hands have made so many women think differently about themselves. You should hear them talk. "Claude Reynaud has changed my life," they say. "I never felt so good as I did in that sequined gown last Saturday night. Even my husband noticed."' She laughed. 'I don't think you realize the stir you create!'

'You flatter me,' he said, bowing his head, his hand awkward in her grasp. He shut his eyes as he gently pushed back her fingers and noticed how far they opened, which, one of his clients had told him, indicated generosity.

The rain fell in sheets outside as the entrées were cleared and the main courses arrived. In between bites, Valentine told Claude about Drouot and her work in the auction house's nineteenth-century painting department, how she had uncovered two fakes the previous year, which had been ready for the auction block valued at millions of euros. He described the designs he had in mind for the fall, how the Parisian social calendar now dictated his hours. Theirs was the talk of intimate, easy friends.

When the waiter returned with the dessert menus, Valentine glanced down at her dress, then at her watch.

'I'd better get going,' she said.

'There's a shop just across the street,' said Claude, placing his credit card on the table.

She dipped into her purse. 'Come, let's split this.'

'All right, but on the condition that you let me

choose another dress. You can't go back to Drouot looking like that.'

She looked down. 'I guess you're right. I have a meeting . . .'

'We'll be fast.' The waiter returned with their credit cards. Neither carried an umbrella. They jumped puddles across the street.

In the shelter of the small boutique, Claude ran his fingers over the racks with his eyes closed, feeling for the right garment as if by instinct. Neither was impressed with the selection. Within five minutes, he had chosen a short navy knit dress with a white ribbon at the waist and a high crew neck.

'Don't worry,' he whispered, holding it up to her. 'The ribbon goes as soon as we're out the door.'

Valentine smiled mischievously, threw a skeptical look at the hanger, and disappeared into the changing room.

'You certainly know my size!' she said, looking pleased as she reemerged. The darkness of the dress, cut so close to her neck, gave her pale face a bright luster.

'I *never* would have chosen this,' she said, as she scrutinized his face. 'Thank you.' The wrinkled ball of the stained wet dress fit miraculously into her purse.

He settled with the shopkeeper and asked if she wanted a ride back to the office.

'I'd love it,' she said.

'About the ribbon.' He boldly inspected the thin white silk ribbon just below her chest. 'It makes the dress look too girlish. We'll need some scissors. I might have some in my car.'

Back in the pouring rain, they half ran, half walked across the pont Saint-Louis and along the rue Notre-Dame to Claude's car. Claude remembered he had parked on a side street, but he had not thought to notice the street name. Running down the rue Chanoinesse, their clothes were drenched and cold within minutes.

'How strange, how strange,' Claude muttered to himself, shaking his head, hardly breathing for his stupidity. They crossed back to the rue Notre-Dame, which bordered an intimate, tidy garden called the square Jean XXIII, behind Notre-Dame.

She looked at her watch, and he heard her take a deep breath. Then, in that way that never failed to surprise him, she laughed, as if she were looking down at the two of them from the top of the world and found what she observed amusing.

'It *must* be somewhere near here.'

'Claude, I will take a taxi.' She laughed, water streaming down her face, a slash of mascara under her eye.

They spotted a lit taxi stand on the other side of the square. As they entered the garden overlooking the buttresses of the cathedral, they left the noisy cars and splashing behind. The soil bordering the freshly washed gravel paths was alive with verdant newborn grass. Robins hopped about with inflated breasts. Claude was struck by the stunning patterns of brown on the wet trunks of the chestnut trees. How curious to be amazed by the abundance of nature in this gray city.

He put his arm around Valentine's waist. Her velvet eyes settled on him briefly, like a butterfly on a bush. Claude turned her to face him, almost as if preparing to dance, and, in the blinding wetness, kissed her smiling lips. He led her to a nearby bench, and they sat down wordlessly, eyes closed and warm lips joined.

'I should be getting back.' She said it quietly, unhurriedly, unwillingly, as if it were rehearsed and had been repeated thousand of times. But her lips stayed with his.

Within moments, she had withdrawn. Still holding hands, they headed back toward the now-visible taxi stand. Several dry people under umbrellas smiled at them.

'Shall we have a quick Pernod before you go back?' he asked quickly.

'Who are you, Claude Reynaud?' She turned to face him and smiled. 'How *can* I have just met you? Why do you make me forget everything? I feel so alive with you, so completely understood from head to toe. How do you do that?'

They had arrived at the taxi stand, the Pernod offer a nameless drop of rain.

'If I knew you so well,' Claude began, as a taxi splashed to the stand, 'I would not have to ask you this one most perplexing question.'

'What?' She smiled, her hand waving at the arriving taxi. She had already left him.

He whispered it to her. 'Do you love your fiancé?'

He wasn't sure if she had heard. She was opening the door of the taxi. 'Why must you spoil our fun, Monsieur Reynaud, after such a lovely rainy afternoon in the garden of Notre-Dame?'

The door was shut; the pelting rain and dark sky swallowed up the black taxi with the pale face and waving hand. As he walked pensively back through the hushed, deserted square behind Notre-Dame, Claude spotted his orange Peugeot, which he had parked within a block of the café.

CHAPTER 7

Back in his studio, Pédant on his shoulder, Claude sat at his desk in his wet clothes and wrote the letter to his wife that he had composed mentally dozens of times in the last few weeks. He would ask his cousin, who had mentioned running into her in Avignon the previous summer, for her address.

> Dear Rose-Marie,
> I hope this finds you well. After all these years apart, I think it is appropriate that we seek a legal divorce. Please have your lawyer call mine, Jacques Delmond, 04 45 98 72 36, who will expedite this matter with the least inconvenience to us both.
> Sincerely,
> Claude

Somewhat cold and unfriendly, he thought, for the woman I married before God. He had not seen her in eight years, but the thought of her still evoked a lurking sense of sorrow and regret.

He had a few good memories, which he had accumulated and stored up to use when they'd been married, to carry him through the rough days. One was gazing at her before she awoke in the morning, before consciousness recontoured the dimensions of her face, before her eyes became alive with scrutiny and her lips pouted in displeasure. There, under the light-red curls on the pillowcase, on the creamy face bespeckled with delicate, vulnerable freckles, rested a sweet upturned smile, seldom seen when she was awake.

Claude would have remained married to Rose-Marie if she hadn't left him. But now he was grateful for her departure. He recalled how, after only six months of marriage, his visits to Juliette and his parents had become solitary events. She derided his family as simple country folk. They lacked sophistication and taste. She dismissed his father as a doddering old fuddy-duddy. She said his mother smelled of potato soup. As time went on, she rarely accompanied him to family events, and he began omitting mentions of his family in their conversations.

He would post the letter proposing divorce tomorrow.

With a load of work piled high on his table and still no sewing help, Claude worked until midnight and rose again at 7 A.M. He worked without passion to get the job done, his energy diverted by nonstop strategizing for his next rendezvous with Valentine.

They had not discussed the color and design of Valentine's nieces' dresses and her nephew's outfit. Time was running out. Her marriage was now only two and a half months away. Even Pédant was an irritation.

'Enough, Pédant, you squawk too much. Why can't you sing like any other bird?'

Only when his four nephews showed up at teatime did he manage to escape his distracted state of alternating despondency and exuberance. The boys provided the combustion he needed to elude, for a short time, the almost inescapable image of Valentine's beckoning blueberry eyes.

Henri, who at fourteen was no longer amused by his uncle's puppet shows, asked if he could play a CD. The rap song repeated the unfortunate words: '*Pourquoi est-ce-qu'il l'aime?* Why does he love her? Who is he to her? . . . She would never, could never, will never . . .'

The same old story for centuries! 'Would you please turn that off?'

'Oh, please, Uncle Claude,' Henri begged. '*Maman* doesn't let me play this at home.'

The other boys ran around the studio, oblivious.

'Henri, why do you like this song?'

'Uncle,' Henri said impatiently, quickly deflated by anticipating the usual grown-up tirade on the good, the bad, and the ugly, 'I don't listen to the words; I know they're stupid, but the music – it's cool. Listen.'

The hard-edged beat muffled the vocalist's words.

For a moment, Claude had the desire to spill his heart's contents to the mature Henri.

'You can listen for a few more minutes,' he told him. 'Then I must get you home and myself back to work.'

As he watched Henri shut his eyes and move his shoulders to the beat, Claude felt dizzy. Was it the music or the same dinner he'd had for four nights in a row or his lack of sleep? Or was this motion sickness a result of the swift passage of time, the clock's ticking irrevocably toward Valentine's wedding? He had always disdained those weak-minded souls who slept wastefully through their lives and complained, 'Where has the time gone?' But now, Claude thought, it has happened to me as well! I wasn't watching, and now I am an old man!

Henri, whom Claude remembered scuffling around in red flannel oversized bedroom slippers, his teddy bear dragging by his side, was now making a case for rap music. On the backs of his own hands, Claude noticed some brown age spots he knew too well as his father's.

He thought of Valentine in the rain, her smiling lips, waiting for him to transform her life. He shut his eyes to retrieve the image of her in the navy knit dress in the rain. How many rainy seasons had he spent without companionship? How many summers of his life remained?

'Come, nephews!' Claude said, impatiently, unusually acridly. 'Uncle Claude must get back to work!'

'But we haven't had our puppet show,' whined the youngest, Arthur.

Henri had found Claude's blue graph paper on his desk and was sketching. He glanced up at the mannequin at the center of the room at regular intervals. 'Let me just finish this drawing, Uncle.'

Claude took a peek over his shoulder. Henri was sketching a girl's figure. She wore wide culottes and bell-shaped sleeves to match.

'Interesting!' said his uncle.

'An outfit my friend Pascale can ride in. I'd like her to wear something like this, like a wild Russian Gypsy, the kind we used to read about, doing handstands and flips on the backs of horses.'

Henri drew a face, erased the eyes, drew them again, erased them again.

'Try not to look at your sketch as you draw.' Claude pulled up a chair. 'There. Now continue with the pencil, not lifting it. No, don't peek! Let your eyes translate the shapes without watching what you're doing.'

The sketch grew confident as the artist looked away.

'Now look!'

'Thanks, Uncle. That's much better.'

With a flick of the pencil, Henri had managed to depict a shimmer in the figure's eyes. His nephew was well acquainted with his subject.

'The show!' begged Arthur, holding the bag of puppets up to his uncle.

'Not today! So sorry! Mui-Mui the baker has a

terrible cold. The others are too busy taking care of her – you know how she complains unbearably – and they don't want to expose you to her microbes. Aren't they thoughtful?'

He tweaked Arthur's nose and watched Henri roll his eyes.

'*A bientôt*. See you soon! Big kisses to your mama and papa! *Au revoir.*'

One, two, three, four, out the thick oak door and into the busy car-beeping late afternoon. Peace. Grandfather clock, ticktock. As usual, Didier had left the small door at the bottom of the clock open, so the clock ticked louder than usual. This time, Claude resisted his inclination to close it. He wanted to be aware of the time passing.

CHAPTER 8

'Claude, live a little! If anyone could use a vacation, it's *you*! The house is yours! Take it for a weekend, a week, a month!'

Claude's friend Richard, Rico for short, with whom he had attended the Fashion Institute in Grenoble and who now designed his own ready-to-wear 'easy-to-wear' fashion line labeled RICHE, had repeatedly invited Claude to visit his house in Vevey, a small resort town on Switzerland's Lake Geneva. Claude saw Rico twice a year, when Rico returned home to Paris from the whirlwind of his life around the world, usually with a new girlfriend on each arm.

The short, dark-skinned, thickly eyebrowed, Italian-French dandy of a dresser loved to tease his friend, whom he had nicknamed Claude Chaud, Hot Claude, during their days together at the institute. Rico had a habit of ascribing to his friends the attributes they did *not* possess.

'You're too cold, Claude!' he scolded now. 'You need heat. You need a lover! That's right, for your circulation, to get your blood going! You're turning into a reptile before my eyes.'

After graduating from the Fashion Institute, Rico

had begged Claude to join him in starting a design company in Paris. He had the perfect name for their outfit: Chaud et Froid: Hot and Cold. Claude declined. His father needed him in the shop. Rico had thrown up his hands in frustration.

'Claude Chaud, you're more talented than I, but you lack ambition. You are so peaceful – too peaceful, in my opinion – and I, I am a man of many conflicts. It is true; my restlessness maims my talent. I'm not happy unless I'm moving, designing, partying, and laughing, always laughing.'

Claude recalled Rico's invitation to use his house. 'You see, Claude, a house is like a gown. You must live in it, laugh in it, dine in it, spill on it, love it enough to make it pulse and vibrate. A house needs human voices like we need air.'

After he had gathered the flattened pillows used as bombs by his nephews, Claude contacted the roaming Rico to ask if he could stay at the house for a short vacation. Claude wondered if he had ever used the word before.

'But of course, Claude! I am so proud of you! Finally!'

He called Valentine when he thought she would be at home, nine o'clock on Wednesday.

'*Bonsoir.* Good evening,' she answered.

'Valentine, it's Claude. A friend has offered me his house in Vevey for the weekend. I know this sounds strange, but might you like a break from Paris?'

His boldness shocked him. A pause.

'What a coincidence! That's so funny. I'm actu-

74

ally going to Geneva on Friday to visit a client. Perhaps we could meet while I'm there. I will get back to you in the morning.' No good-bye, no lingering or hesitation, no sweet voice. She had hung up the phone. Victor must have been in the room. A lion in a lamb's meadow, he would be listening for the pauses, for the heat in his lamb's voice, her unspoken words.

Jealousy added renewed vigor to Claude's work. Madame Blouton needed a hat for a baptism next week. Claude's grandfather was the Reynaud who had extended the family tailoring business to include millinery. Although hat production in the Reynaud home business had trailed off in recent years, many clients continued to request bonnets months in advance, for weddings and for the horse-racing season in nearby Chantilly.

Normally, Claude enjoyed designing hats. The hat was the icing on the cake, an essential part of the whole that added dimension and often delight. Madame Blouton was one of his few clients who could really wear a hat, never treating it as merely an elaborate accessory.

Claude had studied Madame Blouton's head: he noticed how she tipped it to the left when she asked a question and elevated it, as if it were a radio tower antenna, to receive an answer. But, today, as he threw the lace over the top and arranged the orange and red ribbons that he and madame had jointly chosen after giggles and glances in the mirror, he began to wonder if hats weren't silly anachronisms. Wasn't this

75

combination of orange and red garish and unacceptable for church? The wide brim, pinned up with a bright red gauzy ribbon, would be more suitable for a nightclub dancer. He wrapped and rewrapped it, sewed it, and detailed the edges with an eye-length netting.

The telephone.

'Yes? . . . Hello, Valentine,' he said.

'It turns out I *can* meet you. My client told me she wouldn't see me unless I visited Vevey, one of her absolute favorite lakeside towns.'

Enthusiasm in her voice. He tried to control the elation in his response. 'I've heard there's a restaurant on the lake called Café Diderot that is quite good,' he offered. It was set: noon, Saturday. He scribbled her cell phone number. *'A bientôt.'* He hung up the phone.

He placed Madame Blouton's hat on his head and then tossed it in the air. In the mirror across the room, he caught sight of the swirling orange and red ribbons. The image was one of a head on fire.

The train screeched into the Gare de Lyon railway station. Claude revisited his plans: arrive 6 P.M. in Geneva; drive rental car forty-five minutes to Vevey; open the house; next day, check and reserve a table at Café Diderot, where he would lunch with Valentine. Valentine, Valentine, Valentine. Could he ever imagine her choosing *him* over the handsome Victor?

Once seated inside the lurching train, Claude

was taken with childlike wonder by the moving landscape. It had been years since his eyes had fed on terrain other than the humble scene outside his windows at home or on the streets of Paris. Compact one-story houses and orderly farm buildings, greenery in endless horizontal rows, and ceaseless cows sped by. He took note of the brown stripes on green and the eye-catching black-and-white pattern of cows' hides, blurred by the train's speed. From the window, his mind touched the jagged edges of fieldstone on a small house nuzzling a hillside.

A nearby loud cough diverted Claude's attention from the sun-warmed fields. Sitting stiffly across from him was a gaunt gray-haired man, reading a newspaper. With astonishing regularity, he shuffled the newspaper, coughed three times, and slurped noisily from a silver flask, which he lifted to his mouth with trembling fingers.

Having succeeded in attracting his train mate's attention, the stranger asked in a hoarse voice if Claude could give him the name of an inexpensive hotel in Geneva. Claude told the man he was not familiar with Geneva but said he was sure the Geneva train station housed an information booth.

'No matter,' the old man said nonchalantly. 'I'm going there to die, so lodging shouldn't be important.'

'Excuse me, sir?'

'You heard correctly.' The man coughed three

times and put down his trembling newspaper. 'I thought Geneva would be a nice place to die in.'

With the paper withdrawn, Claude could observe the man's bone-exposed body. 'Why not try living there first?'

'Living' – the three coughs – 'it takes too long.'

Claude looked out the window. He noticed a church spire, snug in a distant city in a valley far away. It seemed a mirage, the answer this man sought.

Two short coughs, then a long-drawn-out one. 'I've never liked the wind in Brittany. That's where I'm from, a small town named Presqu'ile de Quiberon. In spring, the wind beats the west coast from the Atlantic.' Double cough. 'In summer, it blows; in winter, it storms. The cliffs are' – cough . . . cough . . . cough . . . swig – 'punished daily by the sea.' Cough, cough. 'It's beaten me. There's no rest, no peace. Now, Geneva!' The old man shut his eyes as his chest convulsed once again.

Claude too had sought the quietude of the muffled earth, clinging to his small home and town. But now, he thought, as he straightened his back, he wanted the wind this frail man was escaping. It was his turn to thrash about in life, in love's thrall. His every muscle strained wildly for Valentine.

The old man coughed until he could no longer hold his newspaper. His already cracked glasses dropped to the floor. Claude picked them up and patted the man's back. Closer up now, the deep lines in this man's face reminded him of his father's wrinkles. Had his father found peace?

'There you go, monsieur. Please, let me help you.'

Claude cleaned the man's glasses on his shirt and handed them and the newspaper back to him. Once his train mate was settled and asleep, Claude found himself monitoring the old man's forceful breathing, in and out, as if the watching would make each gasp more peaceful.

When the first signs of morning arrived in the form of reflected lake shimmer on the white wall opposite Rico's bed, Claude arose gratefully. Rico's elegant house, tucked into arbors that lined the lake, was only a short walk from the one-street town, to which he headed now for a newspaper and coffee.

As he strolled, Claude surrendered himself to the charms of Vevey, surrounded on three sides by softly rising mountains, ringed ephemerally with lofty white clouds, and mirrored in the sheet-glass surface of the lake. Other sun-dappled towns littered the coast to the east. Not a hint of turbulence disturbed the thick parallel brushstrokes of blue lake water.

He stopped in at Café Diderot. The pale yellow tablecloths, the yellow-and-white gingham napkins, the yellowing-from-the-sun lace curtains, puckered at the rod, even the small light oakwood chairs, resembled the fittings of a doll's house, well kept by a dutiful little girl. Claude asked the elderly woman who was fussing with a curtain if he could reserve a particular table for a midday lunch for two.

'*Oui*, monsieur, that table next to the fireplace is the best in the house, just a little light coming in from the south window.'

'Thank you very much,' Claude said. 'I'll take it.'

For the remainder of the brisk morning, Claude thrust himself into the world of joggers, walkers, bikers, and Rollerbladers along the lake path bordering the café. Around the next corner, where the path tightened between the lake and an unusually large and golden-leafed copper beech, he found himself walking behind a couple who unknowingly blocked his passage. They talked busily to each other, unaware of him and his desire to move around them. The tall man's left hand clutched the very slim waist of the woman, who was wearing a pale blue spring suit – good cloth, what looked to be a linen-and-silk combination but lighter material than that – no, it looked fluid, too fluid for linen. She wore boots. Boots at this time of year? He slowed his pace. Boots, beige suede, which had the effect of making her legs appear very long, gazellelike.

He studied the woman's back, her skirt length. Her resemblance to Valentine was like a stab in the heart. Same length of deep brown hair just below the shoulders. The woman twirled the ends of her hair around her fingers!

Claude closed the distance between them. No arm but Victor's would hold a waist like that, as if possessing it. Did she smile? Impossible! She talked, it seemed, with alacrity. Her gait was a skip. She nodded her head. She swung her purse. She swung her purse again!

Claude wiped his brow. Looking only at the man's back, Claude pictured Victor's chest thrust forward, like the first robin of creation pronouncing the arrival of spring.

He forced his legs to double back in the direction of the restaurant. He hated this couple, their dance and the swinging beige purse. How predictable that the purse matched the boots. How pedestrian and unoriginal.

She had forgotten about their lunch. He looked around one last time to catch sight of her chin tilting upward. 'At the very least,' he encouraged her, 'look at your watch!' He checked his: 12:06 P.M. 'Tell him it's time to head back, you must honor your appointment with your true love Claude, the idiotic tailor!'

Hopeless, his heart black, his mind empty, he dragged himself into the pale yellow gingham restaurant overlooking the maddeningly still lake.

He took his preordained seat, prepared to wait out lunchtime. From the window, he glimpsed the top balcony of Rico's retreat. He imagined Rico lounging in the sun there, laughing, champagne flute in hand, with Rico-clad women touching his silk shirtsleeves.

'Throw yourself into life!' Rico would tell him. 'Drink it up!'

But he had, and it had a bitter taste. What *had* he come to, to find himself alone in a restaurant, awaiting a lover who was planning to be married to another man?

A long-legged woman with bleached-blond hair in a pale-yellow gingham apron that matched the napkins approached Claude's table.

'*Qu'est-ce que vous voulez boire, monsieur?* What would you like to drink?' In the sunshine, her eyelashes matched the tawny gold color of the dangling tassels on the window shades.

'*Un Pernod, s'il vous plaît.*'

Valentine would not show up. He wanted to crawl under the table.

Four of the remaining six tables were now occupied, and a gentle bubble of talk floated near his lonely chair. The low-level background chatter was punctuated, at one point, by a thick bronchial cough. Claude craned his neck, seeking his train friend, but the sound had emanated from a buxom elderly lady wearing a red sweater.

How long would he continue to wait, an hour? A night? She would not come. She is running to be here on time. He set himself a half-hour departure time.

He devoted the next ten minutes to reflecting on the ways he detested the restaurant, the town, the lake, and, most particularly, the tomato-red sweater of the woman at the next table. How *could* she choose that red? The color was too bright, too audacious for her large frame. Against the yellow gingham sunlight, the color was surely more of a nauseating lurid orange.

The restaurant door opened to a light-blue skirt, long beige boots, and a man's off-white linen single-pleat pant legs. Valentine and Victor stood looking down at Claude, seated at the romantic lakeview table for two.

'*Bonjour,* Claude, we're so sorry to have kept you waiting,' she said. 'We were walking along the lake.'

'Please, mademoiselle, another chair.' Claude's voice sounded shrill and demanding as he stood abruptly and addressed the mimosa-haired waitress. Victor took the chair from the waitress with one hand, held it up high, and slid it in place. The waitress jangled the silverware loudly as she set another place.

'Victor surprised me!' Valentine said quickly, as she took her chair. 'He jumped out at me at the train station and gave me the scare of a lifetime! I wanted to call you, but Victor insisted we have two surprises today: one for me and one for you.'

Despite his anger, Claude found her blue eyes sweet enough to eat. The light-blue suit – damask, he could see now –was well designed and looked custom-tailored.

Victor pushed a smile into the lower part of his face. 'This seems to be the season for meetings in Switzerland,' he said, winking at Valentine. He placed the gingham napkin in his nap with a flourish.

She glanced quietly at the menu resting on the table.

'But how lovely,' said Claude unconvincingly, 'to have the pleasure of the wedding couple' – he paused – 'together.'

'I'm embarrassed to say,' said Victor, looking only at Valentine, 'it's difficult for me to be away from Valentine for any length of time, even a night.'

He leaned forward and placed his hand over hers on top of the table.

'Just think, darling,' he said, 'in a little over two months we'll be together for a lifetime!' With his right index finger, he caressed the large rectangular sapphire on her ring finger. It was surrounded by small diamonds.

Claude looked at the door.

'You probably don't get to travel that much,' Victor said. 'I would think keeping all those women happily dressed would prove an endless harassment. I *don't* know how you do it.'

He's belittling me, thought Claude, feeling like a shredding scrap of material. He had never been good at rapid-fire witty responses. All their voices seemed fake and disconnected.

Valentine told the two men how exciting it was to have evaluated an Emms painting that morning. 'It's a fox-hunting scene. The painting was very dark, but I'm hoping it's just a matter of lifting years of applied lacquer. It could be worth a lot,' she was saying. Claude noticed that Victor hung on each of Valentine's words, oxygen with which to survive in his breathless, fast-paced world.

While Claude tried to preserve his dignity by nodding his head at the appropriate times and raising the corners of his lips in smiles, his energies were focused on Valentine's face, her gestures, her demeanor.

'Yes, one could say that Valentine's at Drouot because of me.' Victor stroked her hand. 'A secret among the three of us?' Victor grinned. 'I like to keep an eye on her.'

'Victor, give me *some* credit!'

She looked out the window for a flicker of a moment. Claude tried to catch her eye.

'It's true. We're the most fortunate auction house in the world to have secured this woman for our nineteenth-century European painting department. You should see how she lures the buyers and sellers, forges relationships with collectors – like this private collector of Emmses. I'm sure the Emms you evaluated today will bring in a record number this year. Who would think an oil of horses and cocker spaniels would prove so important? My darling will win this consignment with her eyes closed.'

Victor smiled proudly, as if Valentine's attributes were an extension of himself.

One hour into the lunch, Victor alone carried on the discourse. The yellow-gingham afternoon light cast a pallor on Valentine, dulling the blue of her eyes. Her mouth responded, but the look in her eyes seemed far away. Claude deciphered a thin, dark-pink line between her eyebrows. When she lifted a hand to touch her hair, her elbow grazed his jacket. Was this brush unintentional? Claude snapped up the leather folder that enclosed the bill, his hand faster than Victor's.

'If you insist,' Victor said.

As they rose from the table, Victor's leg caught the edge of the tablecloth, unsettling the three wineglasses. Valentine's half-full glass fell to the floor and broke. Victor jumped away from the spray of red wine, brushing his pant leg. He motioned angrily to the waitress.

'There's no room in this place!'

The waitress raised her fringed eyes to the ceiling, then apologized dutifully. Valentine sighed and brushed Claude's cheek with hers. Her cheek felt as soft as the humid lakeside air.

She looked embarrassed, her face pink. 'Thank you for arranging this lunch, Claude. I would still love to talk to you about outfitting our wedding party. Perhaps we could meet tomorrow morning at nine?' She looked across the narrow shop-lined street. 'Let's try another café: that one, Café Turandot au Bord du Lac; yes, that looks just fine. Victor, you may come if you would like to watch Claude – in the throes of yet another harassment.'

'I would enjoy that immensely,' her fiancé replied.

By the time they had separated, Claude had conjured up a dress for Valentine, one that would make all eyes turn, a cream-colored silk crêpe de chine wrapped like a sari; she would be an Indian princess, silk like milk flowing over one shoulder, her eyes the only jewels she needed. Had the furrow between her dark brows reminded him of the red dot, the *bindi,* worn traditionally by married women in India? Dress ideas, suits, accessories solely for Valentine flooded his mind. It occurred to him with the sparkling light of an epiphany: Valentine had become his muse. As Claude headed down the winding streets of Vevey, he found himself retracing his steps on the lakeside path that wound back toward town.

Unbelievably, Claude spotted the couple again, obscured by clusters of strolling adults, dogs on leashes, and running children. He quickened his pace to shorten the distance between them. He kept an eye on Valentine's every motion, her hand at her hair, her elbow moving, the angle of her cheek as she looked up at Victor. He was close enough to observe the ends of her eyelashes, which turned up abruptly, like newly cresting waves. Too close. He drew back. The blue skirt swished back and forth gaily. Victor's walk reminded him of the shuffle of an elderly man in a bathrobe to his shins, wearing slippers, confidently padding his way to the restroom at an outdated seaside resort.

The couple stopped at the white stucco, wood-beamed, pink-geranium-flooded Auberge du Raisin on the place de l'Hôtel de Ville. Claude camouflaged himself among the pedestrians.

When Victor glanced fleetingly in his direction, Claude dashed into a baker's shop to his left. The couple had disappeared when Claude returned to the street.

Had he sunk so low, he thought glumly, that he was stalking Valentine? Was he so hungry for her love that he had to hunt it down, like a beggar for a morsel of bread? What would his father have said? Or Anatole?

Claude had studied bodies all his life. By shadowing Valentine, he had hoped to decipher her state of mind. Despite her occasional laughs and purse-swinging, Claude could not shake the conviction that Valentine was his.

He looked up at the windows of the small inn. Three floors of pale-green-shuttered windows, lined with fuchsia-pink cascading geraniums. Would a shutter open in the few minutes while he looked up? Would Valentine lean out and call, 'Hello, Claude! Come up for some refreshment!' Or would the couple rejoice in the dark privacy of closed shutters, throw back the sheets, and . . . ? Claude shut his eyes. The shutters remained fastened.

Claude thought of his woodpeckered old apple tree. Before he left, he had noticed that the tree's lowest limb leaned heavily downward, almost grazing the grass. Surely, in his absence, this branch had split or broken off from the trunk.

CHAPTER 9

Nine A.M., Café Turandot du Bord du Lac. Valentine was the first to arrive. As if checking the weather, when he first saw her Claude analyzed her outfit: navy cotton skirt to the knees, navy merino crew-neck sweater, silk scarf with beige and gold and light-blue hues entwined, the beige boots, wide slim-framed rectangle sunglasses for the sunny morning. How could she be dressed so simply and look so glamorous? Nothing could shake his delight in her.

'Let's sit outside,' she said cheerfully, as he approached.

They found a table alone outside in a corner, and she nodded to a waiter and ordered quickly, two cafés and two croissants. She turned her now-serious face to his. 'Yesterday, you followed us – Victor and me.'

Claude said nothing.

'You followed us,' she repeated.

There was no going back.

'Claude?'

'Do you love him?'

Her eyebrows knit together as she sipped her coffee. 'Claude,' she said, cup in hand, 'that rainy day outside Notre-Dame . . . I know you must think—' She tried again. 'It's just that you're such a confusion to me . . . You're so sympathetic and responsive and yielding, I could cry. Everything seems so simple with you; everything is so understood.'

She replaced her cup on the saucer. Claude took her hand.

'How is it that you care so much about seemingly insignificant little things?' she asked in a whisper. 'How is it that you care for me?'

'You haven't answered *my* question,' Claude persisted.

'Yes, Claude, yes,' she said, her eyes opened wide. 'There has never been a time when I have not loved Victor. Never. We share a deep love, perhaps a brotherly one, a love that has grown up together. We had romance after romance with each other at different stages of our lives, in school, then out, then in university; after we went our separate ways we were back together again. Victor and I share a love of art, our childhoods, friends, even our families. I adored his mother, who died two years ago. She loved me as the daughter she never had. I can see her face now, when she asked me for grandchildren from the bed she died in. My heart aches at the thought of disappointing her. His father and I are still close, even closer than I am with my own father.

90

'Everything seemed to fit, as if it was meant to be, until – actually, until recently, until the announcement, until the first fitting with you, when the whole thing became so real: the wedding dress, the veil, and you, this lovely person. You've thrown everything into doubt.' She sighed. 'Do I dare change everything?'

Claude placed five euros on the table for the coffees and croissants and took her hand.

'Come with me,' he said.

They left their half-sipped coffee. He led her along the lakeside path to Rico's.

Once inside the front door of Rico's house, the wide-windowed view of the languishing lake embraced them both. In the brilliant shimmer of morning-on-lake sunlight, she dropped into his arms. They kissed: a deep kiss, not the kiss of first-time lovers. He led her to the bedroom. Both seemed to have anticipated the smooth joining of their bodies as a foregone conclusion.

She was silk, soft and pliant, smooth and flowing. The two were nothing more than their bodies with shuttered eyes. Who could say no to such a deep responsive embrace? His mind's eye pictured rolling meadows, one falling over another, grassy, green, rounded hills, another after another, until there was nothing but the vision of moist green, full of morning dew.

He traced the outlines of her full bottom lip, then her smaller upper lip; he placed his index finger on its slight indentation. She smiled, then, as if she had not a care in the world, as if the reality of what was transpiring were irrelevant. Her confidence in the moment confounded him.

Gradually, however, he sensed the change in her. Her legs, her jaw, her shoulders regained definition. He could see the little furrow in her forehead deepening to pink, the color of dusk-brushed roses in his garden.

'This is crazy, isn't it?' she said.

He touched her lips as if to silence them.

'What am I doing?' She turned over and buried her face in the pillow. Out the window, the sun looked worn out.

'Postpone the wedding,' he offered. It seemed the obvious solution.

'But everything's all set, all planned. I feel so at ease with you, as if you're the closest person I've ever known, as if you know every single detail about me and love every detail – but you don't even know me. We've just met. I don't know you.'

He stroked her shiny brown hair. 'I know you.'

'How could you? Do you know, for example' – she lifted her face from the plush pillow – 'that I love nothing better than to lie flat on my back and look up at clouds? In Normandy, where it seems like the clouds have more personality than anywhere else, I could gaze at them for hours. Each one tells tales: about rabbits and men with tall hats and girls jumping rope . . .'

She propped herself up on her elbows.

'But that's me. Dear Claude, what do *you* like

to do, other than falling in love with the women who come to your studio for fittings?'

Claude laughed as he walked his fingertips up her arm to her shoulder. He shut his eyes. 'I suppose I love to stage puppet shows for my nephews. As I stitch the puppet characters out of felt, I imagine the reaction of Didier, who screams with delight, and Arthur, who will be mesmerized to the point of believing they're real. I may have to create a Valentine puppet . . . Mmm . . . what shall she be? A langorous lioness, with a sleek back and ocean-blue eyes that snare her prey?'

Her head sank back on the pillows.

'There, you're doing it again, Claude!' she said, as if from nowhere. 'You keep showing me my reflection, as if you are a lake into which I'm peering. As if your lioness, your wedding gown, your version of me is who I am. But tell me, with all the women in the world at your feet, why are *you* so available at this time of your life? I don't even know how old you are!' She turned to face him. 'Let me guess: forty-two. No; yes, forty-four. That's it.'

'I'm forty-six. I'm married but haven't seen my wife in eight years. I have never been in love before the moment I set eyes on you. Only after I met you did I realize I must seek a divorce.'

'You're married? Claude! You never told me!' She sat up in the bed and narrowed her eyes as she looked into his. 'All this and you're married? Claude, if I had known – well, I don't think we would have . . . you should have told me.' The blueberry eyes became serious and looked deeper into his.

He pulled her down to kiss her. 'I never thought you could love someone simply at the sight of them. I always hated fairy tales, but it has happened to me. The first day I met you, your white face, your sharp chin, your big blue eyes, your weak heart begging, 'Save me, please.' *Et voilà!* I was in love. You see, I'm only doing what you've asked.'

'But – your wife. Where is she? No children? What happened between you?' Her questions erupted.

'I heard from a cousin that she's living in Avignon. That's all I know. We married each other for the wrong reasons. I thought I loved her. She loved me for my talent. When I turned down a job at a major couturier in Paris, she left me. She wanted me in Paris, not in Senlis.'

'Why didn't you take the job?'

Had he heard the question correctly?

'You enjoy the country life, is that it? Paris is too . . . too . . .'

He crafted his words carefully to make sure they would please her. He would do anything for her to love him. 'I thought my life was perfect the way it was. I've changed since then, though.' He told her about his father dying, about Juliette and his nephews. 'My home was who I thought I was. Perhaps I was afraid of Paris; perhaps I was stubborn. My wife pecked at me mercilessly – 'Go, go, go' – until I couldn't tell the difference between her and my parrot.'

'Claude!'

'I still don't know why she has never asked for a divorce. I haven't had a reply to my letter requesting one.'

'You're married!' Valentine repeated to herself. 'I would have thought my friend Charlotte would have told me. Perhaps she doesn't know.' Her hand rested on his chest. 'You married and me almost married,' she said. 'We're a pair, the two of us! The institution is not getting its due respect. I never felt the rush to marry until I turned thirty-five and wished to start a family.'

'But Valentine, you were waiting for *me*.'

She dropped her chin, as if looking for something downward and within.

'I'm confused because I'm all tangled up in you.' She laughed as she tried to unwrap her legs from the sheets and his legs.

'Too late. You're stuck.'

'Please.' She laughed. 'You're right, I am stuck. Okay. What time is it?'

He had wondered when that would come, the arrival of the time. The old watch-checking habit that had comforted him all his life had now turned loathsome.

'No idea,' he said.

'You're impossible.' Her becalmed laugh turned anxious. 'When are you leaving for home?'

'When you do, with you.'

'No wonder your wife couldn't stand you! Come on, you, let me go! I have to look at my watch!

95

Alors.' He could sense her vibrating with a growing panic. He hugged her gently. She hugged him back with ferocity. He felt a scratch on his back. He realized, wincing, that his skin had been scraped by the sharp stone in her engagement ring.

He refrained from calling Valentine the next day. If he sent something, Victor might see it. He searched his mind for the most exquisite gift in the world. Flowers, cliché; a silk scarf, mundane; nothing material could symbolize his love for her – or was it his greed for her, he asked himself, an unrelenting, unsatiable craving? After he packed his bag to return to Senlis, he surveyed the lake. This morning, a misty haze hovered above it, arousing in him a sudden feeling of claustro-phobia. He preferred the rush of the seaside or the breathtaking awe of the mountains to the self-possessed serenity of this lakeside retreat.

Valentine had asked why he hadn't gone to Paris. 'Why Paris, Paris, Paris?' he asked, out loud. Would Paris render him more more attractive, more marketable?

The powder-blue satin cover on Rico's blue-velvet canopy bed was now the crumpled and lonely leftover of the hours before. As Claude tidied up the room and locked the door to the house, he couldn't help thinking that Rico would have been pleased.

CHAPTER 10

Claude's first stop in Senlis was at Juliette's, to pick up Pédant and see his nephews. As he crossed the threshold of the house he loved, he called out, '*Chocolats Suisses!*' Within minutes, four boisterous boys swarmed about him.

Jean-Hugues and Henri pleaded with their uncle to accompany them to the stables to visit the new filly. They didn't own the Belgium-raised Thoroughbred, they explained, but could ride her as much as they wanted. The boys escorted Claude, with Pédant on his shoulder, along the dirt path to the ankle-deep mud of the stable yards. How broad Henri's shoulders had grown!

At the entrance, Pascale, the stable owner's fifteen-year-old daughter, was perched on top of the fence looking blankly in their direction. Henri walked faster when he saw her, leaving his uncle and brother behind.

'Pascale, come with us. Uncle Claude wants to see Marquise,' Henri said, when the others caught up.

Without changing her expression, she jumped off the fence, catching her calf-length skirt on the pole. Pédant screeched and Marquise whinnied and stomped as the four approached.

'Marquise is snorting because she wants to be ridden. She's the most talkative horse. Isn't she beautiful, Uncle Claude?' said Henri. 'And her gait is smoother than ice cream. Pascale, let's give her what she wants and show Uncle how she canters.'

Claude watched Henri hang on Pascale's response.

A quick smile enlivened Pascale's still face. 'I'll go bareback, Henri. Hand me the bridle.' As if repeating an action she'd performed thousands of times, she stretched the leather bridle and bit over the horse's muzzle. Henri, attentive and alert, clasped his hands together to give her foot a lift up.

Now the uncle and two nephews sat atop the railing. Claude glanced over at Henri, who was ingesting every ounce of the rider: the strawlike straggle of hair whipping behind her, the skirt hoisted to reveal legs strongly gripping the Thoroughbred, her eyes and lips, even her nose, quivering and alert.

Horse and girl moved fluidly at a canter around the ring two times. Even without a saddle and stirrups, she took the horse gracefully across two barrel jumps. She smiled brightly at Claude and the boys as she gently pulled the horse to a trot and approached them.

Henri held out his hand to help her down. They laughed over something. 'See you back at the house,' Henri said, waving to his uncle and brother, their cue to leave. Claude watched the couple enter the barn with the horse. For a moment, he was tempted to follow them inside, to witness their sweet exchange as they fed, washed, and curried the shining horse. Instead, he took Jean-Hugues's hand and, with the now-quiet Pédant sleeping on his shoulder, the three retreated up the worn path to the house.

Once in the kitchen, Juliette peppered Claude with questions.

'Where have you been? How is your little love?'

He told Juliette about his weekend in Vevey.

'My poor brother! After all these years! You and Henri should spend more time together! But, Claude, be careful,' Juliette said. 'This could be your wedding-gown woman's last hurrah, a last brief playtime before she takes the leap of faith into marriage. Even I had a meaningless little fling minutes before my marriage.'

'But you were madly in love with Bernard!'

'You told me she said she loved her fiancé.'

'Yes, but I'm convinced she doesn't. I know it as well as I know that your jacket is riding too high on your hips. Juliette, you didn't wear that to work?'

She laughed, pulling the bottom of the jacket down with one hand as she bent to lift a cast-iron skillet from the drawer under the oven.

'Critical brothers must cook dinner,' she said, handing him the pan.

With Pédant screeching, Claude approached his home. Had he forgotten to turn off the hall light in his hurried departure for the train? When he turned the key, the door locked rather than opened. Had he also neglected to lock the front door? He hung his coat in the closet and surveyed the premises. Pédant fluttered to his rest post. A dismaying pile of fabric to be sewn, a stack of unfinished blue-pencil design sketches. What was this? Opened mail on his drafting table? Who had taken his mail inside and opened it? His ears straining, he heard a slight stirring in his bedroom. Pitch-dark. He switched on the light in his bedroom. A shape between his sheets! Tiptoeing closer, he caught a glimpse of red hair on the white pillow. He quickly extinguished the light and quietly withdrew, delicately closing the door. He shushed and grabbed his parrot and his coat and left.

He ran down the crooked, unlit, deserted rue du Châtel, knocked at Anatole's door, then rang the bell impatiently. The night was chilly.

His friend opened the door in an ankle-length brown cotton bathrobe, a book in hand, the dark pupils of his brown eyes surrounded by whites so bright they reminded Claude of eggshells. Anatole smiled when he saw Claude with Pédant in tow.

'What a surprise!' he said. 'The Lord's day is not yet over!'

Anatole closed the space between them and hugged his friend vigorously. Claude had known Anatole since their first day of school, when they had become instant friends. Anatole was the last of three boys, the older two of whom were very athletic. From the age of two, Anatole preferred planting in the garden with his grandfather to kicking a soccer ball with his peers. The young Anatole pulled weeds while his grandfather reminisced lengthily, mostly about his three years as a prisoner of war in Germany.

For as long as Claude could remember, Anatole had spoken about God. As a teenager, Anatole had fallen in love several times, but when he was sixteen he told Claude he wanted to join the church.

'But Anatole' – Claude recalled his anger – 'that means you can't get married! How stupid! What a waste of life! We'll never be friends! And you'll always be telling me what I'm doing wrong.'

He remembered Anatole laughing and then explaining how he had been drawn, 'as if by a magnet,' into church one Saturday afternoon. The monseigneur of the church talked quietly to a small group of people. Without realizing it, Anatole found himself in the first pew, enrapt as the holy man discussed the beauty and sancity of the priesthood. He told Claude that this was the day he was 'called by the Lord.'

'May I stay here tonight, Anatole?'

'Of course, but to what do I owe this pleasure?'

'Anatole, my wife is sleeping in my bed.'

'In most situations, that would be normal.'

'Anatole! I was away. Now I've found her in my bed with no notice, no warning! You know I haven't seen her or had any word from her in eight years. Several weeks ago, I sent her a letter asking for a divorce. I know; I didn't tell you. I didn't feel like it.'

Claude fell into the armchair beside the fireplace's last vestiges of heat. 'She's kept the key all this time! Just as I left, I heard her voice, moaning *Claude.*'

Anatole did not say a word.

'I'm sorry to bother you at this time of night,' Claude continued. Pédant fluttered from his master's shoulder to the top of the dark wood armoire in the corner of the room.

'It would appear that Rose-Marie doesn't want a divorce,' Anatole said quietly.

'Anatole, we weren't meant for each other.' Claude sat at the edge of his chair. 'You know it well. Our marriage was a mistake. Don't look at me with those big eyes of yours. Isn't the fact that we haven't seen each other in all these years evidence enough that the marriage was not meant to be?'

'Unfortunately not. Or fortunately. Are you sure, Claude? Perhaps her heart has changed. What if, after eight years, the wife of your dreams lies under your covers?' Anatole took a seat in the chair facing his friend, his hands clasped under his chin.

'My dream is under covers in Paris.'

Anatole raised his eyebrows and tilted his head.

'Anatole, I love another woman. I've been meaning to tell you. She's about to marry, but the two of us love each other – that is, I do, and I think she does.'

102

The whites of Anatole's eyes now appeared yellow and tired in the dying firelight.

'I've never felt this way,' Claude continued. 'It's as if I'm breathing for the first time in my life.'

'Would you consider giving Rose-Marie a chance?'

'I knew you would ask that! No, no, no! *C'est fini!*'

'Nothing is over once you shine the light of God into your life.'

'Anatole! There is no light in my mind, body, and soul other than the light in Valentine's eyes. I'm a wildfire on the loose. I need to be with her, physically, mentally, completely. She's become an obsession. Sometimes I hide behind the columns of a building near her office and wait for her to leave work. I *follow* her, Anatole, to observe one more time the way she walks with her left hip a little too high, to catch the expression on her lips, to admire the shimmer of her hair in the varying lights of sunset, watch her hand run through it. I sip, I drink her from afar. I stalk her like a criminal. What has become of me?'

Anatole said nothing.

'The worst is when she enters her apartment with her fiancé. It hurts to imagine what happens inside. Why do I torture myself? It's so strange, this life, that it won't offer you what you want the most. But of course, Anatole, you've always known and received the life you wished.'

Anatole leaned back in the old leather chair and glanced up at the ceiling. 'Claude, little do you know how I drive myself just as crazy following on the heels of God.'

'That would be tough,' muttered Claude.

'At times I've been tempted to escape the world entirely and become a monk in a monastery far away in the Atlas Mountains and pray my heart out. Wouldn't that be simple, so divine? In a mountain hut overlooking the eternal sands of the desert, with the midnight sky as my only covering? We torture ourselves because we forget God's answer is always here for us. I'm needed at these crossroads, in Senlis. My work is with people, who, as I think you are discovering, are more challenging than fabric. How I've wished I – we – could be a piece of material, made into *the* perfect garment. But alas, we will always be stained, wrinkled, and constantly in need of tailoring.' He paused. 'Have you ever tried praying to God about your situation?'

'Neither God nor you could persuade me to return to Rose-Marie!'

Anatole sighed. 'You and your pet may hide and reside in my house for as long as you wish.'

'What a relief. Now that the interrogation is over, would you happen to have a Pernod or a cognac to offer your miserable guest?'

The next morning, Anatole convinced Claude to greet his wife of thirteen years, counting their eight years apart.

Heart thumping, Claude opened the unlocked

door of his home. She sat at the center of the room, at *his* desk, telephone in one hand, pen in the other, dark-green glasses perched on the tip of her nose. Despite the glasses, Rose-Marie had not changed. Her brown eyes looked bigger than he remembered; her hair had an artificial copper tint that could only have originated in a bottle. She was dressed in a yellow-checked wool suit he had made for her long ago; it must have been ten years. He congratulated himself – the collar lapel was still fashionable, as was the knee length. Unfortunately, the patch of material at the hips appeared almost threadbare. When she saw him, her lips pushed out in the big red pout he remembered so well. To his surprise, she ran to him, arms outstretched.

'Claude, *mon chéri,* it's been too long! I didn't realize how much I missed you!' She kissed both his cheeks and said, in her familiar whining voice, 'Your request for a divorce nearly broke my heart! Can you imagine that a day before your letter arrived, I had this nagging feeling that I must return to my husband? What an official, loveless letter, Claude!'

Every word Rose-Marie used tasted artificial to him.

'We did have five good years together,' she continued. 'And, you know, I've been collecting your clippings. Oh, the silver evening dress you designed for that Madame Laffon – there was a huge photo of it in *Le Dauphine.* How did you find material like that? It was like she wore diamonds from head to toe! I always knew you were a man of many talents. In Avignon, I told all my friends, 'That's my husband; he's doing what I always knew he could do: becoming a first-class couturier.' You *do* remember that I discovered you in the middle of nowhere? Well' – she reconsidered – 'the middle of *here*.'

She swayed her hips as she walked to the other side of the studio.

'So, is it true or only a rumor that you are moving to Paris? Yes, it is!' she trilled. 'I can see it in your eyes! Isn't that perfect timing, just when I am ready to reestablish our marital affairs? I mean, after all, Claude, we *are* still married. And *I* believe in keeping a commitment sanctified by the church. You won't believe it. I was even missing this cocka-mamie bird; that's right, you, Pédant, *toi*.'

She approached the bird on his stand. The parrot fluttered.

'Why did you wait eight years?' His voice felt as thread-bare as her skirt looked. He reclaimed his desk by sitting in the rolling chair. 'I never knew why you left.'

'It took me eight years to realize what a complete fool I had been in leaving!' she said. 'I thought my path was different from yours. But then I realized your path is and always was my path.' She approached the desk. 'You know it yourself, don't you, sweetheart?' She took his unwilling hand in hers.

He withdrew his hand. 'Rose-Marie, we don't love each other. We never have.'

'But, we're married, Claude.' She touched the back of her hair. 'Love comes if you work on it. We're still young. See?' She pirouetted in front of him. 'My figure hasn't changed a bit.'

'You don't need to stay married to a man you don't love in order to go to Paris.'

'Claude, that's not fair!' she complained. 'You *are* the man I love. *I* can't help it if you're a successful dress designer now and you weren't when I left you. After all, I *chose you*.'

'I'm sure you picked plenty of potential successes over the last eight years. Why didn't you marry one of *them*?'

'Don't speak to me like that! Yes, I went out with a few friends; you can't expect an attractive woman to fester.' She placed her hands on her hips.

'You've waited too long. I have a lawyer who will make the necessary arrangements.'

'I thought you might still love me!'

Claude glanced at the draped mannequin in front of him. The sun dappled the right side of the cream-colored silk moiré.

Rose-Marie advanced toward him again and flashed a plaintive, tragic look. 'Please, Claude, give me a chance! I've changed. You'll see. The time away has made me realize how lucky I was to have you. You are more handsome than I remember you.'

Flatter your subject, he thought.

'I've heard from the grapevine that you're up to your ears in work. You need me now. I'll find you one, two, or twenty seamstresses! You know I'm a great businesswoman, a go-getter! You'll never have to spend another minute of your precious time paying bills, sending invoices . . . Remember when you moved in with me, when we first met and I took care of everything? The apartment was spotless; life was so easy. We talked design at break-fast, lunch, dinner. You even bounced ideas off me. Claude, this will work; we'll be a team.'

So after all these years she was finally ready to get back to work on her unfinished masterpiece; the tailor who would be famous. As if the question were settled, she sat in the chair next to the desk and removed her jacket and her shoes. As she lifted one foot to cross her legs, Claude noticed her beige stocking. He could see the black imprint of her toes dotting the underside. The dye in the lining of her shoes had rubbed off.

'It's over.'

'Claude Reynaud, it is *not* over,' she said calmly, her pout loosening to a faint smile. 'I'm sure you've had some lonely nights.' Her stockinged toes arched to touch the floor. She stood. Her rust-red lips approached.

'I'm sorry, Rose-Marie.' He rose from the chair and headed to the door. Why had he been blind thirteen years ago to what he now saw so clearly in her every motion and word – Rose-Marie's ability to use her voice, words, and body to manipulate him? 'We will *not* go to Paris together. Thank you.'

He left quickly. How he craved a sketch pad, upon which to sketch Valentine's silhouette, wrapped in gossamer, and dispel the image of his wife.

CHAPTER 11

Forty days until the wedding. Claude had moved his old treadle sewing machine, eight bolts of fabric, sketch pads, and duck-clothed mannequin to Anatole's already cramped living room. Scissors, tape measures, sketch pens: his things beckoned to him from every overflowing surface. He worked tirelessly into the night. A traditional lacy wedding dress with a bustle at the back and a daisy lace veil; an emerald-green silk chiffon dress for a friend of Valentine's for the wedding; a beige linen suit with piping along the seams; buttons on the blue blazers of his nephews. God bless Anatole, who had found a lonely elderly seamstress in town to help him with the endless stream of sewing jobs.

After a three-day silence, Claude could no longer resist. He decided to surprise Valentine at work.

In the bustling reception area of Drouot, where private collectors, dealers, *brocanteurs* from the huge Saint-Ouen flea market, and buyers from all over the world flocked daily, Claude approached a tidy blond woman in a gray Chanel jacket with black pockets behind a tall desk. He asked – how

incongruous it felt even to pronounce her name –
for Valentine de Verlay.

'Who may I say is calling?'

'Claude Reynaud,' he said, pining for another
name as he pronounced his own. He would not
be too fussy: it would be nice if the surname had
some hint of stately importance, as if it had traveled in stagecoaches along sixteenth-century
Parisian streets and had perhaps a passing
acquaintance with the likes of the de Verlays.

'She'll be down in a few minutes.'

Valentine's entrance, replete with wide smile,
softened the cacophony in Drouot's lobby. She
wore a lavender cashmere sweater over a deep
magenta long-sleeved shirt with exaggerated cuffs.
A cream-colored jersey skirt skimmed her knees.
She was a flower of magenta petals, her sparkling
eyes the seductive stamens at the center.

'What a nice surprise and perfect timing,' she
said, not stopping to greet him but moving swiftly
to the glass door. 'I'm just out of a meeting and
have an hour before the next one. I wanted to call
you, but then I got busy.'

He jumped in step. She had wanted to call him!
They rounded the corner.

'Let's have a bite here,' she said, outside a café
with a forest-green-and-white striped awning. 'It's
better in summer when you can sit outside, but
let's sit in the back,' she told Claude and the waiter.

They were the first of the lunch crowd. The waiter
arrived and Valentine pushed aside the menus.

'Do you mind if I order?' she asked Claude, then addressed the waiter. '*Merci.* Two salmon and salad. And the house claret.' The waiter left with the menus under his arm. 'You'll love this claret . . . How did you know I was wanting to see you?' she asked, as the waiter returned and poured wine into their glasses. With the glass at her lips, she focused her attention on something in the distance.

'Perfect lighting,' she said quickly, smiling and pointing her finger at the nearby table. 'Look at the angles the glass on that table makes just there with the corner of the blue sky. Now observe very carefully,' she whispered, looking left and right as if to check for spies, then cocking her head to the left. 'Doesn't the table look completely strange from this angle? If you look at the left side of it, the legs look huge. If you look at the right side, the legs look so thin you think they'll break. I think it's the way the light hits the table.'

Claude tried but failed to experience the aberrant proportions as she did. He could only see her, the line of her jaw that paralleled the curve of her brow, the movement of her bottom lip as she spoke. Thoughts of dress shapes, of materials, of bias cuts flooded his head.

'What I appreciate about paintings,' Valentine continued, 'is that they're two-dimensional. What they portray is so much safer and easier than life. For an artist like you, a designer, to be good, I would think you have to be constantly alive to your insides, as if the eyes in your head were turned inward, like searchlights illuminating the most extravagant and hidden places. From what you find, you produce something tangible. Incredible. In your case, I suppose, you must translate two dimensions into three dimensions. Very challenging, I would think!'

The waiter arrived with the salmon and refilled their glasses. He could listen to her voice forever, the slight lilt in the word flow and her bass notes. She continued to surprise him with fresh unexpected insights.

'When did you know you would be a couturier, Claude? From childhood?'

'I can't remember a time when I didn't know I would be a designer.' He chose the word *designer* carefully. 'I admired my father, who loved his profession. He talked with me about his work as if it were his mistress, his escape, his passion. I guess that's what it has been for me.'

'I envy people like you.' She touched the fish with her fork. 'Who work and *live* their work. There's no distance between you and your passion. I've always been so practical. I'm too afraid not to be, I guess. I must learn from you, Claude Reynaud.'

She took a bite.

'Then,' she continued, 'there's the competition for what devours my time: Drouot – you cannot imagine my office, the research piles on the floor, the consultants coming and going, the calendar stretching out of proportion – my social life with Victor, and developing my own modest art collection. Here's the choice: make one hundred and forty phone calls for Drouot, enjoy life with Victor and my friends, or spend the hours mesmerized by the candlelit figures in a de La Tour painting.'

'Show me your art collection.'

She looked surprised and pleased with his request, as though the wind she had been waiting for had finally lifted her kite.

'It's not that special: some things I've bought off the street, some from my grandparents, some from Victor's family. But I'd love to show you what I have. Come to my apartment tomorrow – yes, tomorrow after work. Meet me here – no, better, there. I'll give you the address.'

The salmon was sweet and soft. They ate quickly. The salad arrived. The sun had shifted in the room and their corner had darkened. Claude could feel the excitement of their first moments together waning. He could sense that Valentine was worried about the time. Her hand rose up to touch her hair.

'You have to go,' he said for her.

'I do have to get back. You're so kind to me, Claude, listening to me.'

'You haven't changed your mind – about the wedding?'

She gazed at her plate and shook her head. 'I'm so sorry, Claude.' She paused and he was afraid it was all over then, in the café of strange angles.

'I'm an expert at avoiding changes, so for every day that passes I let what is planned happen. Yesterday, my parents visited for the day from Normandy. I had decided to tell them I needed more time, but there I was, choosing table linens and flowers without saying a word. We spent the day and the night together talking about the reception, the relatives coming from everywhere.' Her almond eyes opened wide and met his. 'This whole thing is totally unfair to you, Claude. Give up on me. Go away so I don't torture the two of us. Or be patient and give me more time.'

'I'm very patient,' he said, relieved the end had not come.

'You see,' she said, 'I worry that we're having fun now, but what about later? Would I fit into your life? There's a part of me that loves Paris and my friends, my life here. You have such an unspoiled, quiet, natural life. I might become too restless. I fear *my* impatience. You're so tender-hearted and kind. I would hate myself for not being the same to you. What if I could not return your love? There, just look at that face.' She smiled at him. 'I adore your face when you look sad for me. It's a sad, puppy-dog face.'

'If it's about Paris,' Claude said quickly, nearly dropping his salad fork, 'we *will* live in Paris. I will be a Parisian couturier; you will have a famous gallery of your collected masterpieces. *Voilà!* A symbiotic relationship.'

'I love being with you,' she said. Did she speak

the truth or did she desire to end their lunch as quickly as possible?

'I am willing to wait, Valentine. Listen to your heart, not the parent-pleasing decision you made when you were fourteen years old.' Wasn't he pleading as his wife had been just days before?

Valentine stood, bill in hand, looking for the waiter and then at her watch. 'I still have a few minutes. Come, have a quick look at my home, which I've renamed my gallery! I live two streets away. That is, if you have the time.'

She paid the bill and he did not resist. He put his arm around her waist as they left the café.

'Anyway, I have a little something special for you at home. Come, walk faster.' She removed his arm from her waist.

As they walked along, he restrained himself from kissing her. Her pink lips were at the right height; her hand was in her hair; her lavender colors lapped up the sunshine. She glided, her fragrance at his shoulder.

He couldn't hold off any longer. He kissed her quickly. She looked away, to the left.

'You're afraid someone's looking?'

'Of course I am!' She continued walking rapidly. 'I am engaged to be married! And, lest you forget, you *are* married.'

Claude followed closely behind her as she ducked into a gray three-story townhouse with tall windows, each underlined with a black wrought-iron balcony. Once inside, he followed her up the narrow black-carpeted staircase, the walls of which were lined with unframed paintings. He stopped in front of one of them, an oil of blue pears, floating happily on a tan background. The color of the pears matched Valentine's eyes.

'I love this! Who is the artist?'

'Silly you!' She paused halfway up the stairs and looked at him carefully, as if to determine if his request was in earnest. 'I painted those in an art class in grad school. Come inside.'

The only door on the narrow third-floor landing opened onto a surprisingly large, brightly lit room, off which he could discern a small kitchen and, to the right, a corridor to what looked like the bedroom. Three floor-to-ceiling curtainless French windows flooded the room with light. Paintings covered the café-au-lait walls. Only two pieces of furniture occupied the space: a modern, square-armed brown suede couch and a dark wood coffee table that matched the floor. In one corner, a tall, paint-spattered easel was pushed up against the wall. The light-filled room reminded him of his sunny studio.

Valentine disappeared down the corridor. Claude took a closer look at the large oil painting on the right-hand wall. It was a landscape not unlike the one that had mesmerized him during his train ride to Geneva: farmland, cows on grassy knolls under a remote blue-gray sky. What struck Claude about the painting was the distance it covered, thousands of acres of lush land, the blue sky peeping in here and there, like the future. Not a bird's-eye view but, rather, a God's-eye view.

'Here it is.' She was at his side, holding a small canvas in both hands, the raw wood back side facing him.

She smiled as she turned it to face him. It was a painting of an apple tree similar to the one outside his studio's window. The painter had used thick brushstrokes. The random white specks were blossoms clustering around the dark brown tunic of the tree.

Claude's throat caught. He coughed until tears came to his eyes. He knew she was the artist. She had captured his tree beautifully, with its arm perpendicular to the swollen trunk, its hollowed top, spring's blossoms thickly dressing the right side.

'I'm not a brilliant artist, but I could not rest until I had captured this.'

'But you were there so briefly.'

'While you were silent at work, your tree spoke to me. In fact, it's still telling me things.' She walked into the small corridor. As she placed the unframed painting on a hook on the wall, she said, 'I painted this for you, but now that I think of it, I'm not quite ready to give it away.'

Her words invited him closer and he kissed her against the wall with his tree on it. She kissed him back. They were in the place again of unknowing knowing. In her small bedroom, the white-sheeted bed was unmade. Thick beige linen curtains were

still pulled; clothes were strewn on a small uphol-
stered bench at the foot of the bed. No visitors
had been expected.

They undressed each other hastily. He watched
her eyes close and open, her eyelashes flutter, her
hips undulate. Her focus was strong. She pulled
his face so close he had to shut his eyes. When he
opened them, she had tears in hers.

'I must go back, but I haven't begun to show
you my little collection.' She pulled the sheet up
over her shoulders. 'And look at us, again! What
is it between us?'

Tears streamed down her face; mascara smudged
her upper cheeks. She dressed quickly, but looked
disheveled, her blue eyes black. She shut the door
to the bathroom in the hall. He heard the tap
screech on. She returned to the bedroom, slipped
into her sandals and laughed at herself, tears still
trailing down her face.

'How can I go back to work looking like this?'
she asked, turning back into the bathroom. When
she reappeared, she said, 'I'm sorry, Claude. As
always with you, I didn't expect this. But now I've
got to run. Will you lock up and put the key on
the top ledge of the door on your way out?'

'I love you, Valentine.'

'It's obvious with you, Claude.' She touched her
hair. 'Everything is so simple, so straightforward.'

In her hurry to leave, she unwittingly knocked
down a framed painting that was leaning against
and facing the bedroom wall. After she had left,

Claude lifted the fallen artwork, turned it around, and stood back: a contemporary head-and-shoulders portrait of Victor. This was not a work by his gentle Valentine. He admired the artist's strong, vivid palette. The painter's name, Théodore Rohan, was scrawled in the bottom left-hand corner. Victor's impressive face snarled in swirls of reds, whites, and pinks; he was angry.

Three mornings and nights and no calls. Every day that passed without his reminding Valentine of his presence felt like a day lost. Had she contacted another couturier for the wedding party's outfits? With little over a month until the wedding, she must have hired someone else. Or perhaps she had left the completion of her wedding plans idling. Hope lingered about him like thin smoke from an extinguished candle.

Claude saw few people socially except for Anatole and his sister's family on the weekends. He avoided his wife, who had taken up life in Senlis as if she had never left it. One day, as Claude scurried past his studio from his temporary abode with Anatole, transporting a bundle of pinned material to the seamstress, he heard the rapping of hammers. Renovations? Had he any control over his life? Why hadn't he heard from his lawyer? How did one eject a wife from her husband's home?

Claude groused and complained to Anatole at night. He grimaced while he worked on yet another resident's blue blazer with gold buttons. How dull! Couldn't people see that everyone wore these? Why the blue blazer? Why not a yellow jacket, the color of the feathers on Pédant's nape?

The small town of Senlis, which had held Claude Reynaud in its warm embrace for forty-six years, was now a source of agitation. Its inhabitants seemed to chatter endlessly about trifling details. The pace of life crawled. Where were the new faces? How had he not noticed until then that most of the people who lived in his hometown were gray-or white-haired and walked with canes? Was Senlis becoming extinct before his eyes? Even his work, including the small sewing tasks he had performed for town friends with pleasure in the old days, felt monotonous. A recurring thought began to tug at his consciousness: he was overqualified to perform the kind of tailoring services his family had so ardently provided for three generations. He was wasting his time.

That afternoon, when his normally loquacious seventy-five-year-old neighbor Monsieur Lassoigne arrived at his doorstep with a button in one tightly clamped hand and a shirt draped over his shaking arm, Claude took the shirt impatiently, and greeted him curtly.

'*Bonjour,* monsieur.'

The man, who had been a friend of his father's, entered the room and sat down in the chair he must have used when Papa Reynaud sewed for him. Claude quickly and irascibly stitched the rusty metal button in place. Looking up as he finished, he was surprised by Monsieur Lassoigne's grimly downturned face.

Claude leaned into the old man's ear. 'I'm so sorry, dear friend of my father's. Forgive my impudence. I need to escape our town.'

'No one has chained your feet to the ground.' The frail man stood with difficulty.

'It's true, monsieur. I have fettered myself!'

In the evening, Anatole scolded his friend. 'Your irritability and frustration are unbecoming, Claude. Even I am having difficulty with you. Things have not turned out the way you would have liked them to. Take your exigence to God, not the people of Senlis and your family.'

'I'd rather pack my bags,' said Claude.

He removed the design projects and fabrics that covered Anatole's dining table and placed them on the unmade couch-turned-bed. Within minutes, he had sloppily packed his clothes and some sewing tools into two large wrinkled brown paper bags.

'Come, Pédant,' he called.

'*Awk!*' The bird ignored his master's order and plucked under his wing.

'On my finger, Pédant!'

Only after fluttering around for some time did the parrot perch on his master's forearm. Anatole said nothing, just watched as Claude opened the door and closed it carefully behind him.

Once outside, Claude addressed his parrot at

eye level. 'What's a friendship that scolds you when you're upset?'

On his way to his Peugeot, he paused at the plaza of Notre-Dame de Senlis and took a deep breath. Standing on the bottom step of the cathedral, looking up at the spire, Claude used his cell phone to call and accept the offer he had ignored for the previous two months: to join the team of lead designers at the Salon de Silvane, one of Paris's top couturiers. He agreed to begin on the Monday after Valentine's wedding.

Immediately after he had finished his conversation with André Lebrais, the director of the salon, his cell phone rang. Claude checked his watch: 6:42 P.M. Valentine's voice. His hand holding the phone trembled. Her voice sounded far off and constricted, almost unrecognizable.

'Claude, pardon my voice. I have a terrible cold. But I need to speak to you. Can you stop by my apartment tonight?' She sneezed.

'À tes souhaits,' he said.

'Thank you. I'll be home from work around nine tonight,' she continued. 'I know it's late, but this week's insane. I've got a huge sale on for the next few days, which means I've got to be available day and night.'

'Please, let me bring you soup, tea, tissues—'

'No, no. I'm okay. Thank you anyway.' Her voice sounded cheerless.

It must be the cold weather, thought Claude. The sniffles, the harsh spring, the rainy day in the park. She wants to talk to me – to tell me we're eloping. She's naturally distressed to be leaving her apartment, her life, her job.

Convincing himself of what he suspected was untrue fatigued him. He dragged his feet to his Peugeot.

'Is this all I am, an old orange Peugeot with everything I need in two brown bags? I'm no better than a bag lady on the street, toting my scraps of material – and with a parrot squawking from my shoulder, no less. Whatever you do, Pédant, don't make a mess!'

Claude left Pédant in the parked car with the windows opened a bit and arrived at Valentine's townhouse at 9 P.M.

He raced to the door and rang the buzzer. No answer. Not back from work yet? He studied the darkened windows facing the street. Claude took a seat in a nearby café and sipped a Pernod while he awaited her return. He observed a well-dressed crowd that laughed and conversed at the next table.

Why was he always on the outside of experience? Why had he never had a group of friends like this garrulous fivesome? His friends were sprinkled here and there, individuals who barely knew one another. At high school and university, he had always felt compelled to rush home to settle in with his expectant parents, to work and eat together. Even at the Fashion Institute in Grenoble, he had had only one good friend, Rico.

Had he been afraid of his peers, of discovering that he was abnormal, unlikable, unworthy? He felt oddly disengaged from life.

Glass emptied and bill paid, he checked Valentine's windows again. Still no light shone from above. Perhaps he had missed her return to her apartment. He rang the intercom again. His watch read 10:30 P.M. He jumped when he received an answer.

'*Oui*. Yes?'

Claude announced himself.

'Claude.' A pause. 'I was sleeping. *Viens*.'

He opened the door as she buzzed him in and he rushed up the stairs, breathless. He glimpsed her before she saw him. Bare feet, pale face, she wore a white cotton piqué bathrobe lined with pink ribbon. The tip of her long nose was red. She motioned him inside with sleepy thick-lidded eyes.

'*Pardonnes-moi*, Claude. I waited for you, then thought you weren't coming, so I got into bed. Don't kiss me. I don't want to give you—'

He ignored her words and kissed both cheeks. Had his lips ever touched anything so soft? 'You have a fever,' he said.

She coughed into a crumpled tissue, welcomed him into the darkened room of her apartment, and swiped clothes off the crowded couch. The tissue fluttered out of her hand. They both reached for it.

'You'll catch my cold.'

125

She laughed then, breaking the tension of the dim cluttered room.

'Thank you for coming,' she called, as she turned on a small light in the corner of the room and headed into the kitchen. He could hear her sniffle and cough and felt sorry for intruding on what could have been a full night's sleep. She reemerged, carrying a cut-crystal glass of amber liquid. How did she know he desired a Pernod? He could not help himself. Despite her cold, he wished to kiss her on the lips.

'Please excuse the mess. I was planning to clean up in the morning. I've been in a blur since I returned from Geneva. We're wrapping up an auction this weekend, the biggest of the year. I've been working from eight in the morning to eleven every night. It's all too much, and then, with this thing happening . . .'

The room was littered with books, magazines, and papers in piles. A jacket was draped on the back of the couch. Newspapers covered the coffee table. He noticed pink lipstick on the rim of a white Styrofoam cup of coffee. No, it was tea.

'Come,' she said, taking a red boiled-wool blanket from the back of a chair, 'let's curl up on the sofa, you with your Pernod and me with my tissues.'

She spread the blanket carefully across their laps as they sat down. He felt suddenly united, as if the blanket were a flag, representing their own country. She coughed.

126

'I need to talk to you, Claude.' She pulled her legs up under the blanket and turned to face him. Her mouth drawn back and serious, she paused and looked at him, as if marking the moment before something significant was to happen. 'First, I want you to know that I *was* planning to stall the wedding – to give us a chance. You' – she took his hand in hers, looked down at it, and stroked it – 'you've been such a gift to me. There's something sincere, something childlike about you, that I want to hold and keep and dream into.' She brought his hand up and looked at it at face level. 'I think you're the most thoughtful person I've ever met.' She let go of his hand quickly and coughed away from him. She blew her red-tipped nose. 'I was trying to work it out. I told Victor and my parents that I needed more time. But something has happened, Claude.

'You see—' She tilted her head and held her tissue to her nose. She sniffled. He said nothing. 'It's Victor. He's lost his job and his auctioneer's license.' Her raspy voice made him think an imposter had occupied her body. 'The *commissaires-priseurs*, the shareholders, have asked him to step down and leave Drouot. I wanted to tell you before you read about it in tomorrow's papers.

'Apparently' – she blew her nose – 'the Comtesse de Beauprenne, a childhood friend of his mother's whom he has known since he was a child, gave Victor for auction a small portrait of a girl by Rembrandt from her renowned private collection.

Rather than bring it to the public market, he sold it privately to another client at her request. The comtesse did not want word to get out that she needed money. The buyer is one of Victor's best clients.' She inhaled deeply and sighed.

'I don't know what he was thinking! It's completely illegal not to bring a work of art, and particularly a masterpiece, to the marketplace. How could he expect a Rembrandt to change hands without some public attention?

'For the last two years, as a top shareholder at Drouot, he's been telling me he had to score a masterpiece. I guess he saw this as his opportunity, and Madame de Beauprenne refused to sell it any other way. When he told me the news the other day, he said he was trying to protect one of his mother's dearest friends. He said he made no commission on the painting; it was a clean sale.'

Valentine stood, rearranged her bathrobe, blew her nose in a new tissue, and sat down again.

'I think the comtesse had even offered him her house in Corsica for our honeymoon. That it came to that! Did he do it for job security, loyalty to his mother's childhood friend, a honeymoon destination? I'm not sure.'

Claude shifted under the blanket, brushing her knee unintentionally with his hand. She coughed into her cupped hands.

'No matter what, Claude, what has happened is this: my heart goes out to this man.' Despite her cold and cough, her voice was now clear. Claude sat motionless. How could he ever have thought he was substantive enough to hold on to this divine sparkle, this burst of star fire? The blanket fell to the floor. All was blank and unimportant.

She pulled three tissues from the box and blew her shiny nose. She wiped her eyes and pulled the blanket up across their legs again.

'I cannot leave Victor at this moment in his life. It's like watching two boats on a stormy sea: one seaworthy that will make it to another side and another that will sink if you don't rescue it. It's hard to explain, but with this happening I realize how deeply connected I am to Victor. I would never forgive myself if I left him. It's a strange alchemy, the feeling I have for him, a mixture of empathy and love that are somehow interchangeable. I realize I would do anything rather than see him suffer.

'I know it's not fair to you – to us, rather. Oh, dear Claude.'

She rose from the couch, her nose red, her blue eyes watery. He could hear her sniffling in the bathroom. When she returned, she sat gently on the couch, pulled the blanket to her chin, and tucked her feet underneath.

'Please forgive me!' She turned to him. 'How strange. It's as if I'm speaking, but disconnected from who I am, speaking outside of myself! Oh, that face, Claude, those warm, inviting eyes. What a shame that they were smitten with me and not someone else!' Suddenly, she hugged him. 'I'm so sorry,' she said quietly, in his ear.

He stood and walked to the door. She rose from the couch and followed him.

'Good-bye, my lovely Claude Reynaud,' she said, lifting the crumpled tissues to her eyes this time. He removed the pale blue handkerchief from his breast pocket and gently touched the silk to her face.

He tried to manage a smile as he averted his eyes from her and opened the door; it seemed somehow expected. But moving his mouth into that sunlit expression felt impossible. She hugged him again to say good-bye, her body rigid.

On his way out the door, Claude noticed the portrait of Victor, this time propped against the right side of the living room and facing out.

'*Au revoir,*' he said, repeating his farewell as he descended the stairs.

He heard her voice echo down the stairwell, a faint, faltering 'I'm so sorry,' but he forced himself not to respond and not to look back up the stairwell for the red-tipped nose and the midnight-blue eyes.

CHAPTER 12

Claude walked Paris by night for hours, without caring where, until he remembered Pédant, still in his car. He ran to retrieve his parrot and a small bag of bird food and roamed the sleeping streets until he spotted a hotel. L'Hôtel des Petits Champs, in the fifth arrondissement, was lit from the ground up to reveal a freshly painted peach-colored stone façade with window boxes dripping with geraniums and cream-colored awnings.

He woke the hotelier to ask for a room for the night. With haughty disdain, the white-haired, bleary-eyed man replied that the hotel was booked; perhaps, if he arrived at an *heure respectable* and if the bird was not messy or loud, he could accommodate him the following night. He pointed down the road to indicate a hotel that might have rooms available. 'So late!' the man reproached, shaking his head.

Rounding the corner, Claude heard loud rap music. He glimpsed a hotel sign above a narrow dark townhouse, squeezed between a throbbing bar and an outdoor café. The barely noticeable black door opened onto beige-carpeted stairs, stained in random places. On the small landing, a woman with black dyed hair and charcoal-rimmed eyes resembling a bulldog's asked him with a suspicious look if he would be having visitors.

'No.'

'Will you have *no* visitors?' she asked again, her right-penciled eyebrow reaching unforeseen heights.

'*Excusez-moi,*' Claude said. 'I will look elsewhere.'

'I thought so!' she said. 'We don't take pets, anyway!'

Six blocks later, he discovered a hanging sign, lit with the words MARIE'S ROOMS TO LET.

He peeked in. They had a room, but checkout time was 8:30 A.M.

'Why so early?' Claude inquired.

'Do you want the room or not?' the white-aproned woman asked gruffly. Claude did not think her half-open eyes had spotted Pédant.

Two-thirty in the morning, with a screeching parrot in hand, was not the ideal time or way for a man unacquainted with Paris to find his first hotel room there. Claude took the room, handing the woman the requested fifty euro. He tucked Pédant under his jacket, whispering shushing sounds as he followed her ankle-length black skirt up the stairs.

Claude awoke to loud voices and a scraping sound, like furniture being moved. Raising the shade, he peered out the painted-shut window, which he had tried to pry open the preceding airless night. Below he found the cream-colored tops of market umbrellas that must have been set up as he slept into the early morning. Wednesday. Of course, market day. In and around the umbrellas, bold combinations of colors collided. Shoppers milled, pinched, weighed, tasted, purchased, and carried. Garlic and onions hung in bunches from one tent; from another, he glimpsed dangling sausages. A wooden tray of tantalizing ripened Camembert cheese rested in the sun on a nearby table.

With Pédant under his arm, he left unnoticed. As he threaded his way through the crowds of shoppers and pedestrians to his car, he thought briefly about the studio and the many client calls he must have missed. How would Rose-Marie have explained his absence? He remembered the emerald-green silk evening gown he had promised Madame de Laye, a friend of Valentine's.

He took his morning coffee in the café abutting the Hôtel des Petits Champs, where he planned to spend that night. He had reserved a room with a small kitchenette and living room.

The café overlooked a small park, in which three children played hide-and-seek. With each *I found you!* the hidden was discovered. Claude reflected on his own game of hide-and-seek with Valentine. He had found her, but she had chosen to hide her love for him for life. How idle and useless was this pursuit of love, this emotional turmoil that drove like a drill through his core, leaving him hollowed.

Taking one last sip of coffee, he gazed up at the hotel's colorful array of balcony flowers. They seemed suddenly too bright. Could they be plastic? He asked the waitress.

'*Oui*, monsieur. It's much too much trouble to water the real ones.'

Before starting his career at the Salon de Silvane, Claude felt obliged to complete the work in Senlis he had ignored. He was his father's son. How could he disappoint his community: the elderly Monsieur Duchamp, who needed a jacket lining resewn, or the barely walking Madame Deluse, who needed a hat with netting for her grandson's wedding? Unfortunately, the seamstress in Senlis whom Anatole had found to help worked at a painstakingly slow pace. After his coffee, Claude strolled his new Parisian neighborhood and spotted a tailor's storefront across the park.

As Claude entered and a bell rang, a slender, hunched-over man with a deeply lined face emerged from a back room. When Claude asked the elderly tailor to show him samples of his work, he caught sight of the man's hands; they resembled his father's, the nails hardened and hatch-marked like battered seashells. Claude was impressed with the tailor's workmanship; the hem on a pair of pants was finely, even artfully stitched. The tailor agreed to start sewing the next day.

Claude returned to Senlis that afternoon to retrieve his messages. Rather than tiptoe into his own home, he decided to stride into it like its rightful owner, pack more sewing tools and clothes, and return to Paris that night.

Thankfully, Rose-Marie was not at home. The house looked cleaner than it had been in eight years. Shiny white tiles replaced the warped, damaged wood on the kitchen counter. Twenty-nine voice-mail messages. Many clients were interested in fall suits and evening gowns; his lawyer had called. Could he smell a plot between his wife and lawyer? No message from Valentine. A young, shy voice asked about a wedding dress.

'No more wedding dresses!' He shouted at the machine. 'Never again will I design a wedding dress!'

Last, a message from Juliette. He played it back: *Claude, please call as soon as you get in. It's Mother; she's had a stroke.* He played it back yet again, his heart skipping beats. The call had come in at 8:28 P.M. the previous night. His sister's normally calm voice sounded panicked.

When he arrived at the hospital room, he found Juliette seated in the hallway, her long loose dress forming a small puddle on the floor. She stood to hug her brother. 'I had to leave the room for a few minutes.' She offered him the chair next to hers in the hall. '*Maman* suffered a stroke. Henri heard her fall out of bed early last night. She was barely conscious when the ambulance arrived. Everything since then has seemed so drawn out, Claude, like slow motion. It began with the ambulance people. They moved so sluggishly; it was as if they carried weights on their arms. The boys told me to calm down, but I kept screaming, "Do something! Do something!"'

'Is this her room?'

Juliette nodded and they entered. His mother lay on the bed in the center of the small room. Her face was pale, her breath was audible, her inhalations labored. As he drew closer, it seemed that her breathing grew louder, raspier. Her eyes remained shut. Was she angered by his presence? He backed against the door.

'What do the doctors say? Did she recognize you after she fell out of bed? Did she speak?'

Juliette shut her eyes, then slowly opened them. 'They say there's little chance she will recover. No, she didn't recognize me. Her eyes didn't even connect with mine. It was so eerie! To have your own mother not know you! We were strangers.'

Claude held his sister.

'She wakes up for ten minutes and then goes back to this dreamy state. She mumbles incoherently. Nothing has changed since we've been here.'

'What about surgery?'

'They're waiting; the doctor doesn't seem optimistic.'

'Why wait?' He felt the panic rising inside of him. 'There must be something the doctor can do.'

He turned from his sister and pressed his hands against the seafoam-colored wall, hoping it would support him.

★ ★ ★

For two days, Claude and Juliette watched over their mother. On the third day, their sister Agnes arrived from Lyon. Each one, in turn, tried to awaken their mother.

'Maman' – Juliette prodded her gently – 'wake up, speak. Tell me, *Maman*, did you ever love Papa? Or did you love only your perfect accounting books, your sharpened pencils, your brooms and cleaning tools, your room away from us all? Oh, *Maman*, wake up, for the children's sake. Yes, you loved your grandchildren! Yes.' Juliette turned to her brother and sister for confirmation. 'For sure, she loved *them*.'

Agnes groaned. 'She never came to visit *my* children. Oh, I guess she did once, but that was only when Constantin was born. No, she didn't love my children. You at least had that, Juliette. Now that you mention it, I've resented it all these years. She was always too busy, or at least that's what she said. Occupied with your children. She told me to come to her. I don't think she ever forgave me for moving to Lyon. *Maman*, wake up. Come on, *Maman*, I know I haven't visited much, but now I'm here.'

Agnes took two photographs from her purse and held them in front of her mother's nose. 'Look!' She shook the images impatiently before her mother's closed eyes. 'Look at my children, your grandchildren whom you didn't care enough to visit. Look!' she persisted aggressively, to the unseeing woman. 'Look at Lisette and her long face, like yours, *Maman*. Doesn't Lisette have the same face, Juliette?' she asked, not turning her head.

The three arranged to take turns, with occasional visits from the four boys, to try to rouse the sleeping figure.

'*Grand-maman*, the house is a mess,' Jean-Hugues announced to her on his way to school one day. 'I couldn't find any socks for school today. Please wake up and come home.'

Didier entreated, '*Grand-mère*, where are you? Why don't you wake up? Even though I don't like it when you guard the fridge, now there's nothing left in it. No carrots for the horses *or* for us!'

'Why won't she wake up?' asked Arthur. He squeezed his grandmother's inert hand.

'Off to school. Come, come!' Juliette commanded, this time persuading the children all too easily to move along.

Juliette's departure left a gaping hole in the room.

'Isn't it funny,' Claude said finally, to Agnes. 'We're brother and sister, and we hardly know each other.'

'You were too old, Claude. Remember? You went away to design school. You were never interested in me. You only wanted Papa. You never wanted to talk to us girls. But I've heard about you, even in Lyon, and read about you. The hot new designer. All the way in Lyon. I hate to admit it, but I was shocked. You've never seemed to want attention, but now you've gotten it anyway. Yves

138

has always said you should go to Paris and really make a career for yourself.

'But now, as I look at you, you're still the same. You're still hiding. I see it in your eyes. You still don't say too much. You don't want life to get at you, get *to* you. But, look: it did! Now it's hit you two times. Oh, Claude.' Her large brown eyes filled with tears. 'I'm sorry. This is probably not the place to discuss this, but' – she wiped her eyes and looked over at their mother – 'it serves you right, *Maman;* it's as good a place as any. Claude, it's your not caring – I mean, no communication! No questions asked. Aren't you curious about my life at all? Why am I saying all this? *Maman,* are you listening? Come on, Claude, let's have the tussle we should have had as children. That might shake her up. Don't look so somber.'

Was it true? Had he never called to ask after his sister Agnes and her husband, Yves, or their children? 'But I do care,' he said.

Agnes rummaged in her purse. For a tissue? Or, did she have a sudden impulse to give her brother something of herself, a form of reconciliation, a gift? She pulled out a set of jingling car keys with the plastic rental identification tag.

'I've got to go back to Lyon, Claude. You're the oldest. Say good-bye to Juliette for me. I told her I'd be leaving tonight. My children need me, and I have to be home by tomorrow morning to host my husband's conference. *Maman* could be in this state for months, years. I'll call tomorrow to check in. *Au revoir, mon frère.*'

Claude spent the remainder of the afternoon and evening with his mother, leaning over her, whispering to her, kissing her cheeks and hands. That night, after Bernard and Juliette had left with their family and Claude returned from a miserable dinner in the hospital cafeteria, he was stunned by the silence in the room.

He tiptoed quickly to his mother's bedside. Her eyes were closed; her hands, cool and still clenched, rested at her sides. Her body lay still as a stone. He felt for the nonexistent pulse, then kissed each cheek and brought her lifeless hand to his heart. *'Maman,'* he whispered, 'good-bye. Say hello to Papa for me.'

Suddenly, he didn't want to be alone with her; her limp face, like unshaped clay, unnerved him. He left the room, calling for the nurse.

When the nurse entered, she gave Claude a knowing nod and sprang into action as if she had long anticipated this moment.

'I will wait out here,' he said, his voice shaking. He phoned Juliette and gave her the message: *'Maman* has died. It is eight-oh-six P.M.'

The nurse began to roll his mother's bed toward the hallway.

'Where are you taking her?'

'To Madame Belgier, monsieur, to take care of the body.'

He remembered from his father's death that

Madame Belgier preserved corpses artfully, masking death with pasty 'life-like' makeup.

'Yes. But no, wait . . . what about a priest?' he asked. 'Please let her stay here in the room until a priest has blessed her body as she is, in her natural state. My friend is a priest, and he will be here in ten minutes. I will call him now.'

'I'm sorry, monsieur,' said the nurse cheerfully. 'They do that *after* the body is beautified.'

The beautification of a corpse. 'One moment,' said Claude, one hand on the bed railing, the other on his cell phone, punching in Anatole's number.

'Anatole, my mother has died. Will you come to the hospital now?'

'He's coming,' he assured the nurse. 'She must have a priest. She was a God-loving woman. She said her rosaries while she watched television.'

'We can wait a few moments, monsieur, but the law requires us to move the body immediately for hospital health reasons. If no one arrives in the next five minutes, we will have to move it.'

'She's only been dead a few moments. Can't you still say *her?*' He turned away from his mother, whose color had all but drained from her face.

'If you please, sir,' the nurse said, as she squeezed between him and the bed and left the room quickly.

The nurse returned five minutes later, her cheerfulness replaced with impatience and annoyance. 'We have waited your five minutes. For reasons of hygiene, we must begin to move the body.' She looked at her watch.

'My mother would love you! *For reasons of hygiene!* How perfect! *Maman,* now it is you who are being cleaned, right out of life. Death can be messy, can't it?' Claude stepped closer to the nurse, as if he were confiding something important to her. 'Yes,' he said loudly. 'Death is messy, but let me tell you, mademoiselle, life is even messier.'

'Sir, we have to move this body.'

'You'll have to move me before you move this body!' he said, putting both hands on the bed's railing, looking away from his dead mother.

The nurse took a step backward and pressed a red button behind the bed. A man in a white jacket, with eyebrows that formed a thick line across his forehead, appeared in the doorway. 'Please, let go of the bed, sir,' he said, approaching Claude.

Claude pushed the bed at the man in the doorway. The man lost his balance and fell. One nurse attended to the fallen attendant, while another tried to pry Claude's hands from the metal bed rails.

Amazed at his own strength, Claude sped the bed quickly down the hall into the elevator, which had conveniently stopped at his floor. He pushed the button for the ground level. When the elevator doors opened, three men dressed in blue-green hospital gowns, either doctors or guards, he couldn't tell, blocked his exit. He aimed his mother's bed at his aggressors as he yelled, 'My mother must see the priest!' The uniformed unit cleared the way for him.

He fled, steering the bed down the glossy white hospital floors.

'She is not your property!' one of the men yelled after him.

Claude pivoted around. 'My own mother is not my property?'

At the end of a blocked-off corridor, the four hospital staff people finally cornered him. He saw Juliette appear. Her big eyes opened wide. He heard her soothing voice addressing someone. With relief, he saw Anatole heading toward him.

'Anatole,' Claude said, 'I wanted you to bless our mother before they took her away. Now you're here. Will you please? But be quick; I'm going to be sick.'

Before he struggled to his feet and rushed into a nearby bathroom, he heard Juliette telling the men and nurses, 'Yes, he took it hard . . . as he should have!' Her words melted around his ears, muffling the harsh hospital sounds.

'Thank God for my sewing,' Claude told Anatole later that week, as he worked in his friend's house. The seamstress he had hired in Senlis and the tailor he employed in Paris were each busily completing multiple jobs. Claude planned to drive to Paris that afternoon to heap eight more pinned garments on the tailor's sewing table. With his fabrics, his sewing machine, his sketch pad, his blue pencil, his scissors, his patterns, and his pins, he had all he needed to feel protected from the outside world of heartache.

I have a hotel room in Paris, he thought, a home I cannot live in, a wife I want to divorce, two employees in two different places, a job with the most famous couturier in France, if not Europe, that begins next week, and I can think of only one thing, one person: Valentine, Valentine, Valentine, the repetitive refrain of my heart.

Had she heard about his mother's death? Would she send him a note of condolence? Offer to visit her grave with him? Of course not. Valentine and he knew people in common, but their worlds were farther apart than the thirty miles that separated Senlis from Paris. He would not mourn or discuss his mother's death in front of his Parisian customers. The only way Valentine would know anything about his personal life was if she asked about it or he filled her in.

Perhaps she would call him now, at this moment, despite everything, to change both their lives. He would tell her about his mother then . . .

Why did he persist in believing in Valentine's love for him? She had told him she was sorry; she had made her decision. Was it because the wedding day had not yet occurred? The time was not up in the hourglass? He had heard of weddings in which the bride or groom had a revelatory moment during the drive to the church or in the dressing room, as the bride's hair was pushed into a chignon, as the groom cut his chin with a razor during his last shave of bachelorhood, as the betrothed's father took her hand to escort her down the lengthy church aisle.

The grand couturiers of his father's day were known to sew the final stitches of the wedding gown *onto* the bride minutes before the church bells signaled the ceremony's beginning. Would that he could bring the needle and thread to stitch a ribbon to her hips, then place a kiss on her slender collarbone and whisper softly in her ear, 'Are you sure, Valentine? Do you have the smallest hesitation? Please listen to my heartbeat and reconsider.'

Or he could slip up and cut the fabric by mistake, rendering the wedding dress un-presentable! Surely, both families would postpone the wedding for the mending of the bridal gown.

Another scenario: Claude, poor inexperienced tailor that he is, has sewn the final seams and – a grand blunder – has stitched himself to the glossy white gown. What a muddle! The thread is so strong and resilient, the tailor cannot be unhitched from his creation. Oh, yes, thousands of strands of thread, criss-crossed in every possible way, must be cut, but not without marring the exquisite dress. Cancel the wedding! The bride and the tailor have been sewn together irreparably, forever!

Even without him by her side, Valentine could come to her senses minutes before the ceremony or even seconds before the groom's kiss. She would declare to her betrothed and the confused congregation, 'I must not continue with this lie. I love another man!' But, no, Claude concluded dolefully, she *will* marry Victor.

Why would you marry, if not for true love? Maybe only simple provincial people thought that way. Of course there were important reasons for tying a loveless knot, but they were completely stupid nonetheless. He thought of his own marriage.

He grabbed his jacket. On his way out of Anatole's house, he nearly knocked over his wife. Had she been listening for him, waiting for the right moment to lure him back to their own loveless marriage?

'*Pardonnes-moi. Bonjour.*'

'Claude! We must speak. Things have changed.'

'Yes, maybe tomorrow.'

'Tomorrow!' she called after him.

He began to run. He didn't care how it looked. He was a child at the seaside, racing, arms stretched horizontally, heading into the wind. He jumped into his Peugeot and drove out of town, with no regard for the thirty-kilometer speed-limit sign he knew so well.

PART II

CHAPTER 13

Claude Reynaud became famous and was ruined on his first day of work at the Salon de Silvane. The photograph of Valentine in her wedding dress, her demure smile in the swanlike gown, sexy yet poised and sophisticated, appeared in all the French newspapers and magazines. *Le Figaro* ran a half-page photo in its style section and labeled Claude Reynaud 'the ingenious couturier from nowhere.' *Paris Match* called the dress 'the wedding invention of the new century! Modern yet classic, simple yet sophisticated.' 'Valentine de Verlay *was* the wedding gown,' gushed the fashion editor of *Le Monde*.

At the Salon de Silvane, Claude was greeted in the reception area by the creative director, André Lebrais.

'Monsieur Claude Reynaud, *l'homme du moment!* Your fame precedes your entrance this morning. Congratulations!' Lebrais was a commanding figure in his fifties, with a short wiry body, sharp dark-brown eyes, a small wide nose that compromised his face's authority, and needle-thin, well-defined lips. He had successfully designed for the salon for over twenty years, maintaining the house's distinctive and respected label. Two years earlier, he had been promoted to oversee all aspects of the business.

Claude winced at every assault of praise.

'*Oui, merci,*' he said. 'It was a good design, but it was the woman who made the dress a success, not the other way around.'

On the conference table, he caught a glimpse of a magazine that lay open to a full-figure color photograph of Valentine. Her beauty made him reel. Could he claim any credit for such grace and elegance? That her wedding dress would be at the same time the symbol of his success and of her grand entrance into Parisian society was too painfully ironic. The dress elongated the gentle curve of her lissome neck and emphasized her height. But her smile seemed to him incongruously melancholic.

In his spacious and freshly painted office, one large window offered a view onto rue des Panoramas, a drab side street off the more commercial place des Victoires. Peering from his window down the street, he spied a women's dress store: the fabric on the clothed mannequins looked cheap, the styles outdated. Three years earlier, the Salon de Silvane had moved to this second-arrondissement 'transitioning neighborhood' known as le Sentier. Over the past year, a number of design companies had staked their ground in the area, but the dilapidated buildings and the nearby red-light district of rue Saint-Denis lent the quarter a distinctly shabby appearance.

As soon as he saw his office, Claude decided to repaint the stark white walls with a peach overlay, or perhaps pink, to add vitality. Cork lined one wall. Four headless mannequins stood lifelessly near the window.

A slender woman with startling red lips entered the room without knocking and introduced herself as Albane Mirelle, Lebrais's secretary. She asked Claude to come at once to Monsieur Lebrais's office so monsieur could introduce him to the staff at the morning meeting.

Albane possessed a jaw that looked like it could crack nuts. She had a short wide forehead and large oval eyes and the thinnest waist Claude had ever seen. She looked every bit the part of a small taut tigress, muscle-bundled to pounce at a given notice.

Claude brushed the back of his jacket uneasily. He was aware that every centimeter of his suit would be analyzed by those representing the eye of *haute couture parisienne*. He entered the office, five steps down the hall from his own, decorated in the style of Louis XIV, complete with intricate moldings, French pastoral landscape paintings, and gilt carved furniture. Intentionally or not, the Versailles replica, designed to manifest royal grandeur and power, appeared more like a stage set.

Two men and one woman occupied the chairs

facing Lebrais's gold inlaid desk. One chair was empty to the far left of the group. As Claude entered, four heads turned toward him. He sensed the group's searing interior calculations, evaluating the length of jacket, cuff, pant hem and the cut of his lapel, down to the shine of his shoe. By the time he was seated in the empty chair, he felt certain that those assembled were slightly disappointed with the hot new designer.

'*Et voilà*,' said Lebrais, standing up from his chair. 'Monsieur Claude Reynaud, first let us congratulate you on this pièce de résistance.' He held up the two newspaper full-size centerfold photographs of Valentine in his gown. Claude had not noticed any photographs of Valentine's nieces and nephew. He wondered who, in the end, had designed their wedding outfits. How had Valentine lured her next couturier?

Lebrais replaced the newspapers on the table, took his seat, and looked up at the standing Claude, his eyes narrowing. 'I expected to see you at the wedding.'

What does he know? thought Claude, gazing back at his inquisitor.

Lebrais broke the uneasy pause. He stood again. 'Allow me to present Charles Sennelier, my protégé. Charles has been with us for five years and, among other distinctions, is currently our head accessory designer.' Charles bowed his full head of artificially streaked blond hair. His overall appearance was round. His face was friendly and open; his red curvaceous lips smacked of little indulgences taken regularly.

'*Voilà* Segolene de la Maze. She's initiating a line for the young twenty to thirty set. Watch her color sense, Claude. She dictates the house's colors. She has teal and orange on her mind for next spring.' Claude took in the woman's frame, her pear shape, her legs tightly crossed. He dressed her in a pantsuit, pink and red pinstripe, to shed her small wrenlike appearance. Large white teeth in her smile produced an unexpected brightness.

'*Et* Alain de Beaumarchais, who has spent much of his life in America and South Africa and heads up a line we aptly labeled Freedom last year. This year he has earned the privilege of designing under his own label. Look to Alain for direction, not to mention exacting measurements, especially below the belt. His bootleg pants are considered revolutionary for their subtle curves.'

Alain's good looks were compromised by his self-consciously black attire and his slicked-back hair. His pants swung low at the hips and covered his shoes, hovering but not quite touching the floor. The effect was that of curtains puddling, a fashion statement, Claude thought, that could be effective if you were embarrassed about your shoes.

'These experienced designers and you will complete our team. Please have a seat. Now tell us, Claude, what inspired such a dress? A return to classicism perhaps?'

Lebrais cocked one eyebrow playfully, as if he

153

knew the answer and held the strings to the marionette in front of him. In that moment, Claude concluded that the creative director of the Salon de Silvane, while no longer in the cutting and sewing rooms, was equally adept at manipulating the material that comprised his mortal counterparts.

'The dress was inspired by nothing more complicated than the woman who wore it,' Claude said.

'Surely you will develop this overstated simplicity of line in our spring collection. Whatever the case, the press is enamored of it and of you,' Lebrais said. 'Today, I have scheduled three interviews for you, the last with the most influential fashion critic at *Le Monde*. We' – Lebrais bowed to those in front of him – 'expect you to announce this dress as the beginning of your design career with the salon. It's the perfect début for your marriage to our company.'

Claude felt the other designers' scrutiny as they awaited his response. Nervousness lingered at the edge of his words. 'I designed the dress before I arrived on these premises. Anything I design hereafter you may say, correctly, has originated from your salon.' Of all the suits, dresses, and gowns he had created in his thirty-year career, this single dress belonged to him.

His fellow designers shifted uneasily in their seats. Lebrais sat back in his chair and raised his feet to his desk so the soles of his shoes faced Claude.

'Certainly we can discuss this later, Claude. Unfortunately for you, the press is under the impression that the dress is your first statement while working for this house.'

'An inaccurate impression,' Claude pointed out.

'We shall discuss this later, alone, Claude,' said Lebrais, in a falsely sanguine tone.

'My decision will not change.'

'Claude Reynaud,' said Lebrais with childish gaiety, 'I can see we're going to get along beautifully here at the Salon de Silvane.' He stood, walked around his desk, and leaned against it in a studied, casual position. 'But how silly. I have introduced you to your co-designers but have yet to familiarize them with you.'

The room breathed again. Lebrais threw a piercing glance at Claude. 'Claude attended the University of Rennes and then the Fashion Institute in Grenoble and has lived all this time in . . . mmm . . . what is the name? Claude, I don't believe I've been there.' He paused, snapping his fingers as if to revive his memory for trivial information. 'Ah, yes, Senlis. Was that it?' Without waiting for an answer, he continued, 'And, Claude, you are married. Do you have any children?'

'No.'

'*Alors.*' Lebrais switched gears. 'Now, Charles, will you please take our new designer around the offices and introduce him to our head seamstress. You will work directly with her and the head sales consultant, who will tell you what our clients are buying.

'You might also like to tell our new designer about our neighborhood and which streets to avoid. He's been so *long* in the countryside.' A sly smile quivered on Lebrais's wire-thin lips. 'What *was* the name of that town again?'

He did not wait for a response.

'I will see you all back here at two-thirty to discuss our spring collection and the rules of our house. I know it is incredibly short notice, but we must have portfolios for the collection a month from this Monday, and I would like you to participate.' He clapped his hands as if dismissing children in a classroom. 'I must be off.'

In his new surroundings, Claude felt comforted by the humming of the hundred or more sewing machines in the massive room at the end of the hall and stimulated by conversations with those he met his first morning on the job. Why *had* he sequestered himself for so long?

His favorite room on the tour was known as the 'color corridor.' It was lined with deep shelves, each of which held hundreds of bolts of fabric, arranged neatly by color – greens on one side and yellows on the other, reds in the middle – in textures ranging from rough leather and supple lamb's wools to silks and organzas. Claude was impressed that Lebrais had renovated the space to include a skylight to show off the true hues of the inhouse fabrics. Standing directly under the window, Claude fancied himself the eye of a hurricane of color.

The tour ended in Claude's office. A wiry and nervous-looking woman with short dark hair molded to her head and red lips that resurrected Coco Chanel slithered between the two men and sat down in the office chair opposite Claude's new desk.

'Allow me to introduce you to Caroline de Falance, our publicist,' Charles said, opening his hand as if introducing a celebrity on a talk show. 'She will interview you and then send your story to the hundreds of magazines and newspapers who are anxiously anticipating the gossip on you. Don't look so worried, Claude. Once your eyes adjust to the limelight, you will never wish for the room to go dark again! No worries. Caroline, be easy on him. We call Caroline the "lean press." She irons out all your wrinkles.'

Charles winked at Caroline as he left the room. Caroline de Falance had a lovely square face with high cheekbones. She wore a bright yellow coat that slit up the back to her waist with a pink button at the top. How delightful a coat! Underneath, she wore a pale green skirt that fell an inch below the knee. Claude would have loved to ask who designed the coat but decided not to reveal his ignorance. Meanwhile, she eyeballed her new subject.

'Monsieur Reynaud,' she said him formally, 'why don't we get started on our little interview – or, as Charles loves to call it, our ironing session?'

'Please, call me Claude.'

'Fine. Claude, I will start the recording now if you don't mind.' She pressed the button on a small recorder in her hand. She then rose from the chair and perched herself next to Claude's shoulder and peeked, to his surprise, at some designs he had removed from his portfolio and placed on his desk earlier that morning.

'Excuse me.' She responded to his lifted eyebrows by retreating back to her chair. 'We publicists are a nosy bunch. But as you probably know, the more information I can collect, the better the story. I can only spin when I have enough yarn!'

She began by asking about Claude's experience as a designer. 'You worked for your father and then yourself? No other houses? First job outside the family? Oh, no, this won't do. Newly moved to Paris, is that so?' She shook her head and muttered under her breath. Her disappointment was palpable.

She tried another tack. 'This wedding dress the magazines and newspapers and fashion critics around the world have leaped on; they call it a *new lexicon of fashion*' – she pulled a newspaper clipping from her stack of papers – '*a simplicity that soars above the clutter*. Monsieur – I mean Claude – this dress was designed under the direction of this house, *n'est-ce pas,* isn't that correct? No? Oh. The idea for the dress? A woman. All right. Is this the beginning of a new line of wedding dresses or a shift to a post-post-modern style? No?

Just for that woman? You refuse to be pinned down, don't you, monsieur – I mean Claude!

'What designer has influenced your work through the years? Your father. But surely, there is someone, Balenciaga, Dior, someone else more – shall we say – noteworthy whose work you have admired? Your father. *Bien. Alors.*'

She frowned.

'I must get back to my work.' Claude shuffled the papers on his desk.

She did not move.

'Let the work speak for itself!' he said finally. 'The point of design is the present: the client who wears the clothes at that moment. Fashion is what we have on our skin, how it feels, pleases, inspires, and changes us and how all of that intermingles with the people in our lives and the places we go. If I can help a woman establish her style, her unique claim to humanity, and feel good about it, then I am happy.'

'When you create the spring ready-to-wear collection, however, you won't know your individual customers. How can you help women claim their individuality when you don't know them?'

She had found a chink in his armor.

'It's something I've never had to do. It will be my greatest challenge. We shall see if I can meet it. I really must get back—'

'About your personal life: your wife's name?'

'I am separated from my wife. I have no more

159

time for this interview, but thank you very much.' Claude stood.

She stared at him, as if waiting for him to add something else. As she left her chair and about-faced, it struck Claude that her silhouette resembled a cardboard cutout.

It took only three working days for Rose-Marie to locate and penetrate her husband's office. The first time she was announced by the receptionist, Claude pretended that he was in a meeting behind closed doors. The second time, Rose-Marie hurried past the reception desk into the office corridor. In her black patent leather high heels and rustling red silk skirt, she called out ostentatiously, 'Monsieur Reynaud? Yes, that's right. I'm his wife.' She was saucer-eyed and smiling when she finally found him.

'My darling, I will *never* divorce you!' she exclaimed loudly, looking around his office, grinning. 'I've always wanted this for you and me! You will be so happy here. I know you're angry with me. But all I wanted for you was this, and now you have it! I was right all those years ago.' She propped herself on the edge of his desk, her red lips too close for comfort, her musky perfume smothering.

'I've already found the perfect apartment for us. It may require a bit of work, but all I need now is a small deposit. Let's see, the amount we need . . .'

She dipped her face into her red faux crocodile purse and raised her eyes.

'This apartment is everything you were meant for: fame and success. They say in time you'll have your own line! Tell me I didn't say so!'

Her cheerfulness drained him.

'If you'll just give me this amount.' From her purse, she produced one of his personal checks, completed except for his signature. She held out a pen.

'It is over between us. I do not love you, nor will I ever.' He sighed loudly. 'I love another woman.'

She retracted the pen and placed her forefinger on her lip, as if she were considering a color to choose for the bedroom walls. 'Who said anything about love? We are *married!* Plenty of couples who've been married as long as we don't expect love, darling. They *learn* to love each other. Claude, it always amazes me how naïve you are!'

'I want a divorce.' Every word he spoke exhausted him. 'Please go,' he said, quietly, gently. He swiveled his chair around and looked out the window.

'I will not leave,' he heard her exclaim sharply from behind him, 'until I have this deposit in my hand! *I* know what's best for you. You *never* have! If it had been up to me, you would have been on your tenth collection already, under your own name!'

He turned back to face her intensity, but Rose-Marie had decided to soften her delivery.

161

'Darling,' she said, in new dulcet tones, 'just give it a chance. Did I marry again? No! Somewhere in this little brain of mine, I knew we would be back together. Come on, Claude, for old times, just a chance? Remember, back in Grenoble, when you were in school and I took you into my apartment after you were forced out of yours? Remember the dinners I cooked, you penniless and me working at a hair salon so I could help your career? I always, always believed in you. Meet me for dinner tonight at Maxim's. Just us. If there's nothing between us tonight, then there's nothing between us.'

She placed herself in his lap and wrapped her arms around his neck.

'I'm not moving until you say yes.'

'Please,' Claude said, the color rising to his face. 'I'd rather you get up than I lift you myself.'

'All right, all right, darling,' she said, laughing awkwardly as she stood, 'I just thought, you know, that after—'

Even for Rose-Marie, she seemed embarrassed. He felt badly for her. She *had* helped him in the old days in Grenoble. But to leave him for years, without a word?

Claude rose and walked to the door, feeling her eyes at his back.

'I'm sorry, Rose-Marie. It's over.' He left the room quickly.

Fifteen minutes later, in the corridor outside his office, Claude was horrified to overhear Lebrais in conversation with a familiar voice. He entered unwillingly.

'Your wife,' said Lebrais, uncoiling from Claude's chair, 'is such a pleasure. You didn't tell me—'

'We're separated to be divorced.'

'Claude, darling, don't go spreading ugly rumors. Monsieur, don't be mistaken, we've just had a little run-in about our new apartment. It's a small thing, darling. Really! I'll let you get back to work. I know an artist needs his space. I've learned that . . . the hard way.' She glanced and winked at Lebrais as she rose from her chair. 'I'll call you later,' she said, blowing Claude a puckered, shiny red kiss.

'I'm sorry for the confusion. We *are* getting a divorce,' said Claude, flushed.

'We had an interesting conversation about you.' Lebrais paused meaningfully. 'Rose-Marie confided in me – well, I guess you could call it that – that there has been another woman—'

'If I had known that the Salon de Silvane cared about—' Claude stopped. He was beginning to understand that Lebrais used many tactics to probe his victims. Claude, still just inside the doorway, lifted his jacket from the hook on the back of it.

Lebrais got up. 'Oh, no, please don't misunderstand. What you *should* know is that word gets around in this fishbowl we call Paris—'

'I would appreciate it if you kept my personal

affairs out of our work dialogue.'

Lebrais paused, smiling, 'Of course, Claude. I didn't realize they were of such a sensitive nature.' He was out the door before Claude. 'Oh, one little thing,' he added casually, 'for your public relations statement that we're delivering to the press tomorrow: I decided to leave in the sentence about the wedding dress having been designed here in the salon. It's best, for you and for us.'

Claude said nothing.

'We have too little to go on with only the paltry interview you gave Caroline. Your bio, you see, Claude, needs Madame Couturier's dress and the accompanying press reviews. Caroline and I realize you need a little help with public relations. Living in a small town for *so* many years, I'm sure, offers little chance for self-promotion.'

He cringed to hear Valentine's new name. 'I designed the dress out of my own atelier. To say otherwise would be a lie.' Claude's voice shook.

'I'm not sure we can keep you without keeping the dress. You have until tomorrow to decide.'

Lebrais's voice had turned cold and professional; the chill spread through the office. On the carpet directly in front of him, Claude spied the deep imprints of Rose-Marie's stiletto heels. He threw on his jacket and escaped the building.

CHAPTER 14

He saw her. Had some love-crazy cupid sent her promenading in his direction, as surely as he would have dreamed it? In her gray cotton suit with three-quarter sleeves and a dramatic white-collared shirt underneath, she was gliding in black open-toed sandals toward the place des Victoires. Perhaps to see him? To tell him she had made a mistake? No, it wasn't her. Yes, it was, high cheekbones, sharp chin, big blue eyes, and long legs that swung comfortably under her skirt. Why was she in Paris, rather than making love on some golden honeymooning beach? July 31. Had so much time gone by? She was back at work, but she would never be the same. Every cell, every speck of her being had been irrevocably changed by wedlock – to the wrong suitor.

She drew nearer, facing him yet not recognizing him, not thinking about him. He did not hesitate but strode quickly up to her and clasped her by the elbow, as an abductor would, forcefully and single-mindedly.

'Valentine.' To hear himself pronounce the name out loud, to its owner! She looked surprised.

Without speaking, without thinking, without looking at her, he guided her, his arm around her waist, to a bench on a narrow side street.

'Valentine,' he said again, sitting down with her.

She looked confused. 'How funny to run into you like this!'

'Everything is funny to you, isn't it?'

She tried to remove his tight grip, which was now attached to her wrist. 'Claude, please, that hurts.'

He released her wrist. 'How you take my breath away. I didn't expect to see you, and then, when I did, I guess . . . I always want to take you places where there is no one to get between us.'

'I haven't seen you since . . . oh, the dress, what a success! Congratulations.'

'I suppose I should be the one congratulating you,' Claude said.

'Claude . . .'

'Marriage. Valentine. Tell me . . .'

A vendor passed, carrying a wheelbarrow of white daisies.

Valentine brought her lovely face closer to his and whispered, 'Claude.' She paused. 'I know I should not say this to you, that it's careless, thoughtless, to say it, but I will! Since we've been apart, I've clung to you, unsuspectingly. Did you know that you've influenced my life hugely, and not just by your wedding dress? Whatever I do, I think of your gentle face, your simplicity. Because you're someone I feel I can tell anything and everything

166

to, I'm telling you this. But, looking at your eyes, perhaps – yes, I can see it – it's better if we never see each other again.'

'First you resurrect me, then you kill me.'

'Claude, come, don't be melodramatic,' she said, rising from the bench. They walked side by side. 'I'm happily married, but you and I will always share a connection, a profound inner communication. The question is, can we see each other like this or will you want more?'

'Valentine.' He grabbed both her hands, pulling her toward him. They looked into each other's eyes. She turned her face.

'You must let me go. I was late even before you kidnapped me,' she said, suddenly smiling. Smiling? How could a smile be so sad? Valentine, his Mona Lisa. How could so many contrasting emotions appear in a face? He released her soft cool hands. As she turned down the street, he watched her touch her hair with her freed hand.

Of course he would want more. He would never give up. He looked at the street sign just above him: rue Drouot. How could it be? His new place of employment was just minutes from her auction house.

Claude did not return to his office that afternoon but drove directly to Senlis. He thought of nothing; his mind was as empty as the white walls of his new office, blank as the future directly facing him. Whatever he cherished from his old life no longer interested him. His sister was at work; his friend Anatole had departed on a retreat with disabled schoolchildren. His nephews were vacationing at their cousin's house in the Loire Valley.

In the middle of the afternoon on a murky summer's day, Senlis looked and felt dull. Was it the heat or the meanderingly slow pace of the Nonette River, the tinny glare of the handrails on the stairs of the summer-forsaken school across the way, or the vacated narrow streets? Even the town's inhabitants had disappeared. Had the water in La Nonette gone bad and poisoned the lot of them?

Why had he cleaved to the very roots of his apple tree in Senlis for so long? Agnes had moved out long ago. Juliette lived only a stone's throw away from her old home but commuted to Paris daily. Her husband, Bernard, seemed to enjoy the quaint village atmosphere of Senlis, but he took many legal cases outside of town and traveled frequently. Claude trudged from his home to his car, loading it once again with books, drafting paper, pens, fabric, and two more suitcases of clothes. He shut the door to his studio without locking it.

When he returned to the faux-flowered hotel in Paris that night, the concierge informed him that his wife, Madame Reynaud, was awaiting him upstairs. How had she found him, his home away from her? He considered turning on his heel, but the raised eyebrows of the concierge forced him into the elevator.

The door to the apartment was open; he smelled garlic.

'Darling?' Rose-Marie called, poking her head out of the kitchen nook like any well-adjusted wife of thirteen years. 'I thought I'd cook you a beautiful dinner tonight. Your work is *so* demanding.' She was at his side, trying unsuccessfully to untie her apron, fiddling with the strings. She turned around with her back to him and said, with a lilt to her energetic voice, 'Will you, Claude?'

He untied her apron.

'Darling, how good it feels to be with you.' She kissed him on both cheeks. She took his hands, not unlike the way he had taken Valentine's that day, in a tight grip. He thought of Valentine responding as he was doing, giving in. 'Sit down, there you go.'

He sat, suddenly too tired to fight.

'You'll see how wonderful it is to be back together,' she said. 'I ran into some old friends of ours today, the Guesquières; they're coming for dinner tonight. You'll remember them when you see them. I met them in Paris many years ago, and they came out for dinner once in Senlis. Daphnée couldn't stop talking about what a genius you are. She wants you to design her daughter a dress for her twentieth birthday party. I said I'd put it on your calendar. I was looking for that, darling, your calendar. I couldn't find it anywhere!'

'I have no calendar,' he said slowly.

'You look tired,' she said, ignoring his response. 'Darling, take a few minutes to relax. They're coming at seven-thirty. You'll love these people. Too bad we all have to be stuffed in these puny rooms. Couldn't you have gone to the Ritz or the George V? I mean, we're famous now, and we're staying in this nasty little flea trap! What *will* the Guesquières *think?* Oh, darling, here I go, harping again, but I must tell you – the apartment I found *is* perfect for us. The location is so chic; from the windows, we'll be able to watch people walking down the street wearing clothes of the top designers, including yours. Oh, my beans! They'll be overdone!' She flew into the kitchen.

'This hotel is fine for me right now,' he said, when she returned.

'Fine for us,' she corrected him. 'I *am* your legal wife.'

He went into his bedroom, shut the door, and lay down. Against his will, he found the sounds of the busy kitchen comforting and fell asleep.

He awoke to the sound of her panicked whispering voice saying, '*Viens,* Claude! Come! Our guests are here. *Viens!*'

'I'm too tired.'

'If you stay in bed, I'll have my guests – our guests – come to you. They're here to see you, the famous designer.'

'I'm not coming. I'm sorry, Rose-Marie, you'll have to entertain them yourself.'

'But, Claude, they'll be so disappointed. Get up,

please, for cocktails at least. Then, go back to bed. Come, baby.' She tried another tactic. 'Can't you smell the dinner I made?'

Fortunately for Rose-Marie, he hadn't eaten that day.

'Well . . .'

'We'll excuse you early. A quick dinner and back to sleep.'

She kissed him brusquely on the lips and scampered from the room. Claude rose from the bed and looked himself over in the mirror above the dresser. His face looked thinner, paler. Dark stubble covered the lower half.

Voices greeted him before he could digest the faces. 'Oh, darling, here he is; hello, Claude.' The woman touched her cheeks to his. 'After all these years, it's so good to see you! Rose-Marie has told us how busy you are. I'm dreaming of the dress you'll make for me. Oh, but I shouldn't be greedy. We're giving our daughter – she's so beautiful and *what* a handful – a birthday . . .'

The woman's thick floral perfume enveloped him. Her face was made up with shiny blue eye shadow, pink rouge in the wrong places, and fuchsia-pink lipstick.

'Daphnée, let the man have a drink before you jump into his lap!' the portly, balding Monsieur Guesquière rebuffed his wife. 'Rose-Marie is in the kitchen. She might like your help.'

But Daphnée preferred to orbit Claude. Her husband introduced himself. 'It's been too long to remember names. Gérard.' He extended his hand.

Neither Guesquière held a drink. Where had Rose-Marie, in her short time in his abode, relocated the small liquor supply he had brought with him from his studio?

'This is *my* hotel room,' Claude said, refusing to take part in his soon-to-be-ex-wife's farce. 'Rose-Marie and I are separating, and I have filed for divorce. And I have no idea where she has stowed the liquor.'

Daphnée's lips formed a large fuchsia oval.

Gérard said, 'Well, well!' The couple laughed awkwardly.

'Daph, why don't you ask Rose-Marie where she's hidden the liquor, so we can fix Claude and me a drink!'

In seconds, Rose-Marie-in-action burst out of the kitchen, her red skirt swishing against her stockinged thighs, her breasts barely stuffed into a pale pink jacket. Like an experienced waitress, she poured the Pernod and wine, passed green olives, and popped one into her red mouth at the same time. The four sat around the small, round, chipped brown coffee table.

'Don't think by any stretch of the imagination that this outfit has been designed by my husband or that it pleases his designer's eye! Claude is too busy to think of his own wife!' she complained. 'This month, darling, will you include your devoted wife in your schedule?' She sidled up to him.

Claude looked down at the olives. He caught a flicker of anger on Rose-Marie's face, her narrowing eyes reminding him that other people were present, that he was required to act the part she had given him in her play. Daphnée sipped noisily from her glass.

Something sizzled loudly, and Rose-Marie jumped up and disappeared into the kitchen.

Daphnée took advantage of the Rose-Marie-less moment. 'I realize how busy you must be, Claude, but – well, now, lately, I love myself in reds, as you can see. I had my colors done last year: yes, red. I'm autumn, if you couldn't already tell! But what would my friends say if I had dinner with you and did not ask you, did not at the very least suggest, that you design the dress of a lifetime for me and my daughter? What would that say about me? About you?'

'Daphnée, Daphnée,' her husband interrupted. 'Give Claude a moment to speak. I'm sure he will fit you into his tight schedule.'

'I'm in the middle of designing the spring collection, which means I won't have time for individual requests until mid-fall.'

'There you have it, Daph. A dress as a Christmas present. You'll wow all your friends at the parties.'

'My Gérard. You're the best. Should I schedule a fitting now, for September, so the dress will be ready before December first?'

Rose-Marie appeared in the room again. He desperately wanted to excuse himself but did not wish to be rude to the Guesquières. He was also hungry. He allowed his mind to wander and reflect on his chance meeting with Valentine that day. He tried to convince himself that Valentine *must* have wanted to see him. He reminded himself that she was now married. He no longer heard the voices or words that surrounded him at the small chatty dinner table. As he nodded and smiled appropriately, his mind yearned for Valentine, to dress and undress Valentine, only Valentine. Always Valentine.

In the meantime, Rose-Marie had applied more red to her lips. She passed him a demitasse of coffee. He imagined himself looking down from above. In the blur, he heard himself say, 'Yes, I'll make you a dress. As you wish. Call the salon and they'll set up an appointment. Purple, short and sassy? Yes, a wonderful idea.'

By evening's end, Claude had promised a dress to Daphnée Guesquière (recognizing how over-loaded Claude's schedule was, she had quickly given up the request for her daughter's birthday) and a gown for Rose-Marie. He excused himself from the table at 10 P.M. and closed the door to the bedroom. No lock on the door. If he weren't so fatigued, he would have left the hotel. But go where?

He threw off his clothes and dove into bed, hoping sleep would protect him from any advances from Rose-Marie. He awoke to her nuzzling against him. He had forgotten how silky her breasts and skin felt. In his drowsiness, he remembered the strawberry freckles that speckled her creamy skin. Strawberries and cream. Her hair cascaded across his face. She had closed in, an octopus using every tentacle. He was too weary to fight.

Besides, Rose-Marie was an expert. The softness of her skin lured him. The pleasure was too rich to deny. He was impressed with her skills, the way her body moved in slow motion, as if underwater, confidently, stealthily, over his.

'I have missed you,' she whispered.

As he touched her, he discovered places where her body had changed over the years, how her belly and hips had rounded, how her breasts resided farther down. But her skin! Her skin was more supple than he remembered, as fine as the most luxurious silk the salon owned, and when he opened his eyes for a moment, in the darkness, its creamy whiteness shone like the moon. She moved on top of him, tickling, probing, and stroking. He let himself go, feeling a twinge of guilt at intervals of consciousness, guilty for responding to his wife's caresses.

That night, as she had intended, Rose-Marie stole her husband back – his body, his talent, his money, everything he had – except, of course, his heart.

CHAPTER 15

Rose-Marie dictated a relentless social life. Every night of the week she dragged Claude to receptions, dinners, charity events, and dances. The frenetic schedule was an effective distraction, but Claude felt ill equipped to engage in the essential art of small talk. At every function, he arrived late and escaped early.

At the salon, he worked from his early arrival to his late departure. As if hypnotized, he capitulated to all around him. Without a word of dissent, he had surrendered ownership of the beloved wedding dress to the Salon de Silvane. Chatting in the hall or grabbing a bite with his co-workers did not interest him. He shut his door and designed dress after dress.

With attention to the smallest detail, Claude oversaw all procedures. He covered his cork-covered wall with his sketches and with fabric swatches, color charts, photographs from art magazines, newspapers, and advertisements that inspired him. Every morning, he phoned his new contacts at the textile factories in Paris, Milan, Hong Kong, and Kuala Lumpur, discussing the newest fabrics, designs, and colors. He took advantage of the salon's far-reaching prestige to buy the largest assortment of materials and accessories possible, to gain access to the boldest and most creative vendors. One morning, he asked the Italian representative for a material that resembled linoleum.

'*Vous êtes fou!* You are crazy!' Marco Bennetto, from Milan, yelled into the receiver. 'Linoleum?'

'Yes,' insisted Claude. 'It's a fascinating material, all the grooves, specks, patterns! It will be the favorite fabric of the year. Trust me!'

Claude left meetings early, resenting anything that kept him from designing. Only while he was sketching, contriving, contouring, envisioning color combinations, was he able to lose himself and his recurring thoughts of Valentine.

Two months into the job, Claude won the French Couture Award for the wedding dress of the year. Again, the dress and Valentine in it blanketed the city's fashion press. Again, their names appeared side by side in the same sentences. Claude cringed when he saw her face, her eyes still so blue; was there ever a more melancholic blue? Did his own eyes play tricks on him to make him think so?

As a present, one publicist had enlarged the wedding photograph to life size. Claude placed the thick cardboard figure behind his door. He refused to peek. How could he expel the source of his torture from his office? He considered throwing it out the window. One late night at work, he gave it to the cleaning crew.

Claude had completed ten out of the twenty designs he needed to participate in the spring collections. The clothes would carry the label of the Salon de Silvane. Who cared about a name, anyway?

An assertive call to the accounting office 'to settle a tax question' was all it took for Rose-Marie to learn the details of Claude's starting salary at the salon. The apartment she chose to buy with her husband's money cost eight times his annual pay. After shrewdly calculating mortgages and bank loans, she told the realtor she would have the deposit in a week.

The battalions were in place, as were the mounted cavalry, the snipers, and the most accurate gunners. Claude's defensive stand did not last more than a day and a half. He collapsed under the barrage of calls to his office, the embarrassing 'dropins,' the siren entreaties at night, the pressure from her friends when they went out to dinner parties. She had him surrounded on all sides.

Claude was buried in the seemingly never-ending folds of midnight-blue velvet, the color of Valentine's eyes, from which he was constructing a suit of three layers, when he finally admitted defeat. He signed the check.

The purchase of the apartment was the best investment Claude had ever made – in his freedom. Rose-Marie busied herself with life-or-death decorating decisions, tortured herself over recent trends and the differing opinions of two decorators, and exhausted herself shopping to furnish the spacious rooms.

Claude had provided his social-climbing wife one more leg up on the ladder: the right address. He began to regard her ambition as the way to his escape. When she had clambered as high as Claude could take her, she might find someone higher up on whom she could work her circus tricks. She *was* artful.

With new motivation, Claude designed Rose-Marie's gowns to excite attention. He would execute a delicately plunging neckline to reveal only the tantalizing brink of cleavage, choose a material that would reflect her superbly warm and creamy skin and hope to win her the attention of an older viscount on the lookout for a sexy redhead. She lived in the new apartment during the renovations, while he stayed at his hotel and worked undisturbed into the night. Without her threats and bribes swarming about him, he declined all invitations, declaring from then on that he was on deadline for the spring collections.

Assembling a first-time collection in one month required impassioned creativity, enormous attention to detail, and back-breaking speed. Lebrais understood the enormity of the task and assigned his new designer two assistants and a team of eight aging seamstresses, who worked tirelesslessly under klieg lights with magnifying glasses: two for *flou,* soft material, two for *tailleur,* tailored fabrics, and four for collars and hems. Claude sketched and designed dress after dress, suit after suit, jacket after jacket, hour after hour. He plumbed the depths of his talent, conceiving ideas that surprised even him. In only one week, the first photographs of the line would be taken for previews in the fashion rags. Shoes, hairstyles, accessories, and the set for the show still had to be chosen.

The model Claude used was Valentine, of course. He showed his assistants recent newspaper and magazine photographs and asked them to find him her neck, her torso, her legs, her replica. His assistants returned with poor results.

'Non!' he shouted in aggravation, becoming the prima donna he had once detested. *'Non!* This collection needs a woman with long arms, long torso, eyebrows that curve at this angle.' With his brown pencil, he sketched the line with ferocity. 'A long neck is essential, the longest neck you can find!'

His collection, as dictated by Lebrais, was to consist of four formal gowns, four casual dresses, three pantsuits, three lightweight skirt suits, and two bathing suit designs with cover-ups, with four variations in different colors. Claude had balked at a wedding dress, the grand-finale white confection of most shows.

'It would be anticlimactic after the de Verlay wedding dress.'

Lebrais agreed. Lebrais informed Claude that Charles, the head accessory designer, would provide the belts, hats, and shoes. Claude resisted.

'How can I design a dress without the accessories?' he asked.

'Remember, my enthusiastic *new* designer,' Lebrais said loftily, 'this is not *your* collection. I must rely on my Charles, who knows our standards and our priorities, to maintain consistency throughout the show.'

The next day, as Lebrais made his office rounds, Claude told him he'd like to title his particular segment of the collection 'Valentine in Spring.' Lebrais cocked his head, a glint in his eye. 'We've decided on the name already. Are you so naïve as to think *you* would be naming this collection?'

'What is the name?'

'Simply Spring. Isn't it lovely? We like to think it says it all.'

'It sounds like a cheap perfume.'

'Claude Reynaud, tailor's son from the small town of – is it Senlis? – has grand ideas about himself, doesn't he? Someone with so little experience, yet such—'

'The title "Valentine in Spring" will accompany my work.'

'I'm beginning to see a connection here,' Lebrais said with a mischievous smile. 'Perhaps it would be appropriate to ask Valentine *Couturier* for permission before we engage further in this discussion. After all, it is *she* after whom you're naming the collection? Now that I think of it, we might be better advised to ask her devoted husband, Victor—'

'The name stays.'

Claude owed this collection to Valentine. Secretly, he hoped the collection and the press's response to it would entice her back to him. He could not shake the conviction that one day Valentine might forsake Victor for the man she truly loved. He had observed how fragmented she appeared with Victor, as if a part of her did not participate. Yet, with him, was it not the same? Despite his confusion, frustration, and bitterness, he would not stop loving her.

'We will discuss this later,' said Lebrais, keenly aware that his designer was on deadline. 'Now we need to discuss the music you are considering.' Lebrais's cell phone rang from his pocket. Phone to ear, he headed quickly out of the office. 'Get back to me on the *music*, Claude.'

Henri and Jean-Hugues would know what music he should choose. They were tuned in to what was hip and current. He called his sister's home and left a message asking his two nephews to visit his offices this Friday after school and to bring with them what they considered the coolest music to accompany his new collection. He asked for 'a new sound, something people will remember after the show, a melody that will remind them of the color blue.'

When fourteen-year-old Henri and thirteen-year-old Jean-Hugues burst into the Salon de Silvane,

Claude winced, first at the sight of two people he loved so much, but second at the appearance of the bedraggled-looking boys in their unhemmed pants and soiled and crumpled navy blazers. Could not his sister have found something more presentable for them to wear to one of the major salons of haute couture?

'Uncle Claude!' said Henri. 'This office is cool. It's so modern!'

Claude rose from his desk and hugged his nephews, a hug that felt so good he let it continue until they became embarrassed and shook him off.

'Anyone can have modernity,' Claude said. 'It's charm that's a challenge to produce or to purchase. How are you? How is your *maman*? Your papa? Come sit down! I've been missing you!'

'It's strange not having you around, Uncle Claude. We walk by your empty house every day on the way home from school. We miss Pédant!'

'How is your mother? I worry about her with no extra help.'

'She's okay, but it's hard without *grand-maman*,' said Henri. '*Maman* hired someone to help in the afternoons, but she's terrible! She wears these dust mops on her feet so she can dust the floors while she walks around, and she's so stingy. If we have dessert, she gives us a teaspoonful, not a bowl.'

'By now,' added Jean-Hugues, 'we can tell when she's about to lose it, so we do the "freakout" countdown. Didier counts down on his watch – five, four, three, two, one – and before you know it she's yelling at the top of her lungs about some little thing. She won't even let Pascale in the house unless she takes off her riding boots. Pascale never wears socks, so she has to go barefoot.'

'That's not acceptable.' Their uncle was always on their side. 'I will talk to your mother tonight.'

'Will you please, Uncle?' begged Henri. 'We don't need anybody. I could take care of everything after school. It's a waste of money. Tell her that.'

'Okay.'

'Do you want to hear our music now?' asked Jean-Hugues.

Claude drank in the color of his nephews' skin. The color wasn't pink or peach; it was the color of the inside of a conch shell, the beigeish shiny part that coils inside, protected by the outer ridges. He detected a hint of pimples on Henri's forehead.

'Here, Uncle.' Henri's voice cracked as he handed over the headphones of the portable CD player. Claude donned the headset.

'The first song is the Shelalas, an American band. It's my favorite,' said Jean-Hugues. Henri pressed the button.

I will never stop, I will never stop, not even for the cops, let 'em come to me, rough me up, I will never stop, never stop, loving you.

Claude spoke enough English to understand the simple words. Why did everything that spoke, sang, hissed, or roared have to do with love?

He pressed the forward button to the next song, which was more melodic. *It doesn't look good, when you look too good, means you're not who you are*. At least a little philosophy in that one, but the beat was too heavy and repetitive. Claude could not decipher a word from the next song. The words flew out like cars on a roller coaster, gathering speed as he listened. He removed the headphone from one ear.

'How do you know what he's singing about?'

'One of my friends wrote out the words and we translated them,' Henri said. 'Here's a French one I think you'll like.'

A soft female voice that sailed on high notes. The country ballad described the wilderness of the ocean. Loneliness echoed on the waves of the singer's voice. As Claude listened, looking at the attentive boys seated opposite him, he thought of Valentine. The music, like everything in his show, would be Valentine. Valentine in the ocean. Valentine in her apartment. Valentine in the sheets.

Since he could not have her, he would cling to the idea of her, her gentility, her naturalness, her almond-shaped eyes, the way she held her hair, so it fit inside her palm, the arch in the back of the neck that was the same as the arch in her foot-step, who she was on the inside, who she appeared to be from the outside. Her scarves, her sweaters, her look, her look, her look. It would take him a year to describe her every nuance.

The longing in this voice, as if from the inside

of the abyss, reminded Claude of his own voice and its yearning for Valentine, but it was too disheartening for this, his first collection.

The realization hit him as he looked into the wide eyes of his nephews seated across from him. The sound of Valentine was bright and carefree. The music that suited her best was bells, her charming laugh, their echo. That was it! The sound track for his first collection would encompass bells of all kinds, bells waking up children from unencumbered dewy slumber, Spanish bells, handbells, carillons, chiming, pealing, ringing, mammoth bells, tinkling bells, bells where the tone stretched for a mile, for an hour, where the last echo communed with the air on a breeze.

'Thank you, Jean-Hugues and Henri!' he said, ripping off the headphones. 'I've got it. Thank you! I will start with school bells and end with church bells. Don't look so worried, Henri.'

'I am. How could you choose bells when you need music?'

Jean-Hugues agreed. 'Bells, Uncle? Not cool. Bells can drive you crazy, like the ones at school. Bells mean school time, church time, the end of sleep or fun. I don't think so.'

'But bells are beautiful. In the old days, they rang them to drive away the evil spirits, to bless the crops, to send the sonorous truth out over the world. Listen today when you go home.'

'No, please. Whatever you do, don't use bells!' said Henri. 'What a waste!'

'Promise me to listen, tonight, with an open mind.'

The boys looked at each other and shook their heads slowly.

'Uncle Claude, *Maman* said I shouldn't forget to ask if you could design her a Christmas dress for a party at work,' said Jean-Hugues. 'Uncle Claude, are you all right?'

'Oh, yes, I just forgot where I was for a moment. A dress for your *maman*. Ah. Both of you draw the design and color your mother would look best in.' He pushed sketch paper and pencils in front of the two boys.

Henri grabbed the paper and went to work. Jean-Hugues looked up at his uncle. 'Can I write a description instead?'

'No – well, why not? A simple drawing and full description if you wish. Remember, the dress must be appropriate for work and also highlight her best qualities so she will appear brilliant no matter where she is. We three know, of course, that no matter what your *maman* wears, she will always draw attention. Color, always think about the color as you draw. You can also choose a material, but draw the lines first.'

The boys bent over their paper. Henri was finished before Jean-Hugues.

'Not bad, Henri,' said Claude. 'What color?'

'Green.'

'What kind of green?'

'Blue-green.'

'Excellent.' Claude stood up as Jean-Hugues

finished his drawing. 'Green-green wouldn't be good at all,' he advised, 'but blue-green changes everything. Bravo! With this straight line, does the slit go up to the knee or rest just below?'

'For *Maman*, I think just below.'

'You've got it! To the knee would be too short for your mother; she has long calves. I also like the V-neck.'

Claude picked up Jean-Hugues's less detailed rendition.

'You're coming along, Jean Hugues. What color?'

'Red, I think *Maman* looks great in red.'

'She does, but look, I think with this kind of dress with such sharp lines, you need a gentler color, perhaps a pink, a transparent very light rose. What about the belt? You choose the color and texture of the belt.'

The two boys huddled over the drawing until they came to a consensus: a black leather belt.

'A black leather belt on a pink dress? Are you sure?'

'It's original,' Henri said.

'You can't have it *too* pretty,' said Jean-Hugues.

'I'm not sure. Let's see, it could be leather, but perhaps a pink suede, covered randomly with black beads or sequins?'

'*Oui, oui,* I like it,' said Henri.

Jean-Hugues was not convinced.

Claude showed the boys the fabric room. He watched Henri's mouth drop at the enormous bolts of rolled multicolored material.

'I believe this room contains just about every color in the world for silk, moiré, linen, and satin,' Claude said.

'It's a city of color!' cried Jean-Hugues.

When they returned to his office, they found Lebrais at the threshold, looking at his watch.

'Claude, how's the collection coming?' he asked quickly, without waiting for an answer. 'I have some comments. Do you have a moment?' Lebrais looked at Henri and Jean-Hugues with an impatient smile.

'Allow me to introduce my nephews. Monsieur Lebrais, Henri and Jean-Hugues Roche.' He watched Lebrais absorb the frayed hems on Henri's pants and the stain on Jean-Hugues's wrinkled yellow tie.

Claude interrupted Lebrais's leaping judgments. 'Henri and Jean-Hugues have given me some suggestions for the collection's sound track. Boys, have a seat while I talk with Monsieur Lebrais. We'll grab a bite after that.'

Lebrais sat in the chair opposite Claude's desk. 'I've looked at your first two skirts for the collection, Claude. They're too short. The skirt and dress length for this collection is mid-calf. The other designers have cut the length that way, and of course I expect our entire collection to coalesce on the same hem length.'

'Mid-calf?'

'That's where Italy has gone for spring. Knee hem length is tired and over. Focusing on the calf will set us apart from others who are still indecisive.'

'André,' Claude asked, 'do you know any woman under five feet eight inches tall who looks good with a skirt or dress at the calf? It cuts the leg in half and shortens it. Who likes to look at a woman's calf muscle, especially on the runway? Now a transparent dress, perhaps, or a *coat* to mid-calf, but a skirt, a dress?'

'My naïve Claude, I always forget, although I shouldn't.' Lebrais paused to glance at Henri and Jean-Hugues perusing magazines in the corner. 'I shouldn't forget from where you come, so *little* experience of haute couture. Allow me to educate you. The length of the dress is something that is decided by many factors, many influences—'

'Do these influences,' Claude interrupted, 'the stock market, the Italians, have anything to do with whether a dress looks good on a woman or not? Are visuals merely secondary?'

'Claude, we're not in fashion school anymore. It would save us all a lot of time if you would remember that.' Lebrais emptied the chair of himself. 'The length,' he said loudly, 'will be to the calf. The entire collection from this house will show calf-length dresses, suits, and skirts. There is no discussion on this matter.' He glared at Claude and left the room without good-byes.

'Boys, you have hereby witnessed the silliness of the grown-up world! To the calf! I might as well work as hard as possible to design the ugliest garments I can think of. What a success I would be, *n'est-ce pas?* To the calf! What next?'

He laughed.

'Come, let's get a bite to eat outside, where I can show you the importance of the hemline, where the fabric ends and the body begins. To the calf! He might as well have said, 'I'm sorry, you'll have to design only brown-colored clothing.' To the calf! We'll see. I suppose I'm going to have to be sneaky about this one.'

CHAPTER 16

His hands shook as he opened the invitation. The contemporary portrait of Victor, which had scowled at Claude on his last exit from Valentine's apartment, glowered at him once again, this time reproduced on a glossy white heavy card stock. Although it was Victor's portrait, the likeness was not obvious: Victor's eyes were not so large; the real Victor's chin bore a more pronounced cleft, his lips were thinner, more determined and pursed than in the portrait's version.

Claude remembered Valentine mentioning that she was hanging a show for an old friend of hers and that a co-worker had lent them gallery space. But to feature the portrait of Victor Couturier on the invitation, the man who had most recently been expelled by the art establishment, appeared extremely aggressive, if not risky for the show's popularity and for Valentine's job. She did have a new boss. Did the artist, Théodore Rohan, and Valentine concur that this work, despite the scandal created by its subject matter, was the artist's most significant to date? Perhaps Valentine wished to prove that, despite all, Victor was alive and well in the art world.

She must not have sought approval from the new *commissaire-priseur* of Drouot. What new director would assent to an invitation sent to the entire art community that celebrated a portrait of his shamed predecessor? The persistent yet twisted hope of a lover sprang forth: Victor *must* have influenced Valentine's decision. He turned the card over and studied the formal engraved script.

A Collection
of
Contemporary Portraits and Works
by
Théodore Rohan

A Cocktail Reception

Friday, September 11,
6:30–8:30 p.m.
Assembled by Valentine de Verlay
La Gallerie des Oiseaux

16, quai Voltaire
Paris
RSVP: Marie Gilbert, 01 14 42 35 99

Valentine had not used her married name! Lebrais entered Claude's office. 'Ah,' he said, glimpsing the invitation that Claude had hastily replaced on his desk. 'I see you've received one also. I think it's quite a good likeness of Victor. Although the artist did not quite get the cleft in his chin. Have you met the man?'

'At their engagement party.' Claude shuffled the papers on his desk.

'Must be rather awkward, I would think,' said Lebrais. 'A portrait of Victor, the Drouot disappointment, now featured in a show that should attract major attention from the art world. I've heard the artist is an intimate friend of Victor's family, and although I haven't seen any of Rohan's work except for this,' he pointed to the invitation, 'he's supposed to be an impressive talent.'

Engaging in the morning's gossip seemed to elicit an unusually cheerful mood from Lebrais. 'By the way, Claude, I've done the impossible for you.'

'Yes?'

'I've decided to grant your wish. Your collection will be reintroduced under the name Valentine in Spring. It will fit nicely as a subheading of our Simply Spring collection, and the name has a nice ring to it. Tomorrow, you will be given five of the most coveted invitations of the season for your personal guests. Please send them out as quickly as possible.'

The next day, despite the taunts he expected from Lebrais, Claude escorted the chatty Pédant from his apartment to his Salon de Silvane office. Pédant's occasional squawk and the messy, soothing sounds of his scratching and fluttering wings were the company Claude needed in the intense and lonely designing period ahead.

Rose-Marie shared Lebrais's habit of popping in unannounced to visit Claude. Every so-called sojourn had a purpose and a routine. The act began with the attempted guilt trip – 'Why do I never see you?' – followed by an ample peek of cleavage and ended with the complaint, 'All the other husbands accompany *their* wives to these events!'

Claude waited patiently for the dénouement of this afternoon's visit, which was, 'But really, darling, the whole world is going to the Côte d'Azur for August, and I've found the perfect house for us to rent outside Saint-Tropez. It's just come on the market because these very wealthy people canceled. I can't believe our luck! It's just up the road from the chic Club Fifty-five, which is the most perfect location, and the Trouvés have rented on the same road. Darling, it's such a steal, too. We'd be *stupides* not to jump at this!'

Her act's grand finale was to thrust a pen into Claude's hand and a check under his nose. If he hesitated to sign his name, she would repeat the performance from the first scene onward. To escape her perfume (he made a mental note to buy her a scent he liked) and return to the solace of his work, Claude signed without question.

Rose-Marie usually added an epilogue on her way out the door.

'Oh, how *could* I have forgotten? If I'm going south, where I will be seen by absolutely everyone who *is* anyone, I must have a dress or just a few new outfits, darling. Could you? I know how impossibly busy you are, but yes . . . I knew you'd say yes!'

Holding the check out carefully between her red fingernails, Rose-Marie would blow him a stage kiss from the doorway and whisper, 'Keep working, Claude!'

August arrived and Paris emptied. The bustling noises of the city faded to echoes in the unin-habited heat. Despite the oppressive humidity, which took him unawares – in Senlis, a slight breeze from the North Sea cooled even the hottest days – Claude sauntered comfortably down the avenues from his wifeless Parisian apartment to the Salon de Silvane. The summer leftovers at the salon included the receptionist, Anne; Lebrais's secretary; the eight seamstresses hired specifically for Claude; and a woman who smelled strongly of cigars, who organized and ironed the material in the fabric room.

The other designers had completed their collec-tions earlier in the spring or planned to return in mid to late August. Their offices were evacuated warrens, abandoned for summer beaches or alpine views.

By mid-month, Claude's seamstresses were basting; by August 25 he had completed the requisite twenty designs; bolts of fabric, pinned with instructions to the seamstresses, were lined up like soldiers ready for battle. Claude hewed to Lebrais's hemline dictate by designing a to-the-calf jacket to accompany all his daywear, under which *his* hemline reigned. Claude brimmed over with pleasure at the creative compromise and the original result.

Claude's daywear designs consisted of simple classical knitwear, molded perfectly to his models' bodies. Few seventeen-year-old models can achieve the intelligent maturity Claude sought in a woman wearing his designs, so he hired older models to display them.

The gray-green and heather-piped bouclé wool suit with its oversized hip-hugging belt of the same material was one of Claude's favorites. The model's gray-green eyes melted into the suit color like evening sunset on a grassy field. A scarf crafted of the same splendid wool in powder pink mirrored the sheer breeze blouse under the suit jacket.

Evening wear was left as bare as possible; his sinuous gowns were mostly floor-length, simple colorful sheaths of silk-rayon blends with dipping V-necks. The more practical dresses were buttoned up with rhinestones to a starchy white collar; the dreamier ones were encircled with Japanese-inspired crimson cummerbunds or with thick lavender fringe. Fringe! Claude Reynaud would never have conjured up fringe in his tailor shop at home. Had his wife corrupted his sense of fashion? A lowslung, emerald-green, rayon-cashmere pantsuit embodied freedom and comfort combined with elegance.

Of all the designs in his collection, Claude was convinced his white Spanish lace gown would seize the most attention. The swirling lace pirouetted around the white fitted silk-satin-weave gown; long lace sleeves buttoned to mid-finger. He tucked a white camellia between the model's ear and her dark side-swept chignon. He hungered to behold Valentine in this dress. He imagined her as a swan, gliding in a still lake. The slight rise in her left hip would set off a quivering motion of white lace.

The neckline was crucial to Claude. Either the neck arose from a sharp V in his evening wear or from a *bateau* neck across the collarbone in his day wear. Occasionally, he used soft ruffles. He avoided scoop necks, which he thought thickened the neck.

Claude also emphasized the waist, cinching, wrapping, cuddling, and encircling the curve in suits, dresses, and gowns. Above all, he aspired to design garments that *disappeared,* so the viewer experienced the woman, radiantly herself, rather than the clothes she wore.

Claude slept four hours a night. So much to order, cut, pin, sew, arrange, discuss. Lebrais supplied his designers with cots for sleepover work nights. Claude was the only one who took advantage of the extra furniture. Dozing off in the same room with his designs tacked to the wall and his fabric-pinned mannequins as company reminded him of waking up to his creations in his sunlit studio in Senlis. He could dream about them day and night.

Claude decamped from his work for only one weekend to visit his sister and family in a house they had rented on the Île de Ré, a small island off Bordeaux's coast. The stark landscape of white salt marshes bordering light-infused horizons supplied Claude with a renewed appreciation of blended grays, whites, and beiges. Every experience fed his work. His nephew Henri helped him address his personal invitations to the show. He wanted to draw a horse on every envelope.

'A horse?' asked his uncle.

'You're in a stable, aren't you?' Henri began sketching the horse. 'See, something like this.' His horse's nostrils flared; the eyes were too small for the head. 'Oh, and Uncle, don't forget to put a strand of hay in each envelope!'

'What's a sailboat doing in the background?' Claude asked his furiously sketching nephew.

'I'm not sure! I guess I was thinking of what Anatole told us the other night, that the mast of the ship is our cross in a storm. It holds the sails that keep us moving through life. Something like that.'

Henri sketched a cross on the boat's deck. 'Your buddy Anatole has some pretty interesting ideas.

I wouldn't mind having a mast in front of me right now.' He lifted his arms, signaling for imaginary help. 'My ship is tossing!'

Claude's invitation list included his sister and brother-in-law, Anatole, Rico, and, of course, Valentine. Claude did not extend the invitation to Valentine's husband. Although he was tempted, he could not exclude Rose-Marie. He would ask Lebrais for an extra invitation.

CHAPTER 17

Paris woke up during the first week of September. She beamed with vacation-warmed skins, bustled with purpose, and overflowed with movement, color, and noise. Parisian women threw off their espadrilles and string bikinis and donned heels and tight skirts, determined to recapture lost time and recover their city-speed pace. The clamor of traffic and sirens resumed.

Lebrais had chosen Le Salon Impérial of the Hotel Intercontinental, the *grande dame de Paris,* to show the collections. When Claude viewed the gilded ballroom with its huge marble columns, he grew disheartened. The room was decorated lavishly, replete with sculptures of gilt stucco and a ceiling fresco depicting nymphs and satyrs in a pastoral setting.

He tried to imagine ways to modify the room's extravagance and thought of Henri's horse sketches and his suggestion to enclose hay in each invitation's envelope. Inspiration struck; he called the stables inside the Bois de Boulogne where a client of his rode and, without asking Lebrais for permission, ordered hay to be delivered to the hotel's service entrance. Fortunately, six ten-foot-high, floor-to-ceiling windows accented the grand ball-room. To reduce the daytime glare and hide the gilt window molding, Claude instructed his workers to arrange the hay so it cascaded gently from the top of each window. He draped the enormous chandeliers with white tulle to create luminescent clouds.

To Claude's surprise, Lebrais approved of the hay; he even suggested including some stray mice-catching cats and adding a few fistfuls of straw to the models' meticulously arranged hair.

'But, please, Claude,' Lebrais warned, 'don't go too horsey, too country, on me! Like just about everything, it *has* been done.'

Preparations for the room were almost complete. Claude and the workers affixed tulle the color of hay onto the walls, then covered the tulle with different-sized leaf shapes in light-green crushed silk.

For the music, Claude searched for bells with different tones. He found and bought four gongs in a Korean shop down the street from his office. He discovered a cassette tape of church bells not unlike the bells that clanged inside the belfry of Notre-Dame de Senlis. Lebrais's receptionist helped him locate alpine bells, which suggested the incongruous melody of the tinkling clatter of goats moving up the side of a craggy mountain. After many inquiries, he was sent a recording of bells from a Tibetan monastery.

More sewing, adjusting material to bodies, locating lost accessories. The shoes for one suit had not arrived. There was no place or time for Claude's anguished heart. No matter. Since he had chosen models who captured Valentine's profile and height, he had succeeded in creating a world in which he was surrounded by his obsession.

The show opened on September 8. Claude, in his modest black Senlis work coat, directed from backstage and helped the models button, zip up, and look the part. Pédant had been left behind in the apartment, rejected from the repertoire.

'Please, give the models some air; it's too hot!' he chided the technical assistants. The air-conditioning was not functioning. Never in his life had Claude dealt with so many details at once: lights, setting, acoustics, makeup, hair, shoes, belts, ribbons, stockings, not to mention the attitudes of his models.

One model tripped on a bale of hay and went sailing. She cut her knee on a high-heeled shoe that had been left on the runway. She needed a Band-Aid, and her white dress was soiled.

Enter Madame de Rénier, Lebrais's veteran showroom assistant. In her bejeweled red sneakers, she administered from her first aid and sewing kit and from the makeup case, with its hairbrush, on her belt.

Another model was found in the bathroom, sick from the previous night's alcoholic binge. Or was she pregnant? Madame de Rénier, head bent, punched numbers on one of the two cell phones on her belt in search of a replacement.

'Mon-sieur Rey-naud,' she said, in her authoritative staccato, 'I can reach only one model to replace Leila. Her name is Amanda, and that's all I'm going to say. You've never seen a better runway stride in your life.'

Claude had no time for further questioning. 'Very well.'

Out of the corner of his eye, he saw Lebrais popping open a champagne bottle. 'To lift the spirit of the dark backstage,' he heard his boss pronounce loudly. The *première main,* first seamstress in the well-delineated pecking order of sewers, slipped on a microphone headset and began a roll call of the models. Céline, Saskia, Chlöe, Leila – 'She's left!' called another model from a back room. The models stumbled out of the dressing room.

'Her replacement will be here in five minutes,' yelled Madame de Rénier.

The photographers clicked and flashed for brief pre-runway poses. Claude told each of the models to practice *breathing* before they began their walk.

'Please don't hold in your stomachs!' he said. 'Try to experience the clothing on your skin. Smile if the material tickles you as you walk and air comes into the folds. Whatever you do, no *attitude!* Wake up, show your intelligence, be the great women you are, lionesses after the hunt, serene yet powerful.'

He discovered that a model in one of his sleeveless gowns had a dragon tattoo on a forearm that would be seen. He tucked straw into the dress's V-neck and shoulder, hoping it would obscure the green image.

Claude's heart beat out the hours like a drum. Lebrais wandered the premises, checking for loose threads, ripped hems, and unbrushed hair, asking questions, watching, witnessing. He answered queries from those of the press who had found their way backstage and closed in on the arm-flinging Claude for a quick pose and interview.

'But Lebrais, I must – the model who was absent . . .'

Although Lebrais knew enough not to interrupt his designer just minutes before a show, he could not resist commenting on Claude's appearance.

'You can't wear that old thing when you come out from backstage.'

'I'm not planning to appear onstage.' Claude adjusted a model's scarf.

'Please excuse me. I continue to forget your *inexperience*, Claude. You *will* appear onstage. As a rule, we exhibit the collection *and* at the finale, the couturier. If you wish, your models can accompany you. The press *must* relate to the person behind the collection.'

'I do not plan to walk on the runway,' Claude repeated, now gratefully interrupted by a model with a torn stocking.

'I can't find Madame de Rénier,' she said. She

bore a facial resemblance to Valentine but looked half drugged. She spoke listlessly, slurring her words.

'This man will help you find another pair of stockings,' Claude said, nodding at Lebrais. 'He's the maestro of this orchestra!'

Another model ran up, breathless. Her shoes were too tight. She showed him a blister from shoes at another show. 'There's Madame de Rénier. She'll find another pair,' Claude said calmly. 'If you can't walk, jump or dance barefoot down the runway!'

Madame de Rénier had returned with Amanda, the new model. Madame had spoken correctly: the girl's walk toward Claude was attention-riveting, a combination of masculine swagger and streetwalker's stalk.

Claude took a deep breath. Valentine in Spring? Impossible. He needed advice; Lebrais would know what to do. He would omit the dresses scheduled for that model. But then it occurred to him: the evening gown with the red silk sweater slung around the waist. With Amanda's attitude and long swinging stride, the garment would soar. He called out to the *première main* to change the clothing lineup.

Claude felt the vibrations of people gathering, pushing in through the ballroom doors. He imagined them threading their way among the meticulously dressed invitation takers and the larger-than-life bouncers, hired to instill order in the soon-to-be-teeming outer salon. He sprinted to the empty seating area to check the view from the back row of custard-colored silk chairs, to ascertain that the hay looked thick enough, the runway was clear, the lights were not too bright. He paused there for a few moments, before his first collection would be exposed to the most discerning fashion critics of the world. His body quivered nervously, but he savored the stir and fuss, the moment just before creation meets its judges.

He careened backstage as he glimpsed the light from outside bursting through the dark doors. He felt the heat in the room accumulate. Heat? The air conditioner had been fixed, hadn't it? The clicking sounds of cameras. What were they photographing? Where were the bells?

'The bells!' he yelled through his cupped hands.

Tibetan bells began the show. Claude remembered Rico saying, 'A collection must be delivered like a baby, smoothly, carefully, surely.' With a wink, Rico had told him he normally *massaged* his models into the mood.

Out stepped the models, one by one.

'Saunter slowly, please, but with life, animation. *Feel* the clothes,' Claude pleaded at the edge of the curtain. 'What does the fabric say to you? *Now?* Be yourself! Use *your* style!'

The model who had complained about the tight shoes addressed him on the threshold of light. Her neck in the light – he had to contain himself – matched almost exactly Valentine's arc of whiteness. 'I will fall. I know it! These shoes, that hay . . .'

Claude asked for her shoes and scraped the shiny new bottoms with a nail file he found on a makeup table. 'If you slip,' Claude whispered to her, 'don't hold back. Tumble one hundred percent, lie there in the hay, roll around a bit! But please, whatever you have to do, do it with luxurious smiles! Smiles that melt in your mouth!'

Claude dropped a chocolate truffle into each model's mouth as she waited for her cue. He heard the cameras, the buzz, the bells. He tied belts, arranged scarves, scratched bottoms of shoes, adjusted straw in hair, smoothed the wrinkles in a scarf, glued a loose white bead onto a model's bodice, rubbed off rouge, imitated carrying his head high, listened agonizingly to the silence, and exhaled with relief at the bursts of applause, thunder out of nowhere on a hot sultry day.

After the last model came back smiling, naturally – was it possible – happy, her eyes sparkling in the white lace gown, Claude heard what sounded like an explosion. Was it applause or denunciation? Claude *knew* the press would be smitten with the white Spanish lace gown. Lebrais approached him, his white teeth gleaming in the backstage dimness, his hands outstretched. Claude took a moment to peek at the videoscreen that offered a panoramic view of the house, his audience. During the show, unlike Lebrais, who was fixated by each viewer's response, Claude had avoided the screen. Now his eyes went to the brightest color on the display: red lips.

His wife. He looked away. He'd rather receive the approaching Lebrais.

'You must take a bow,' Lebrais shouted over the applause. 'They want you to.'

'You go for me.'

'Now's not the time for modesty or stage fright, Claude Reynaud.' It hardly seemed possible, but the applause grew louder.

'You must go out,' Lebrais yelled again, his face reddening. 'They want to congratulate you personally.'

Claude was immovable.

'For heaven's sake!' Lebrais yelled, as he charged out from behind the curtain.

Claude peeked again. This time, he spotted Valentine in the center front seat he had reserved for her. She wore a shiny red halter dress. Who had designed such a thing? In that instant, despite the noise and congratulations from models, from backstage assistants, he was overcome with jealousy. How could she wear a dress designed by someone else, a dress in shiny garish red that drew all life from her face?

Lebrais was back and this time pulling him, saying 'Now! Enough of this childishness!'

Claude pulled back. 'Non.'

Lebrais repeated, 'Now!'

The clapping had not abated. The tension

thickened. Claude was not prepared, had not considered this. He thought of Anatole, of his sister and brother-in-law in the crowd. He scowled at Lebrais and then dashed into the spotlight as if diving into a pool. Claude Reynaud, his tattered black work coat down to his shins. Perspiration dotted his upper lip and his forehead. He did not smile luxuriously as he had compelled his models to do. Amid the throbbing flashes of brilliance from cameras, he blinked and bowed. When he looked up, he saw the flutter of hands, a mass migration on the brink of flight. He bowed again and nodded, repeating, *'Merci, merci,'* and jogged off the hay-strewn walkway of his first collection.

Claude had prepared for every detail of the show, from the color and texture of stockings, the stable-yard lighting, the padding on the runway, even the shade of mascara. What he had neglected to anticipate was Lebrais's well-attended post-show reception.

After the applause had died down and the models began to dismantle themselves and Claude had received congratulations from everyone backstage, Lebrais escorted him quickly by the elbow into the neighboring reception room. Microphones were at his mouth, a man in a black leather shirt shouted in his ear.

'Monsieur Reynaud, what or who inspired your show? Your models looked so relaxed, so happy, so round, not bone-thin and frazzled. Is this a new concept of beauty? Is the white lace dress a return to the Victorian era? Why the hay, monsieur? These surely aren't stable clothes! And, please, what about the bells? Is a religious theme running through your work?'

Claude nodded, smiled, frowned, and muttered insufficient answers to the inquiries.

C'est ridicule! he thought, laughing to the faraway Juliette, whom he motioned to join him. 'This is ridiculous! They ask me questions and hear the answers they have already decided would look best in print!'

His laughter stopped. Out of the corner of his eye, he saw Valentine. The poorly chosen crimson satin halter dress made her skin appear ghostly pale. The halter shortened her long neck. How could his elegant muse have chosen something so tawdry on the occasion of his first collection? As she approached, she put out her hands – to protect herself? No, to take his in hers.

'You've really done it, Claude Reynaud,' she said. 'You've wowed the crowds; you've produced the best collection of the decade, perhaps the century!'

He couldn't help himself, 'Your dress—'

'You don't like it,' she said, and glanced down. 'Victor insisted I wear it . . . But Claude, forget the dress. I'm here to support you, like a good friend.'

'Good friend,' he repeated, as if not understanding.

Brigitte de Savoie, a client who had visited

Claude's studio in Senlis, arrived at Valentine's side, wearing a cream sheer silk blouse and a rust-and-cream-print crinkle-pleated skirt. Claude noticed a thin sheen of perspiration above her upper lip. The room had been uncomfortably hot.

'Valentine, hello! Claude, you *are* the real thing, so original! Brilliant! I can't wait until I get my hands on that white lace dress, but then, again, the world will be wearing it.'

More people arrived at his side, beautifully dressed admirers wearing clothes he never would have imagined brushing against or touching. He watched as the pale Valentine, in her red dress that exaggerated the dark circles under her eyes, began to fall away from the circle.

'Valentine,' said Brigitte, not letting her go, 'the color of your dress is amazing! Claude, *you* must have designed it.'

A laugh was his reply. Seeing another wave heading his way, Claude excused himself briskly, took Valentine's hand, and steered her toward an EMERGENCY EXIT ONLY fire door.

'I have a present for you, Valentine,' he said to her turned cheek, as she looked behind her. He led her through a fluorescent-lit narrow corridor to a darkened back room. As his eyes adjusted, he could make out, in the back corner of the room, a ceiling-high pile of filled black plastic bags that looked like garbage containers. He moved her to the wall and leaned into her. Was it the vulgarity of the red dress that drove him to this behavior?

'Stop, Claude, really.'

He held her shoulders.

'Claude, really. Please. What are you doing?'

He let her go and said he was sorry, that he did have a present for her. Before he could retrieve it from his pocket, she was gone, the red dress oscillating in the glaring fluorescent light. He could hear the muffled tumult of the party beyond the fire doors, the noisy cries of swallows in the first flush of spring.

It's all about mating, in the end, he thought. I'm mating madly but incorrectly. He touched the gift in his pocket that he had wrapped that day, a silver framed invitation to his show, which he had signed *To my muse, forever*. Then the Salon de Silvane's newest couturier sank to the floor . . .

Claude left the dark trash storage room only because of the persistent thought that Lebrais or a search party would discover him. As he rose to go, he felt an ache in his lower back. Had he aged twenty years as he crouched there? Would he enter the gilded reception room and find that two decades had passed and the room was empty of the people who had swarmed to interview Claude Reynaud?

As he drew nearer to the door, he tried to possess and prepare himself, as he had learned to do in life, against all that was rude and inappropriate, against crimson satin dresses designed by other people. Against the noise.

'If it isn't Claude himself!' Lebrais, on the

lookout, was the first to spot his couturier in hiding. 'Gone for a break, no doubt, or a cigarette. What, in this little corridor?'

Was a photographer nearby? A videocamera? Claude looked around.

'You have the world at your feet! Everyone wants a piece of you; the orders are into the hundreds now. And,' said the mocking Lebrais, 'you rush to the back corridors. Will wonders never stop? The cameramen were careening down the rue de Rivoli, assuming you had escaped. But, I knew it; I knew you were close by. I knew you wouldn't leave, now that the collection is out, now that you are truly a Salon de Silvane couturier, and' – Lebrais paused meaningfully – 'more importantly, because Valentine de Verlay is in the next room!'

Claude answered many questions, posed for photographs with his models and clients, and managed to escape the room after a pummeling publicity lunch. In the entrance hall, he overheard two tourists discussing the hotel. 'This is where King Louis the Sixteenth and Marie Antoinette spent their last days together and where the king was condemned to death!'

I too have been condemned here! thought Claude.

Rather than return to his apartment, where he feared the unending glare of his wife and her dozen friends' congratulations, he unearthed his Peugeot from the basement garage on the place de la Concorde and drove north toward Senlis.

Lebrais would be angry that Claude had made an early exit. Lebrais's job was to accompany the moment, ensure that it was *happening*, prod it, love it up, coerce and threaten it, even bribe it; be everywhere, do whatever it took to make the moment last. 'The most important time for a designer,' Lebrais had patronizingly instructed Claude earlier that day, 'is directly after his collection is shown.'

Back at his office, Claude would be fielding publicity people, giving interviews, elaborating on his next collection, dodging Lebrais and that night's invitations. Unfortunately for Lebrais, his newly acclaimed designer desired only the comfort of his nephews and the quiet peace of his garden.

As Claude drove into Senlis that late afternoon, he took comfort in the cicadas' leg-rubbing sonata and the soothing rumble of tires over worn cobblestone. He wished Pédant were with him. He doubted Rose-Marie would remember to feed him, but Pédant was smart enough to find his own food or else to announce annoyingly every few minutes, *'Feed the parrot! Feed the parrot!'*

When he entered his studio, it seemed as small as a rodent's hole, the impoverished relative of the opulent Hotel Intercontinental. The creamy wall paint was graying; cracks he had never noticed formed a delta in the right-hand corner of the ceiling. His pantry contained a sack of onions, a few dirty potatoes. In his refrigerator, he found an old carton of milk gone sour, a bottle of uncorked wine, a few now soft and wrinkled apples, a piece of chocolate.

How pathetic is this creature who lives here! he thought.

He recalled Valentine's visits to his lowly studio, her hesitation over where to place her coat, which she had dropped on the only chair, next to his desk. Had he thought this quaint setting would uplift him? He turned off his cell phone and lay down on the unmade bed, too tired to undress or to bring the sheets that dragged on the floor up to meet his stubbly chin.

CHAPTER 18

The room throbbed with sunlight. He had slept as if for two lifetimes. Renewed shame filled him as he remembered the way he had behaved with Valentine the day before. He tried to obliterate from his mind the awful red dress that punctuated every thought.

'Oh, sadness!' he said, as he looked at his watch. Nine minutes after nine o'clock! He had missed his nephews, Juliette, and Bernard. They were at school or at work; their house would be empty.

He could drive to the salon and incur the wrath of Lebrais for his exit the day before or he could meet his nephews after school. A jolt of the boys was what he needed to forget his idiotic behavior with Valentine. If he took the day off, he could design, garden, visit his parents' grave, lunch with Anatole, and greet the boys after school, perhaps stage one of Didier's favorite puppet shows.

He had designed his first collection. He had appeared onstage in his dowdy old black work coat. He had degraded himself to the basest level of humanity with the woman he loved, and then he had hidden in a storeroom like a wounded animal.

As much as he disliked the idea of disappointing Lebrais, Claude decided that, after months of arduous and single-minded work and preparation, this day was his. The press would not disappear. He could answer their questions the following morning and from then on. In any case, today he had no answers.

The memory of his afternoons with his young nephews returned to him in full color, and he wished forlornly, absent-mindedly, that he had never been introduced to the devastating pleasures of Valentine. He called Lebrais's office. The secretary informed Claude that he needed to be at the salon at 11 A.M.

'Please tell Monsieur Lebrais I'll be in tomorrow,' Claude said.

'But, Monsieur Reynaud, I know he has many appointments planned for you,' she trilled. 'At eleven, the fashion-page editor of *The International Herald Tribune* will be here for an interview. *Vogue* at three P.M. Congratulations, monsieur.' Another pause. He imagined her eyes zipping around the green-screened computer. 'There's a television station coming also and a radio interview.'

'These were not on my schedule.'

'Monsieur Lebrais made the appointments after the success of the show; he's been on the phone all night and this morning.'

'Please tell him I will call at one P.M., but I will not be available for interviews until tomorrow.'

The bells rang at the lycée across the street with

a fuller and more rounded sound, a more purposeful ringing than the Hotel Intercontinetal's sound system could muster. He bought *Le Monde* and *Le Journal de Senlis* and a coffee at the sun-laced café down the street.

'Claude!' cried George, a massive man with hands that resembled mitts and wiry hair springing from the back of them. He bowed and held out a chair to his loyal customer as if he were welcoming a royal personage.

'We've been following your success in the news! Thank you for the privilege of your company – only the day after your show! Anatole was here fifteen minutes ago, talking, as always, about you. He was on his way to the church, as always, too!'

'Yes, yes, I'll visit him soon,' said Claude, perusing the headlines of the newspapers. His name occupied the top four inches of both style sections.

CLAUDE REYNAUD RINGS IN A NEW ERA OF DESIGN. CLASSICISM AU NATUREL another title read. Below the first full-page article, he saw a color photograph of himself alone on the blinding stage, his face in a tight grimace. One photograph featured the model wearing the white lace. A tremor ran through him. She was Valentine, more Valentine than the woman herself! *Le Monde*'s style editor had chosen to feature the lavender fringe-waisted evening gown.

On a subsequent page of the arts section of *Le Figaro,* his eye caught a small photograph of him at the reception with Valentine, her right shoulder cut off.

We were never meant to be in the same frame, he thought bitterly. At second glance, Claude could not help but admit that they looked good together. Could he detect a glimmer in their eyes, a bold smile, a shared romance? He felt it as clearly as the blue brightness of sky outside.

The article quoted Lebrais:

> The spring themes of the Salon de Silvane were cleverly interpreted by M. Reynaud. Since Claude Reynaud and the salon shook hands in partnership, we have enjoyed a symbiosis of inspired collaboration.

Claude cringed as he read about 'the reticent designer who hid behind the curtain when it was time to make the final runway appearance.'

The article commended Claude for the new natural look of his models, for his

> eye for accuracy and his subtle tricks of tailoring. M. Reynaud brings to tailoring a new rigor. The semantics of dress have never been more refined. Despite skepticism that the neophyte Reynaud would not have had enough time to establish an identity in Silvane's nuanced company, the couturier has, instead, introduced in the salon a brand-new reductive elegance, deceptively

simple, to enhance the wearer and not the couturier or the garment. In his work, we encounter femininity with intelligence.

George read the article over Claude's shoulder. The man's physical proximity and the smell of onions on his overused, underwashed apron was distracting. He straightened his newspaper briskly, to dispel the smell. George continued to read. Claude felt George's hot breath on his neck.

'Can't believe it, our town's tailor, you see, there's our town in print: Senlis. The whole town is talking about you. But go see Anatole,' George said thickly, his breath also smelling of onions.

Could he ever return to the simple roosting ground that he had loved so dearly? He was no longer a man of the dead-end countryside. Paris had lifted him into another category of lifestyle: bigger, fuller, where café owners were too busy to advise their customers to visit the local priest. The church bells pealed outside, then inside his head.

As he approached the steps of the lycée, Claude spied three of his nephews dashing from different doors. He ran up the stairs to surprise and greet them.

'*Bon après-midi!*' he said, as he caught the hand of the youngest, Arthur, just as he was preparing to swing his knapsack at his older brother. The wide-cheeked, Pédant-loving Arthur grinned at his uncle and at the large box of *pâtisseries* in his uncle's other hand.

'Can we come over to see Pédant?' Arthur asked.

'You like my parrot better than me. Where is Henri?'

'As usual, he's talking to the girls. We have to wait.'

'Come here, Didier and Jean-Hugues, I want a big hug. I've been missing you.' The school bells rang. 'Your uncle has been off in Paris getting famous. Come, did your mother show you the paper this morning?'

'She had to go to work early, so we didn't see her.'

'*Alors,* who took you to school?'

'We walked on our own like we do all the time.'

'What about your papa? He must have read the newspaper?'

'Papa was sleeping when we left.'

'Your papa was sleeping!'

'He was out late last night with *Maman* and he had an appointment later today. He wrote us a note to be quiet this morning, to eat and go on our own.'

'Your uncle famous in one day and his family doesn't even know! But your *maman* and papa were there last night. I'll beat them to the punch line. Where is that Henri? I'll have to talk to him about making his brothers wait.'

'Will you please?' pleaded Jean-Hugues. 'It's such a pain, especially since I've got so much homework these days.'

'Everyone is gone and we're still waiting,' said Didier. Their voices echoed on the empty marble staircases.

'Here he comes!' yelled Arthur.

Henri and Jean-Hugues had visited their uncle's offices only three weeks earlier, but this afternoon Henri's chest looked broader, his smile less eager, more reserved. No big hug.

'Hi, Uncle. What are you doing here?'

'What about a hug for your uncle instead of that ridiculous question? I decided to come and share my fame with my favorite people in the world, you four! Come to my studio for *pâtisseries*!'

Once inside, Claude placed the box of confections on the kitchen table. 'You should see the apartment I own in Paris,' he said, realizing he had never slept there. 'It's so grand: the ceilings are—'

'But we like it here!' said Didier, running to the grandfather clock. 'Uncle Claude,' he called a minute later, 'the clock has stopped. It says it's ten in the morning. Can I fix it, please? I know how. Remember? You showed me!'

Claude had not noticed the stopped clock. He opened the windows and pulled the afternoon sunshine in. The thick scent of ripening apples from the nearby tree suddenly reminded him of his departed parents.

'Can we open the box?' The boys were at the kitchen table, already settling down, eyes glued to the white butter-stained box.

'Uncle, the *pâtisseries*!'

'Of course! They're for you. So tell me, what do you think of your uncle's accomplishments?'

They were eating, so they weren't thinking of him at all. He placed the morning's newspaper, folded to his photograph, on the table in front of the quietly munching cluster.

'There's your Uncle Claude.'

'Wow,' Henri said, between bites. 'That's awesome! You *are* famous.'

Claude read them the article. They sat and listened.

'Which dress do you like the best out of these?' he asked, proud for the first time since the show had ended.

'I like that dress, the white one,' said Arthur, as he disappeared under the table and came out the other end with a ball that he hurled across the room.

'I like the green one with the pants,' said Henri. 'I really like the belt and the color. It's very cool.'

Jean-Hugues and Didier were fighting over the extra éclair.

'It's for Uncle, Didier!'

'No, it isn't! He never eats them!'

'Uncle, isn't that one for you?'

'You two split it,' said Claude, moving his head just in time to avoid a collision with the soccer ball as it flew across the room. The ball hit the counter, toppling but not breaking two empty coffee cups.

Didier held his breath, watching for his uncle's reaction.

'Didier, you haven't told me which dress you like best.' Claude held out the ball and the newspaper. 'I'll give this back to you only after you tell me.'

'I guess I like the green one.'

'He's saying that because Henri did, and he copies Henri in everything,' said Jean-Hugues.

'Do you really like the green one?' Claude asked Didier in a whisper.

'I think . . . that one,' he whispered back.

Didier pointed to Valentine in her red dress. Claude's heart sank.

'You really like that color on that woman? Or do you like the woman more than the dress?'

'She's pretty,' Didier said.

'You and I have the same taste in women,' said Claude, looking away quickly, handing Didier his ball.

'Uncle Claude,' Henri said. 'I have to go home. I have loads of homework.'

Without waiting for an answer, he burst out the door. Noises erupted from all directions in the modest studio. The phone rang.

He started to say, '*No* one—'

But before Claude could stop him. Jean-Hugues held the phone to his ear.

'Yes, he's here . . . *Uncle Claude, c'est pour toi. Qui?* Who? It's a Monsieur Le Vrais.'

Claude held the receiver two inches from his ear to dull the attack.

'*Where the hell are you?* The television crew has

225

been waiting here for two hours! *Get back here now!*'
Claude heard Lebrais yelling at someone in the background. 'A car service from the next town – it's Chantilly?' he was yelling to his assistant – 'will be there in fifteen minutes to pick you up and bring you here.'

'I'm busy this afternoon. It will have to wait until tomorrow.'

'There will be *no* tomorrow for you at this salon if you don't get into that car in ten minutes.'

Lebrais's voice shook; Claude pictured the redness in his face.

'I'm sorry,' he said quietly. 'I cannot be there today or tonight.'

Claude planned to dine that night with Juliette and Bernard; he was not willing to relinquish the first ounce of relief he had felt in a month.

The line went dead.

Claude switched off his cell phone. When Didier threw the ball, again at Claude's head, Claude caught it.

'The phone call upset you, Uncle,' offered the ever-insightful Jean-Hugues.

'Yes, it did. Don't you think it's enough that I delivered a well-received collection without having to work the very next day to sell it? I've designed a collection for the salon, but now I have to *be* it, wear it, look good and say the right things, give the right answers, act the right way, so the world over will be satisfied. With what? With what the salon thinks is the right thing!

'They want to know how you tick, so they ask, 'Where do you find your inspiration, and at what times of the day do you do your best work?' They want you to hand over the key to open you up and peek into your closets, especially the dark ones. Once they've flashed you with full light, they take what they want, leaving you exposed, blinded by the flash, and empty!'

'Don't let them see your closets, Uncle!'

'Why don't you live here anymore?' asked Didier, tossing the ball back. 'We want you and Pédant to come back. We miss our snack time.'

'I miss you too,' said Claude. 'This will always be home to me, but for the next little bit of the future, I have to get to know Paris. It's—'

'It's more sophisticated,' said Jean-Hugues. 'That's what Henri says. He's dying to graduate so he can go to university there.'

'Please, Uncle, the puppets,' said Arthur, jumping up and down and fetching the puppet bag attached to the closet door across the room.

After a brief show in which the elephant's trunk was damaged once more and then repaired by the compassionate poodle, Claude escorted his nephews home. They dashed inside to excavate the refrigerator, pulling out milk, ice cream, yogurt, and a day-old baguette. Claude removed the tangle of school bags, jackets, hats, and shoes from the doorway. Juliette's rebellion against their mother's fastidiousness was still alive and well.

Henri asked his uncle to accompany him to the stables, claiming he needed a break from his homework. They walked to the chipped, graying white fence at the back of the property, muddying their shoes. An almost full moon was visible in the quickly fading daylight. As they drew closer, Claude smelled the hay. His show trailed him everywhere he went.

A few horses snorted and stamped hooves at their entrance. Henri walked quickly toward a girl – no, a young woman: it was Pascale. Claude hadn't seen her in months. At fifteen, she was now taller than the fourteen-year-old Henri; her body was still slim like a schoolgirl's, but it had developed incipient curves; her smile was less acerbic than he had remembered, more rounded and loose. Her eyes brightened at the sight of Henri.

'*Bonsoir.*' She cheek-kissed Henri naturally and quickly, her arms at her sides.

'Ah . . . Monsieur Reynaud,' she murmured quietly. 'Congratulations. I read about you today. My father showed me the article.'

'Uncle, won't you make a dress for Pascale? Uncle can take one look at your size and never take a measurement,' Henri said. 'The dress will fit you perfectly!'

'No. Monsieur is too busy for me. It would be too expensive.'

'Please, Uncle, make her a dress. I know, a dress for the school's Christmas dance! I'm taking Pascale.'

Pascale blushed; Claude noticed that her long mane of light-brown hair was knotted in places.

What color, Claude thought, already blending hues, for such pale skin? Ah, but she has bright hazel eyes. 'It would be my pleasure,' he said.

She smiled shyly and moved closer to Henri.

Cobalt blue immediately came to Claude's mind. Cobalt blue with a red trim to bring out the copper strands in her brown hair.

'Henri,' he said, 'you can help me design it and choose the color. Before you say anything, look at Pascale's palette; every face is a palette.'

Nearby, a horse stamped and whinnied gently.

'I think a soft pastel color,' Henri said.

'What color?'

'Blue, pastel blue.'

'Like what color that you've seen before?'

'I guess, the light blue in the sky at the Île de Ré, in the morning just before the sun rises. Remember when we stayed up all night, Uncle? It was worth it just to see that color.'

'Excellent choice, Henri, because that blue had yellow in it, which is essential in this case.'

'Uncle,' said Henri, turning to Pascale, 'thinks each color should have a time and place.'

'What lines?' continued Claude.

'Curves, I think.'

'When you get home, will you draw it for me? You're on the right track.'

Pascale looked down at Henri's hand by her side and took it in hers. Claude noticed Henri's hand close tightly around hers; their arms touched.

'Let's go see Marquise,' she said abruptly. Claude could make out the deep chestnut's steamy breath above the stall door as they approached in the cool darkness. The horse was admirably strong and tall, a shining chestnut. Pascale rested her head on the steed's neck. Henri took a curry brush from the stall's ledge and began brushing the forelegs. Pascale rearranged the hay in the corner and then offered a handful to the horse's muzzle. As the horse munched, she peeked up at Henri, patting the horse's neck.

'Marquise looks so happy,' Claude said, 'As do you two. I'm going back to the house. Perhaps your mother or father has arrived.'

Claude departed to the sounds of their voices, a duet accompanied by the stirrings of the horse in the hay.

Was there anything in this world more romantic and unaffected than these two in the stable? Claude calculated Pascale's lithe, uncomplicated fifteen-year-old measurements. He wouldn't need her to 'stand' for him until, perhaps, the last fitting.

Juliette did not arrive until seven-thirty that night, her husband not until eleven. In the meantime, Claude rummaged through the overloaded and disorganized pantry. Green shoots three inches long had sprouted unabashedly from the onions. He threw these out and found some long-abandoned, also sprouting potatoes that he managed to salvage after a scrubbing. In the refrigerator, he discovered six leftover chicken legs that would barely feed the four hungry boys. He tossed the soggy lettuce into the garbage and washed and dried off the twenty or more limp carrots.

Two boys had given up on homework and were throwing lemons from a distance at a fruit bowl towering with oranges.

'Watch me knock off the top one, Uncle. I did it yesterday!'

'I'll throw from this side,' announced Didier.

'No, no me first,' Arthur cried out, as he threw a lemon at the bowl and missed. Didier hit from the other side and knocked the bowl off the counter. Claude closed his eyes. Ignoring the oranges rolling from one end of the floor to the other, Didier picked up the intact ceramic bowl.

'Now, pick up the oranges,' said Claude.

'Arthur has to help me.'

'*Both* of you, please pick them up.'

Jean-Hugues, in his dirty socks, slid into the kitchen from the dining room. He held the freezer open with one hand and with a spoon in the other, began digging a hole in the lidless ice cream container.

'We'll be eating dinner soon,' said Claude.

'But Mama and Papa aren't home yet. It could be hours. Just a bite!' Jean-Hugues lifted a spoonful of the ice cream from the container in the freezer. Claude pointed to his own mouth and

Jean-Hugues obediently dropped the spoonful on Claude's tongue.

'Mmmm. Not bad. But this is soft.'

'The freezer's broken, but it's perfect for ice cream.'

When Juliette arrived with three baguettes under one arm and the other hand clutching her bag of manuscripts, the chicken, potatoes, and carrots were heating in the oven. She shouted with surprise to see her brother.

'Claude, hello, what a surprise! What an honor! I'm so proud of you. My brother, so famous! Congratulations! But what on earth are you doing here? I would think they would want to toast you, wine you, and dine you for weeks!'

'They do, but this is my reward to myself. Through all this hard work, I've missed you and my nephews.'

'All the better for us! That white dress, how fabulous! You're so good, Claude! How did you think of that lace dress? It's my favorite! You'll go down in history for that one, for sure.' She washed her hands and ran up the stairs, calling, 'I'll be down in a moment after I change. I'm so glad you're getting the recognition you deserve.' From upstairs, she shouted, 'Now that you're so famous, you'll never have time to make me a suit for the Christmas season, will you? Hint hint. Christmas *is* coming!'

Claude heard her greeting Henri. She returned in wool pants and a lamb's-wool gray turtleneck sweater.

'Henri asked me to design a dress for Pascale,' Claude said. 'They're very sweet together.'

'It's true, Claude. There's no doubt about it. Henri is smitten.' Juliette began emptying the dishwasher. 'Oh, that reminds me. Before I forget, I wanted to ask you a favor. Bernard and I are leaving for London next Wednesday for a night. Could you stay over? I wanted to ask you earlier but was afraid to bother you just before your show. Oh, and by the way, speaking of Henri, Bernard and I have yet to give him some lessons on you-know-what. At the same time, I don't want to suggest that they . . . Perhaps you're the one who could—'

'*Non, non,* Bernard should. Where is he?'

'Working too hard these days. He lost his partner two weeks ago to a higher-paying law firm. Bernard's taken on the man's clients until he finds someone to replace him. He hasn't been getting home until ten-thirty or eleven every night. *Alors,* enough complaints!'

Miraculously, Juliette had found and was sautéeing garlic, fennel, and spinach. 'I have the famous Claude Reynaud in my kitchen! Imagine what Father would say! And Mother! No, they wouldn't like it. Father would be convinced the outside world would destroy your integrity, your work would suffer, and the people in Paris would corrupt your soul so you could never be true to yourself. And, poor Senlis; he would shed a tear for his old friends and their broken zippers and lost buttons!'

'Mother,' Claude joined in, 'would be suspicious of my every move. Remember how she never trusted anyone from Paris? She would ask me how much they charge per dress and how much I am paid, and am I spending it or saving it.'

'Then she would shake her head with a look of disgust,' continued Juliette, 'and say, "I thought as much." Didn't she always say that: "I thought as much"? Could it be that she really *did* know everything and thought as much, or did she say that to make herself feel better when she knew absolutely nothing?'

'If she didn't think of it, it didn't happen.' Claude laughed.

'She wanted us to think she was on top of everything,' said Juliette, 'which is actually funny because she never left this town in her entire life. You're right. She would be disapproving, but on second thought she wouldn't mind the accolades and attention she'd be getting from her friends. Secretly, I bet she'd be titillated by the fanfare. She'd probably say it was all due to the way she had trained you.'

After Juliette had called the children to the table, she said casually, 'I noticed the collection was titled "Valentine in Spring."'

'To answer your next question, yes, despite all my efforts, I continue to be as possessed as ever. The dresses in the collection were designed with her in mind. As you could see, the models bore a slight resemblance.'

'As if it weren't obvious!'

'I tried to kiss her at the show when she came up to congratulate me. I behaved like an idiot. She rejected me.'

'Claude, she *is* married!'

'I know what you're thinking, Juliette, but something about her, about me – call it an addiction if you wish – won't let go of the idea that she loves and wants me. I need you to witness it! Come to a show tomorrow that Valentine has assembled for a friend of hers. I think the artist, Rohan, is pretty good. If you detect nothing tomorrow night, not a bewitching glance in her eye nor a meaningful embrace, then you have every right to call me a complete idiot.'

'I heard about her show, and of course I read about her husband losing his job at Drouot. How tough the publicity must be for both of them and their careers! To think they were at the center of the international art world. It's got to be hard to be shunted aside like that.'

'Meet me after work.' Claude changed the subject. 'Stay by my side, protect me from dreaming Valentine into my arms.'

'You're crazy to think of going.'

'I can't not go.'

'You're stronger than that! Set your sights elsewhere.'

'On my wife?'

'Well, perhaps not her, but why don't you travel a bit, get out of the country, meet other people. Visit the Delannoys in Brittany. Constance would love to see you. Hasn't it been years? Remember the vacations we took together as kids? She's always asking after you.'

'Yes, that's a good idea – after you come with me to the show.'

Juliette thanked him for the invitation but demurred. Bernard would be out of town that night, and she needed to be with the children.

After dinner, Claude entered Henri's room and sat in the chair near his desk. He asked his nephew about his schoolwork and the soccer games of the week.

He could not help himself. 'You seem to like Pascale very much.'

Henri turned his head to his book.

'An older woman! Fifteen.'

'You should see her on Marquise, Uncle.' Henri looked up. 'She *becomes* the horse; they move in sync. You can't tell where she begins and the horse ends.'

Claude could detect the flush in Henri's face, could almost feel the quickened heartbeat. Those two were so free and young, Claude thought. And he so middle-aged and fettered. How did that happen?

'Is she good at schoolwork?' He was taking a chance; he was digging too deeply.

'She skips school a lot. The horses are more important to her. Her father doesn't care if she doesn't do her homework. She says she only does it if she's interested. She's not like anyone I know.'

'Your mother tells me *you* skipped school last week. The teacher called her.'

'I didn't know *Maman* knew!'

'Why did you?'

'Pascale invited me to have a picnic with her. We biked out to the Forêt d'Halatte and sat under this massive pine tree. Then we read to each other, from a book about Joan of Arc that she is reading, then we chased each other around the pine trees and swam in La Nonette. It was freezing! Even though I tried to stop her, she gave almost our whole picnic away to this mangy brown dog. His ear was half cut off. We named him Chocolat and he followed us home. She has this way with animals. He was gone yesterday, but Pascale knows he'll come back.'

'A picnic and a new friend!'

'Pascale says her father has a girlfriend,' Henri added. 'She says she can smell her perfume on his shirts when she does the laundry.'

'Maybe he's looking for a mother for Pascale.'

'She says she's never needed a mother.'

'Ah, well, Henri.' Claude sighed. 'She does seem a bit lonely. Like your mother's garden out there, she needs weeding, love, and care. But just make sure you take care, too . . .'

'Too serious, Uncle.'

Claude stood. 'Too serious, yes. Yes, that's me,' he said, smiling but saddened. The description fit him all too well.

CHAPTER 19

Two kinds of invitees attended Valentine's reception for her friend Théodore Rohan: those genuinely interested in art and the artist and those wishing to partake of the social scene and the accompanying wine and canapés. When Claude entered the spacious studio on the quai Voltaire, he immediately noticed Victor holding court among members of the second camp.

No art was visible from the entrance of the exhibition space. The large monotone-gray room had been partitioned into a mazelike design of small alcoves that allowed for private viewings of each painting. Claude was disappointed; he would have liked to experience the entirety of Rohan's art with one sweep of the eye.

He peered around the first alcove and saw the portrait from the invitation. Claude admired the use of red, the flat perspective. The thick, imposing texture conjured the artist's subject, his larger-than-life presence, his prodigious laugh; the use of the color purple at his temple accentuated his broad but short forehead.

A laugh, not the typical light titter expected in a gallery space, erupted from the center of the room. Claude walked around the next alcove. He froze: a gentle light from above illuminated the small painting of the apple tree – his apple tree, his father's, his grandfather's apple tree – from which he could almost smell the blossoms. The title read, REYNAUD'S APPLE TREE.

He backed up. What was *her* painting doing there, in the midst of Théodore Rohan's? Her painting, *his* apple tree? Such a passive, vulnerable small scene, embarrassingly simple, bearing his name. She could have asked! He wavered between feeling flattered and mocked. When he turned, he caught Valentine looking at him, then returning her gaze to the center of the room. Was she asking for help?

Victor's voice and laughter resounded in the room. The former *commissaire-priseur* of Drouot did not appear to be very interested in Rohan's collection. Lebrais's insistent, wiry figure blocked his view of Valentine. Although Claude had been answering questions and smiling into cameras at the salon all day, he had not seen Lebrais until then.

'Monsieur Reynaud.' Lebrais smiled wryly. 'You're becoming all too predictable! I should have known that only Valentine Couturier could lure *our* couturier out of his home-grown woods.'

Claude expected scowls, reprimands, and threats. Instead, Lebrais was disconcertingly polite.

'After our conversation yesterday' – Lebrais cleared his throat; obviously this was not easy – 'I thought that perhaps you were right; after working so hard, you deserved a day of rest. I'm amazed we succeeded in pushing the press off for a day. You owe your co-designer Charles for this one. I thought I had explained that the most crucial time is the period immediately *after* the show, when editors of magazines, newspapers, and television programs interpret and choose their favorite works. It's your job to steer them to your best work, to organize their thoughts, to bring them down on our side, our philosophy, and always, *always* to have the last word. Your untimely departure sent them into a tizzy. They were not sure if they felt insulted or titillated. This time last night, they imagined that you had been incapacitated by a devastating illness, brought on by the genius you had to extract for this collection. I think you did yourself and your work much discredit not to receive them immediately . . . much discredit. I – why, hello, Valentine.'

Valentine's beauty was striking. Her dark hair gathered in a chignon framed her full white face, just as her black eyelashes framed the sparkle of her dark blue eyes. Her lightly glossed lips were inviting. She wore a camel pantsuit with a black turtleneck and her beige boots: simple and chic, but the cut of the jacket was wrong for her. Never a short jacket with a long torso! The velvet camel-colored ribbon at the back of her head saved the day. No matter what she wore, her look was mesmerizing.

'I'm happy you came, Claude . . . and André,' she said. She looked directly into Claude's eyes. 'You should know that Théodore begged me to include two of my paintings in the show – it's embarrassing, such amateurish dabbling compared to his work. I can't believe I conceded. I think you saw one of them, Claude. Unfortunately, the other piece wasn't finished for this show. It's the portrait I'm painting of you.'

'Oh-la-la. What a subject,' said Lebrais. 'The dressmaker has a portrait painter. Please don't leave out the stubborn chin, Valentine. Can you imagine that Claude ran all the way home after his collection was presented? I tried everything to get him back. The only thing I forgot to use was you. You would have brought him back in a flash.'

The three turned when they heard another loud guffaw from the center of the room and a booming voice calling for Valentine.

'*Pardonnez-moi,*' she said hesitatingly, reluctantly, but she did not move.

A high woman's voice shrieked, '*Noooooo!*'

'Valentine.' Claude steered her by her elbow toward the voice.

She stopped him as they rounded the corner and caught sight of Victor on the couch. Out of hearing distance from Lebrais, she whispered, 'He's started drinking . . . without a job. For him to be here is impossible. I told him not to come, with people from Drouot bound to stop by. I never should have let him, never! How stupid of me and how humiliating for him!' As she gazed toward the floor, hair fell from the crown of her head over her face. 'But enough of that.' She looked up at Claude. 'Before I go to him, I have something to tell you. I must tell you now! It will only take a minute. Come.'

They heard a woman laugh as loudly as Victor.

Valentine led him into a darkened corner of the large room. On the way, he examined the marble floor, its gray-white color interrupted by veins of darker gray and brighter white.

'You're the first person I wanted to tell.'

Her lips were close to him. He tried not to think of his joy.

'I'm expecting,' she whispered.

His child? But no.

'You look so sad. You didn't think – oh, no! Claude, that you – my sweet Claude. No, it's since I've been married. Smile, Claude! It's great, isn't it? I was so worried I wouldn't be able to conceive. You know, I *am* getting older. I was so happy, I wanted you to know.'

No words came to him.

'The only problem is Victor,' she continued. 'It's the strangest thing. I haven't told him yet. I wanted to tell him at the right time, and now he's going through such a rough patch. It seems to be getting worse rather than better: the alcohol.'

He tried to swallow.

'It's a nightmare every time we go out,' she continued.

He said nothing.

'If I want to see a friend at night, I've begun to sneak out.' She rubbed her eyes. 'This is so strange. Such a happy thing for Victor and me, this baby, but I feel I'm treading water, waiting for Victor to get better, waiting to share my news with him. I'm afraid that if I tell him about my condition, it will put him under more pressure.'

Of course a woman in her thirty-sixth year would be thrilled to be expecting a child. But *how* could she, after all they had experienced, expect him to be overjoyed to hear of her carrying a child by another man? Victor the victor? How could he have so hugely miscalculated the nature of their relationship?

She was newly pregnant. Even so, her dress took on a different shape today; her breasts looked fuller.

'I must confess,' he said, in a forced, slightly angry whisper. 'This news is not easy for me, considering my feelings for you. Why do I persist in thinking we are more than friends?'

'Come, Claude.' She lowered her voice. 'We were lovers in a different sense, not for marriage and babies but for something else, something above all that. Even though I haven't known you for long, I feel you are such a rare, true friend. That's why I wanted you to be the first to know. I feel I can share everything with you, as if I am you or you are me.'

Her words coaxed him back to life. Against his will and his forceful intellect, he perceived a slight glimmer of hope.

'Valentine!' The voice from the other end of the room had grown impatient and demanding.

She left him, then, to quench the dragon fire waiting for her at the gallery's epicenter, the beige velvet ribbon bobbing at the back of her long and graceful neck.

On his walk to work the next morning, a sudden wind loosened a cluster of stiffened yellow-brown leaves from a row of sycamore trees. They rained down on him, awakening him to the last gasp of autumnal colors. Even on the gray sidewalks of Paris, autumn's brilliance, mixed with a slight chill, was exhilarating. A dancing red leaf on the pavement caught his eye, and he picked it up to study it. He hadn't seen that shade of red in years, the color of scarlet velvet with a slight hint of orange. He pressed it into his jacket pocket.

At this time of year especially, Claude felt a yearning for the trees of Senlis, the massive beech groves, the oaks, the pine trees, and the hornbeams. His grandfather used to tell him that every tumbling leaf told a story. He remembered the one about the boy who lived on a yellow leaf and raced the other leaves to the ground.

'Son, watch how nature colors our lives,' his father had advised. 'Each day, the color swells into a deeper color, but the world can't take the intensity, so the leaves must crinkle up, turn brown, and tumble. If they didn't fall and leave us, their beauty would overwhelm us and burden our hearts.'

Claude treasured the textures of fall clothing, the thick wools, tweeds, fine twilled cashmeres, heavy cotton velvets, even the cruder flannels and leathers. However, cutting and sewing the thicker materials presented challenges.

'*Anyone* can sew a silk,' his father would explain. 'But it takes a man of experience and great skill to stitch a tweed to last a lifetime.'

Claude greeted the salon's upright black-clad receptionist. Her smile reminded him of the grimace of a gargoyle hanging over the portal of the Paris Notre-Dame. How had she trained her facial muscles to arouse guilt? Every time Claude entered the reception area, her haughty expression needled him: *It's about time you got to work!*

As if he had been awaiting Claude's arrival, Lebrais met him in the hall and followed promptly into Claude's office. Lebrais carried a manila envelope. Claude noticed perspiration on his boss's upper lip and prepared himself. It was rare to witness a crack in the Lebraisian composure.

'Big assignment, Claude! We're so excited for you. The prime minister's wife has asked you to design her wardrobe for a three-day trip to Algiers next month. The look must be conservative and modest, preferably with Moroccan textiles and colors.' Lebrais took a breath and held out the envelope. 'This is *very* important, our first government assignment in two decades. I want you to begin today. Here's her photograph and a brief biography. You'll find she has an interesting background: Saudi great-grandfather on one side, French politicians from the eighteenth century on the other. Think perfect politician's wife: conservative, diplomatic, pleasing, practical, and French inside and out.'

The prime minister's wife! Sophie Lorieux had a pale face with hazy brown eyes and dark brown hair, cut to mid-neck. Her eyes were glazed over and her coloring pasty, as if the life had been sucked out of her. Claude knew his challenge immediately: to inject sparkle into Madame Lorieux's staid, matronly appearance.

'I've asked Charles to draw up a few ideas. Here they—'

'I'd prefer not to see anything,' said Claude. 'I will show you my designs by the end of tomorrow.'

Lebrais rolled up Charles's drawings, visibly shocked at Claude's response. 'Excuse me,' he said, in a tone that bordered on respect. 'In that case, I look forward to tomorrow evening.'

Claude looked upward after Lebrais departed. 'Now you must be very proud, Papa.'

In the few moments that it took Claude to hook his jacket on the door, Lebrais had poked his head back into the office. 'By the way, have you heard the news?'

'More news?'

Lebrais smiled his mischievous smile. 'Your

friends Valentine and Victor are moving to the United States. Victor has accepted a job at a leading art gallery in New York. I thought you might have read or heard about it.' He paused meaningfully. 'I'm sorry to be the one to tell you.' His head vanished from the room like one of Claude's puppets disappearing behind their makeshift stage.

Valentine leaving Paris! Claude retreated to the window. The falling leaves on the sycamore tree outside summoned him. Claude grabbed his jacket.

'Monsieur Reynaud.' The receptionist interrupted his swift exit. 'Monsieur Lebrais instructed me you're not to leave without telling me when you'll be back . . . The calls . . . I see here you have an appointment in an hour—'

'Thank you,' Claude said.

Outside was full of noise.

What good is all this? he asked himself. What good is designing the prime minister's wife's dress? Despite her Saudi background, the Algerians will continue to shun her and her colonially myopic opinions. What good is it to be the couturier for the prime minister's wife? Another chance to prove myself? For what? To whom?

After continuing down another few streets, he realized he was heading in the direction of Valentine's workplace, rue Drouot. In a sweat, he strode inside, past the main reception desk.

Valentine had once pointed out her office window from the street. He exited the elevator on the second floor but found the landing doors locked. He knew that even Valentine had keys for only a few rooms at Drouot. The *commissaire-priseur,* the queen chess piece, was the only player with the ability to unlock any door. He waited. When a young man in a navy suit emerged from a door with a box full of papers, Claude held the door open for him and then entered the inner sanctum. The corridor contained four doors, one of which was unlocked. He entered the unlocked office and shut the door behind him.

Five half-packed boxes sat in the middle of the floor. Valentine's office. It had to be. It smelled of Valentine's lilacs, her skin. Artwork was propped against the walls. Large coffee-table books were piled precariously on her office chair. The room looked as if it had been vacated quickly, as if something urgent had called the occupant from the work at hand. No jacket or purse. He swung the chair behind the desk around irascibly, waiting for the books to topple. They didn't. The entire Drouot concern appeared asleep. Where was everyone?

Eleven-twenty-three A.M. Too early for lunch. Perhaps a meeting down the hall? A good-bye party on the rooftop? Should he stay? His hands were clammy.

Beside her darkened computer, he found a notepad. He hesitated before opening the top drawer to find a pen. A violation. The drawer was neatly organized. Cough drops, pens, pencils, ruler, pad of invoice slips, a bottle of perfume:

1000 by Patou. That she should spray herself for the world to enjoy her made him immediately jealous. He sniffed the bottle. She'd never worn this heavy scent around him.

Voices outside. He shut the drawer. More voices. He hurriedly composed his note.

Valentine, came to help you move. A lie. He tore the paper off the pad.

Valentine, stopped by to see you.

Why could he never bring himself to blame her – for continually dashing his hopes, for changing his life? Was it her eyes that weakened him, that asked for forgiveness before anything was said or done? Surely, they were the watering hole in which he drowned every time. After he signed his name, he tore a tortoise-shell button off the right cuff of his tweed jacket and placed it on his note.

Claude hailed a taxi and sped to his wife's sixteenth arrondissement apartment building. He decided not to wait for the elevator but, instead, took the red-carpeted stairs two by two to the third floor. He tried the door, rang the bell, and knocked. A white-aproned housekeeper greeted him. A few moments later, his wife of the red-orange lips appeared. She was wrapped in white towels of the most luxurious cotton and wore white terry-cloth slippers that suggested oversized rabbit feet. With her pout in full flower, she shook her hands in little up-down movements to dry her freshly painted nails.

'Claude, *alors*,' she cried. 'What a terrible time for you to come. I have a lunch and I'm already half an hour late. What *are* you doing here?'

The telephone rang. Her eyes darted to the right. 'Amélie!' she called. 'Oh, that woman can't hear!' she said to him as she headed down the hall. 'Wait here.'

He poked his head into the living room. To his surprise, he found that Rose-Marie had hired a decorator with taste. He liked the brown velvet curtains with cream taffeta lining. The unusually textured beige-and-black geometric design in African *Kuba* cloth piqued his interest. He quickly shut his eyes, however, when he entered the dining room. The lurid red-orange walls clashed hideously with the gold suede upholstery on the chairs.

Rose-Marie was back with combed hair, wearing a red silk bathrobe under which her bunny feet shuffled.

'I can't believe, out of all the days in this entire year, you arrive *now*! I don't have *one moment*! This luncheon is very important. I'll already be late, and the cocktail hour is de rigueur! My friend has promised to introduce me to Madame de Laye!'

'I want a divorce,' Claude said.

'Well, of all the . . . now?'

He watched Rose-Marie's face flame with indignation and seconds later turn calculatingly calm. 'I'm so sorry, Claude, but I cannot discuss this now.' She turned to leave with her head lifted high.

'You must discuss this now.' The phone rang.

'Amélie!' Rose-Marie called shrilly. 'Amélie! Is she deaf? Amélie!' she shrieked.

The phone rang again.

The housekeeper arrived, her worried eyes blinking. 'Amélie! Answer the phone! Can't you hear?'

It rang again.

'*Now!* Answer the phone!'

Rose-Marie turned on him, tossing her head and narrowing her eyes. 'If you think you can barge in here, ask for a divorce, and cause me to be late for my lunch, without having bothered about me for the last two months, you're wrong, absolutely wrong. Please leave me to get dressed. We'll discuss this . . . at a more appropriate time.'

'You are giving me a divorce today. You can keep everything you have, and you will be given enough alimony to keep you happy. Our marriage is over. My lawyer will send the final documents tomorrow.'

When he closed the door behind him, Claude knew with certainty that his wife would sign the divorce papers, so long as she could keep her winnings. The new arrangement would suit her nicely.

CHAPTER 20

Claude enjoyed completing the designs for Madame Lorieux's November voyage to Algiers. The work challenged his imagination and kept his mind off Valentine's looming absence. Using an enlarged photograph of his subject for his palette, Claude had chosen a transparent cotton mossgreen and dusty-pink combination for a one-shouldered evening dress. For the travel suit, he broadened the shoulders to compensate for madame's slight hip heaviness. He selected a raw silk in shiny deep terra-cotta, the color of a ceramic pot. Claude pinned a flowing beige silk scarf to the right shoulder of the suit, so madame could drape it on her head or wrap it across her face during a Muslim ceremony.

For her hat, he chose a small beret in beige with a transparent brown veil attached to its back. For the second day of the trip, he designed a knee-length cream-colored tunic to be worn over a sleeveless ankle-length day dress of tango-orange light-weight knit cotton. A rope belt draped loosely around the waist; a cream-colored silk scarf enveloped the neck.

Lebrais swept into Claude's office to check on his progress. He made little indecipherable sounds as he looked over the portfolio. 'My only problem,' he said, after a few moments of serious examination, 'is the cream-colored tunic. It might look like a religious vestment – many religious figures wear white. And for November? How about another color? You don't have any blue in here. Apparently, she likes blue.'

'This woman should never wear blue.'

'You choose, then: perhaps in the red family.'

'When will she come in for a fitting?'

'My dear Claude, I always forget you're a man from the provinces! Madame Lorieux would never 'stand' for a designer! A model of her figure arrived yesterday. I'm surprised it hasn't made it to your office. I'll have it brought in immediately.'

When Lebrais left the room, Claude sketched the design for another dress: a sheer silk blouse in sunset colors with a pink crêpe-de-chine skirt flowing to the ankles. A casual and slimming cardigan of the same multicolored cotton, tied at the waist with dangling rose-colored tassels. The consummate evening dress for the consummated Valentine.

Claude's designs were met with quiet adulation from the prime minister's wife. Sophie Lorieux called Lebrais herself from an unidentified location, conveying her deep gratitude *and* her desire for a ball gown for a gala at the White House in January.

To make the most of these illustrious assignments, Lebrais demanded that Claude spend more 'face time' with the press. He placed six invitations on Claude's desk, with the words MUST ATTEND printed across the top of three.

Claude designed a long black-and-gray pinstripe skirt with a daringly flirtatious thick black lace top for Madame Lorieux's Washington event. When he counted four more orders to be filled the following week for four new clients, Claude felt weary. With all the press exposure and high expectations, he began for the first time in his life to doubt his abilities.

Claude had always prided himself on his talent for intuiting a client's individual style. But on two recent occasions he had been mistaken on color choice and the type of décolletage. And when Anne d'Orsay requested an evening gown like the one he had designed for Isabelle Montand, he would not accept the assignment.

'I would prefer to design your own dress,' he suggested gently. 'Madame Montand's gown would not suit you.'

She insisted, cajoled, smiled, laughed, and would not let him have his way. 'I want *that* dress and I want *you* to make it.'

'Madame, I cannot create a dress that will not enhance your own fine coloring. I have a—'

'If you can't copy your own work, I'll find someone who can!'

'As you wish,' he said, clenching his hand into

a tight fist as he felt his father's presence in the room.

She walked out the door, her shoulders squared. The lurking Lebrais discovered the disgruntled customer in the reception area and flew into Claude's room.

'You may have just lost our biggest client! She has been a loyal customer for over a decade. She has never had any problems with this house. Charles designs what she likes. It's *that* simple. She wanted you because of your reputation, and now, unless I can bring her back to Charles, you'll have lost her entirely.' Lebrais resorted to his low-toned ultimatum voice. 'You must call her to apologize.'

'I refuse to make a dress that I know will not compliment her. If I copied the white dress with the black moiré stripe down the middle that I created for Madame Montand, Madame d'Orsay, with those thick blond streaks in her hair, would resemble a skunk. The thing would be laughable.'

'Let her be laughable.'

'You must tell her there are other styles that would suit her better,' Claude said. 'You, André, can convince anyone of anything.'

Lebrais shook his head and shut the door tightly behind him. Claude saw it as clearly as the empty sidewalk outside his window: he concluded with a sense of horror that in only a short time his work had become predictable.

Journalists called him 'the line man.' 'Claude Reynaud urges the lines of his creations to curve, coil, and slither, sometimes jiggle, sometimes dance, to suit and flatter any body,' wrote the fashion editor of *Le Figaro*.

'I'm the "line man," the "classicist"; I've been labeled!' he muttered to himself. 'How constricting to be known for one's own defining style! Why must we lazy humans categorize everything?'

The thought of Valentine interrupted him, overturned his mind: her thickening figure, the waste of her pregnancy on a man who would not notice. How could she, whom he loved, be so foolish and careless? He tried to consume the fire of his anger by working harder, but all that he produced looked imitative and dull. He growled at Pédant for making a mess on the floor. He worked late but inefficiently. He slept while he designed; he designed while he slept.

One midweek morning, Lebrais entered Claude's office, as usual without knocking. 'Hello, Claude,' he said, eyes twinkling, as he handed an envelope across the desk.

Inside were round-trip airline tickets to New York, a press pass to the New York fashion shows, and an oversized, heavily embossed invitation to the Costume Gala at the Metropolitan Museum of Art. Claude scrutinized Lebrais, waiting for an explanation.

'It would seem that our workaholic Claude could profit from a vacation. I've reserved a flight for tomorrow morning, so you can catch tomorrow evening's glamorous party at the Metropolitan

Museum and then attend the shows in the following few days. This pass will get you anywhere you want.'

Claude's listless response astonished even Lebrais.

'I have to complete four more designs,' he said.

'I don't want to see another of your design portfolios until you get back,' said Lebrais. Did Claude detect a spark of mischief in Lebrais's voice, as if the man were holding a glass of champagne in front of an alcoholic? Was Lebrais using Valentine to inspire better work from his top designer? He had to laugh.

'I am onto your tricks, André, and this time you are completely and appallingly on target.'

He would leave in a heartbeat to be near Valentine, pregnant or not, loving him or not. Willingly, he hooked himself on his boss's lure.

Claude spent the night before his flight to New York at his sister's house while she and Bernard enjoyed their night in London. He managed to dodge soccer balls and flying horseshoes and still produce a satisfactory dinner of steak, scalloped potatoes, and beets, despite the fact that beets were shunned and considered 'devil food.' (Woe to the adjacent food that was tainted with beet juice.) As always, Claude gave in to his nephews' wishes, and they conspired in whispers to save the beets for the rabbits at the farmhouse nearby.

Once the table was cleared and the floor was swept, Pascale poked her head into the dining room.

'I've come to practice,' she said. She did not appear surprised to see Henri's uncle presiding over the household. As soon as Claude had said, 'Of course,' he could hear Henri's chair scraping the floor. Henri was at her side within seconds.

'Pascale, I need to ask you a question about your phrasing in the Haydn piece.'

As she left the room with Henri's hand on her elbow, she nodded her head and said, '*Bonsoir, Monsieur Reynaud.*'

Pascale's voice sounded decidedly different from the last time. As Didier asked his uncle how to balance a soccer ball on the back of his heel as his friend had done at school, Claude put his finger on the change. Pascale's simple voice had become a woman's, deeper, textured, and rich with complexity.

From the other room, they heard a simple minuet by Mozart, then a piece by Haydn – the nimble fingers must have been hers – followed by no sound at all. Didier and Jean-Hugues elbowed each other knowingly and urged their uncle to interrupt the couple's silent music making. Claude refrained; the duet was perfect without another meddling instrument.

Didier headed out of the kitchen. 'I have to get a paper for you to sign from the hall,' he said over his shoulder.

Claude was at the door in seconds. '*Non, non,* not so fast! Didn't I tell you what I brought for dessert? Ice cream and cones for us to pretend we're at the beach in summertime! Come, all of you. They're in the—' Claude was almost knocked over as the three boys ran to the freezer door.

When he allowed his nephews out of the kitchen, they found the piano bench deserted. Pascale and Henri dangled their legs from the fence outside. In the glow of the outside light, the couple's heads bobbed in unison, Pascale turning to Henri, then he to her. Claude visualized their conversation as an intricate tapestry, formed by the weaving of emotions and words.

CHAPTER 21

Autumn in New York City was more colorful than Paris could ever hope to be. Against the crisp blue backdrop, the city's autumnal skyscape stunned Claude. In Paris at this time of year, a more mature gray prevailed, as if the blue of its youth had aged over the years. The sky here was young, its heart docile and ready for passion, its mind unencumbered by centuries of history gone awry. Claude stared upward, trying to imprint the color on his mind so he could reproduce it in his next collection.

In New York City, time leaned forward. In Paris it lingered, sitting down for coffee and a croissant. As he gazed out of the locked window of his midtown boutique hotel, he saw people dashing about, slanted against the wind.

The Manhattan Hotel was known for its minimalism. The built-in low bed covered in beige was the sole object in the room. A large white canvas with a single black dot in its center held the above-the-bed position.

By the end of this trip, Claude thought, I will either love or detest that dot. The adjoining room featured a desk, a chair, a coffee table, and a couch covered in beige.

The first event on his itinerary was the evening Spring Fashion Parade, modeled after a rabble-rousing Mardi Gras celebration, in which the more avant-garde designers marched with their models down Spring Street in Soho in their latest spring designs.

As Claude left the taxi, he heard a saxophone blasting a long cool note. Layers of crowds lined the streets, but somehow he managed to find an area labeled DESIGNERS AND PRESS, equipped with space heaters.

The parade had begun. Willowy-thin models, clad in the wildest garments Claude had ever seen, were followed by or walked hand in hand with their designers. The originality of the designs reduced Claude to tears! How long had it been since he had experienced clothing that demanded an answer to 'So what do you think of *this*?'

One model sported a porcelain plate on each breast. How ever had they been attached? At her waist she wore a chain belt, from which hung cooking utensils, big silver slotted spoons, a wood spatula, a carving fork, and a cake knife. How ridiculous and rousing at the same time! Her pants resembled upside-down chef's toques.

Another American designer, whose work Claude had always admired, was followed by a model wearing a transparent American flag, her long legs completely revealed. A mohair knitted star fit perfectly over each breast. The wind blew. Those around him applauded energetically. Everything in this city felt as if it had been created for the first time.

An hour later, a taxi let him off at the Metropolitan Museum of Art. He stood gazing at the imposing columned building for a few moments, taking in the colorful gowns flowing up the stairs. Claude quickly realized he was not properly attired: the men wore black tie. In his halting English, he asked a young man in formal attire skipping up the stairs if it was acceptable for him to enter wearing suit and tie.

'Of course it is,' the man said. 'Dress codes are obnoxious.'

Once inside, Claude's eye consumed the dresses that swished about and skimmed the marble floor of the colossal room housing the Temple of Dendur. Well-designed small bodices, beaded and plain, with overflowing full skirts rustled past him. Black ruled the room. Except for one . . .

In the right corner of the room, a purple jacket over a red dress caught his eye. The scarlet sequined tunic layered with the darker purple jacket was riveting. He propelled himself through the voices and gesticulating hands and the jittery waiters. Never in his life had he seen so many dazzling jewels on display, so many sumptuous silks, taffetas, and velvets.

As he moved closer to the enticing purple-red combination, he could see that the purple jacket was cut too short for the torso. What a shame. The shoulder fit was well tailored. The red dress underneath held its form with every movement. How smashing to mix the red and purple; he loved the audacity of color and the extra dimensions the combination created.

He froze. The hair swung in a shiny brown curtain just below the shoulders; the arms were long. A hand reached to touch the hair, a hand that fit perfectly into the shining wave.

She turned. His eyes were fastened on their subject; she had not seen him. From where he stood, he could see that her belly looked slightly bigger; the short jacket barely covered it. Her face, her hair, and her eyes shone. She was a crystal chandelier lighting the crowds.

'Dinner is served,' announced a waiter behind him.

Claude stood still, like a stalking tiger gathering heat to pounce on his prey. His legs would not move; her beauty paralyzed him. In this great room, in this dress that cried for attention, Valentine looked more spectacular than ever.

She saw him then and, before he knew it, was rushing toward him, her smile wide.

'*Mon cher Claude, quelle surprise!* What brings you to New York?' she asked.

A little crowd gathered around them. Valentine waited, focused intently on his response. Did she expect him to say that he had followed her here?

'A visit to the spring shows,' he said. He tried

to make his voice glide casually, like his nephews down a newly polished banister.

'You must sit at my table,' she called over the clamor. 'I haven't been away that long, but I already miss Paris! New York is wild; it's on the go all the time. Claude.' She was at his shoulder; he dipped his nose to inhale her lilac fragrance. 'You should see the art. These artists aren't holding anything back! There's so much originality. You have the feeling that everything is *huge* and new. Here, *tradition* is just a word; it doesn't carry the baggage, the history, the generations of expectation that it does at home. I have so much to tell you. When did you arrive?'

The crowds began pushing through to the tables; the waiters were arriving with trays.

'Here, please sit with me,' she said, as she drifted, with Claude at her side, to her table. She plucked the name card out of a tiny silver pheasant at the place setting next to hers and, with a smile, deposited it on the neighboring table.

The other seat beside Valentine had already been occupied by a man in a purple bow tie, matching, surprisingly, the color of Valentine's jacket.

'Come, sit,' she said, laughing. 'No one will notice. Who would try to separate two reunited friends from abroad? I need to hear all about you, and the news from Paris. Who knows when we'll be back?'

Waiters appeared behind each chair, pouring white wine, serving up a concoction of lobster tail on endives with a celery-carrot remoulade. A group clustered near Valentine's chair, resting hands near her hair, talking to her and to one another. Her waiter became increasingly agitated as he tried to serve.

'Excuse me,' he said. He bumped a woman's back with his tray.

'Valentine!' came in a commanding American voice from a man who looked to be in his late fifties. He wore small rectangular metal-framed glasses that only slightly muted the piercing blue eyes beneath. 'I was told I was sitting next to you.'

'Stop your whining, Ian.' Claude was surprised by Valentine's good English. Of course, he reminded himself, English was de rigeur for work at Drouot. 'This is my great good friend Claude Reynaud, who's just arrived from Paris. I know Ian's been wanting to meet you, Claude. He's *more* than an avid admirer. Ian Day. Ian designed this dress and is a sculptor in his spare time.'

'Spare time is a gem in a box of rocks,' Ian said, as the two shook hands.

The waiter, barely visible under two trays, asked Ian to take a seat.

'Yes, well, of course I *would* take a seat if I *had* one,' he said, his eyes darting at Claude.

'Valentine, where do you suggest I sit?' he asked.

'Ian, please forgive me,' Valentine said calmly, confident her will would be done. 'Allow me the luxury of catching up with my friend Claude here. He has to fill me in on our mutual friends and family and the beloved city that my heart pines for! I placed your name card on that table.'

He glanced at the indicated table and pursed his lips in a frown. It was full.

'I suppose the thing to do is to find Mr Reynaud's seat,' he said.

'Sir, please, a seat,' said the waiter. 'I cannot serve if you remain standing.'

Ian bent down to Valentine and whispered something in her ear. Valentine looked unsettled, undecided, then put her hands to her mouth and laughed.

'*Oui, oui*. Okay.'

Ian Day left them.

'What did he ask?' Claude asked.

'He said he'd only give up his seat if he could sculpt me naked.'

'You said *yes*!'

'I was tired of his whining. He won't want to sculpt me when he finds out I'm expecting, and then, after the baby, he's sure to forget.'

'To his dying day, he will never forget.'

As the waiters spun around, unfolding dinner before them, Claude looked closely at the design of Valentine's dress. No wonder he liked it. It resembled the wedding gown he'd designed for her, but the sheer veils of bold colors softened the straight column underneath and at the same time enlivened the material. The jacket had been added. Designers copied one another often, but this likeness was extremely obvious.

'Do you notice anything familiar about the dress you're wearing?' he asked her.

'Of course, Claude, it's a replica of my – your – wedding dress. Ian asked if I minded if he copied it. I was meaning to ask you, but there was so much going on. I thought you'd consider it a compliment. I hope that's okay. It's obviously your design. And, it *is* good on me, isn't it?'

As long as he was with her, anything would be acceptable. No wonder Ian had burned with color as they were introduced. *He* was the imposter at the table, not Claude.

Valentine spoke with the handsome man to her left. The man laughed. From Claude's angle, her teeth sparkled.

Claude tried to converse in his halting English with the woman to his right, a very thin model with unnaturally large lips. After they had eaten the main course, Valentine leaned over to him and whispered in his ear. Her warm breath tickled. '*Allons-y!* Let's get out of here. I will meet you on the stairs outside in ten minutes. I'll go first; then you follow. Okay?'

Her breath in his ear was like smooth dripping honey. He shut his eyes, felt her movement from the table, and watched her coast seamlessly out through the massive doorways.

He glanced at his watch three times, navigated through one more conversation, and excused himself from the table. As he walked among the Egyptian sphinxes and the bejeweled mummies, design ideas began hatching in his mind. His next dress would hang from a gold Egyptian necklace and feature a lowslung gold and enamel belt at the waist. Flat strappy gold sandals would finish the look. He would name his new line Sphinx.

Claude found Valentine outside at the top of the stairs in the shadow between the spotlights. Her rounded belly caught his eye as he walked toward her. The silhouette formed such a perfect arc that he had to pull his gaze away from it to look at her face. She surprised him by gently putting her arms around him. He felt her belly against his.

'Do you know how happy I am to see my friend Claude Reynaud?' she asked, pulling away from the hug. 'We will always be friends, won't we, Claude? It's such a comfort to see your face, your sweet face!' She hugged him again as if she couldn't get enough. A wind stirred a cluster of crusty brown leaves on the steps.

He reached for her hands. 'You're freezing. Come, let's get out of the cold.'

'No,' she said, resisting his tug. 'I'll tell you where I want to go. Over there, on the ledge.' She pointed to a landing to the right of the top step, about twenty-five feet above the pavement below. 'I've been standing here analyzing how to get to it. You see, right here, you jump over that little crack and there you'd be, so high up, looking down. Come on! It will be fun.'

'Valentine, what are you talking about?' he said.

'It's just' – she gazed at the ledge – 'that it would feel so liberating to walk out there and feel the cool air under us and see the city and bright lights at eye level.'

'You like going to the edge of things, don't you? It's too cold.'

'Just for a moment. Humor me!'

'Your condition . . .' He looked down and she followed his eyes. 'Let's get a drink, a coffee, across the street.'

With his arm around her shoulders, he walked her out of the edge of the spotlight and down the stairs.

'I just wanted to see what it felt like,' she said. A second later, she had broken free from his hand and had run back up the steps. He ran after her. She jumped the gap to the ledge. Aghast, he followed.

She turned to face him, now on the edge, the whites of her eyes lit by the spotlight. 'I'm always pulling myself *away* from the edge, Claude! Always going the appropriate route. I'm tired of it!' She laughed. 'Doesn't it feel great, being up here?'

'You're too close to the edge. Hold my hand.'

The wind whipped against the side of the building.

'Okay, I'm ready to jump!' she yelled, her eyes wild. He caught her hand.

'Valentine!' Her fragrance, the feel of her hand in his, her beckoning face: he kissed her. She kissed him back. She laughed to break the embrace. 'Claude, I was just joking! My dear Claude, you're so concerned. I'm just playing. Life can get so serious!'

She laughed again, then quickly grew quiet. She kicked off a shoe and watched it fall out of sight in the darkness. They heard a dull clatter below. She picked up her other shoe, but he caught it in her hand before she threw it.

'Come on, it's fun! These things are killing my feet anyway. I'm tired of teetering around off balance.'

'This shoe stays in my pocket.'

'Then here goes my jacket.'

She began unbuttoning the rhinestones on her jacket.

'No!' Claude said. 'It's cold! Are you going to strip entirely? What has New York City done to you? I'll have to carry you down as it is, and . . . you're heavier than you were.'

'Carry me, Claude, carry me,' she said merrily.

'We have to jump back over the gap. I'll do it first, then you.'

'No, let's not go down yet! Don't be so responsible! All I want is a bit of an escape, a break from the weight of life. The air is so fresh and the night so close to us up here. Night, come and be with us!'

'Your feet must be freezing! Come,' he said, jumping the small gap and holding his arms out for her.

She sat down and dangled her feet over the edge. She was a bird of paradise on the verge of flying.

Suddenly she got up again. 'Claude! Forgive me! Aren't I behaving like a spoiled child?' In her stocking feet, she jumped over the opening in the ledge effortlessly and melted in his arms. He carried her down the stairs as gently as he could. Her head nestled under his as he imagined a swan's would, seeking warmth in her mate on a chilly night.

Slightly winded, he put her down carefully to retrieve her other shoe, then gathered her up again. The swirling disconnected leaves and wind pushed them across the street into the doors of the Stanhope Hotel.

'Here's one shoe, but I've decided to keep the other,' he said.

'Do you think I'll run away for fear my carriage will turn into a pumpkin?'

'I will never let you go.'

She grabbed the shoe from his hand and slid it on, smiling. 'Faster than you!'

She walked ahead of him into the hotel's cozy corner bar overlooking Fifth Avenue. Claude asked what she would like to drink.

'Nothing alcoholic,' she said.

He closed his eyes to shut out the thought that he was protecting another man's baby. 'Just minutes ago, you wanted to jump off the edge. Now, you are watching your alcohol!'

He ordered an espresso for himself and a Perrier for Valentine.

'Claude, you're the only one who understands me,' she said, laughing.

'That's the problem.'

'*Non.*' She cupped her dark hair in her hand. 'Can I count on you for it, from now to forever?'

'You aren't with Victor tonight,' he said, hating to mention the name, to sever all that had been theirs until then.

'Victor, Victor, Victor,' she said, with a sigh. Did the mention of his name bring forth the dark blue circles that resembled shadows under her eyes? Her brow pinched together. 'He's worse than ever.' She paused and took a deep breath. 'I thought the move would do him good. Last week, I discovered he was dismissed from his position at the art gallery, but he hasn't told me yet. He leaves in the morning, saying he's going to work, and comes home in the middle of the night, so drunk he falls asleep in the living room with his clothes on.'

The waiter arrived with their drinks.

'When he sees me in the morning, he's grouchy, for I don't know what reason, being awake, I guess. He gets mad over little things, tells me I should not look at him like that, that I disdain him, that I act as if I'm better than he, that I'm thinking of leaving him. I used to defend myself and we would argue. Now, I leave the apartment early in the morning so I'm not there when he wakes up.

'I feel so sorry for him, Claude. He feels like an outcast everywhere he goes. His parents say he has sullied their name. I still can't believe how little compassion they show him. The auction house was his entire world, everything he had worked toward.'

Valentine ignored her Perrier and took a sip of his espresso.

'Then, when I see him in the afternoon, he's a pussycat, his loving self, doing anything in the world for me.'

Claude caught the slight roundness at her navel in the periphery of his vision. Unconsciously, he had already designed a maternity dress, Josephine Bonaparte style, but instead of a fluid gauzy gossamer, falling from the bottom of the breast-bone, Claude drew rectangles and overlapping flaps of stiff taffeta.

'If I go out with him, he makes a fool of us both. If anything, it's good we're here in New York. We don't know many people. And in this city, everyone's slightly crazy anyway. That's what I love about this place. I feel freer in this city than anywhere else I've ever been.'

'In one of his drunken states, he hasn't . . . been physical?' He winced.

'No, no, no,' she said, inhaling. 'He would not . . . It's only if I happen to be in . . . When he gets angry, he can be like a tornado that will take anything in its path. He doesn't know I'm here tonight. He's usually out until two or three o'clock in the morning. I guess, one time he did return early and I wasn't home yet. It was eleven at night, and I had gone to a birthday party of an old friend, Annette from Paris, who moved here two years ago. He wouldn't let me in the door! He yelled through the peephole into the hallway, "Go back to wherever you were! No wife of mine tramps around town at night!" I slept at Annette's. The next morning, he came to Annette's apartment with flowers and apologies. It's so confusing.'

She took another sip from his espresso, sat back in her chair, and shut her eyes. 'That's warming me up.' A drop glistened on her bottom lip for a second.

'When we were in our teens, Victor talked endlessly about paintings and art of all kinds and how he loved certain artists. He couldn't get enough of Titian; when he grew up, he was going to know and own the Titians of our day. He was always dreaming and talking about the future, but strangely enough it was as if he were reminiscing, looking back on how glorious it was. Every time we went out riding, he'd compare me on my horse or the landscape behind me to a painting he'd studied. I would run home and find the painting in my art history book. It still amazes me how knowledgable about art he is.

'Unfortunately, his father had other ideas for him. He thought his son should follow his career in business. The summer Victor worked for his father, he spent most of his time analyzing the eighteenth-century landscape prints that lined the halls.' She laughed. 'His father dismissed Victor's career choice as *soft*. So there you have it! My goodness, I've never told anyone so much in one sitting! You're such a kind friend to listen. The problem for me is I think I'm a reminder to Victor of all that he was and wished, yet failed to be.'

'You're in a difficult situation,' Claude said finally, sitting back, wishing he could place his hand on her brow to smooth the crease.

'It's the drinking that makes him so unpredictable.'

'Perhaps you should move out, stay with your friend, at least until the baby . . .'

Valentine had a way of pausing before responding, as if to give significance to each spoken word.

'No, no, I could never do that! I'm the only one Victor has here.'

She sipped her Perrier.

'He's too proud to confess to his parents and friends in Paris that he's lost another job. His sister calls, but he won't respond. He's losing New York friends every time he goes out and overdrinks. Annette also thinks I should get out of his way. And – what? Leave him to become a drunk in the gutters of New York City? Remember, I've known Victor since we were children. You don't know how sweet, how truly good-hearted, he is. I've tried to get him to a meeting of this AA organization that I've heard so much about. Just one meeting. Of course, he refuses. People say it's a midlife crisis, and then it's over and everyone's smarter. Oh, but this is all so dreary, Claude. You thought you'd have fun, seeing me! But you, what about you?'

Laughter and boisterous voices invaded their intimate corner.

'Oh, look, honey, Claude Reynaud from Paris.' Claude looked up at a woman in a gown of marigold-yellow ruffled chiffon layers. Unfortunately, the bodice was a size too small for the woman's upper body.

'We loved your collection!' She tittered. 'I'm Harriet Stillman and this is my husband, Ollie. I've followed you since that amazing wedding dress, haven't I, Ollie . . . Oh, it's the woman herself!' she whispered to her mate. 'How funny! Would you mind if we sat right here? That party drove us out. It's as loud as an overpopulated aviary! Carpets would help tremendously. But really, they should carpet the walls. One day that temple will fall down with all the commotion.

'Come, let us treat you to the next round.' The woman lifted her large arm to call the waiter.

'Thank you very much,' said Claude, rising. 'But we were about to leave.'

When Valentine rose from the table, all three took notice of her belly.

'Did you design that dress?' the woman asked.

'Unfortunately, I did not.' He looked at Valentine.

'Oh, before you leave, please do take my name and phone number. I would go gaga if you would design me a dress, whatever the price.' She busied her hands in her large black-sequined evening bag, found a pen and blank card, scribbled her details, and gave it to him.

Claude bowed formally and left with Valentine,

paying on the way out. The red-carpeted stairs outside the Metropolitan were dotted with departing guests.

'I should get you back home quickly,' Claude said, glancing at his watch as the wind pushed them from behind. He looked uptown for a taxi.

'What time is it?'

'Eleven-thirty.'

'Here's a taxi,' Valentine said. 'Hop in with me. Then you can continue on to your hotel.'

She gave her address to the taxi driver. Her voice in English was edible.

'We're renting an apartment from a friend from home. I wish I could show you the view down Park Avenue. It's mesmerizing to watch the street activity, even at two in the morning.'

'Valentine.' He wrote a phone number for her on the back of his Salon de Silvane card. Before his departure, Lebrais had given Claude an international cell phone for the trip, 'to stay in touch.' 'Take this and call me in the morning for a cup of coffee. Then you can have your own espresso.' The taxi stopped.

'Please, Claude, no need to get out. It's better if you don't.' He could hear anxiety in her voice. 'Go on . . . I'll be fine.' She slid out of the taxi, and he waved to her. How he wished he could press his cheek against hers, now out in the cold and rosy with the wind.

CHAPTER 22

U nder a massive white tent behind the New York Public Library, the designers Gallencia and Sorbu staged an extensive amusement park to introduce their Sheer Swing into Spring collection. Unfortunately, because of the models' skeletal bodies, the event became an ugly spectacle of malnourished young women flung about by churning machinery. The towering Ferris wheel beamed with blue-tinted floodlights that drained color from the models' already dour faces.

What a shame, thought Claude. All this excellent work and fine fabric draped on the wrong bodies!

Even from afar, in Senlis, Claude had admired Gallencia's respect for the flow of material. But exhibiting the dresses in bumper cars and other metal contraptions made the fabrics and designs look cheap, even tawdry. Claude imagined his father shaking his head as the cars bumped and the satin quivered, saying, '*C'est affreux!* Take a lesson from this! Every fabric must be allowed its *own* movement. Especially satin. It's a disgrace to mistreat satin!'

As the woman seated next to him rose to go, Claude admired her exciting tapestry jacket, an Aubusson replica. Within a few seconds, her seat had been taken by none other than Lebrais.

'Let me introduce you,' Lebrais said, never missing a beat. He nodded at the man to Claude's right. 'Claude, I would like you to meet Tom Powers, curator of the DeWitt Museum, one of the most cutting-edge museums in New York. Tom, one of my top designers, Claude Reynaud.'

Claude leaned over to shake the man's hand. The applause began for Gallencia and Sorbu. Lebrais and Powers rose from their seats with the rest of the audience to give the show a standing ovation. Claude stood reluctantly.

'I'm certainly familiar with your work, Claude,' said Powers, as the clapping died down. 'I must admit, I studied the wedding gown that won you much admiration. What I especially appreciated was the way you gave the garment a visible underlying structure, a column. We haven't seen such architectural underpinning since the hoop skirt.'

The crowd pushed toward the exits. Amid the crush of voices and bodies, Lebrais spoke for Claude. 'Yes, yes, that's what we promote in our salon – girding in every garment.'

The next day, Claude felt the tug of France. Was it his pile of unfinished work that begged for his return or was it Didier's birthday party, scheduled for the next weekend? Juliette had left a message reminding him of the event. Celebrating his nephews' birthdays was one of his great joys. At each boy's party, Juliette served champagne for the adults to mark a year passed without injury. Cake and frosting-faced children of all ages raced and slid in and out of doors. Laughter echoed in the halls as the house was ravaged; stable feet muddied the wooden floors and sent the threadbare Persian rugs flying. The taste of Juliette's *quatre-quarts à l'orange* cake with orange-zest icing lingered in the memory until the next celebration.

Claude longed for his nephews. At this very moment, their bones were thickening and lengthening without him. Henri was boasting a slight hint of facial hair. Would he shave for the first time without his uncle present? But nothing would take Claude from Valentine. He would stall as long as he could to be with her.

After the show that morning, an atrocious display of models dressed as bawdy prostitutes, replete with red mouths that mimed the words 'Go away,' he informed Lebrais that he planned to stay on a few days longer to follow up on some contacts. He also wanted to sort through his growing heap of crinkled napkins scribbled with design ideas.

Lebrais's mission was accomplished. He had inspired his designer. It was next to impossible to leave New York without a calamity of impressions, without ideas stampeding out of the brain.

'Claude Reynaud,' Lebrais said, 'don't think I don't know the real reason you wish to stay.'

As if on cue, Claude's cell phone rang. Valentine's soft voice.

'Please excuse me.' Claude moved off to a corner of the showroom, pressing the phone against his ear.

'Claude,' Valentine began. 'I hate to ask this question on a phone, but I know you will understand. Would you be able to lend me five hundred dollars? There's no more cash . . . My credit cards were rejected. I think Victor has taken all the money from my wallet and has had our savings wired to him here. I'm not sure how he did that without my signature. I just need to pay this one doctor . . .'

'Of course,' he said, trying to remember where he had last spotted a bank. 'Meet me for lunch at the Palm Court of the Plaza Hotel on Fifty-ninth Street and Fifth Avenue, and I'll give it to you then.' He had visited the grand old hotel earlier that day.

Lebrais was at the door as Claude rushed to leave. 'Be in Paris at the designers' meeting in our offices on Friday, four o'clock sharp. We'll be expecting you.'

Four extra days in New York City! Was that the expiration date Lebrais had calculated for his troubled romance?

CHAPTER 23

Everything about the Plaza's Palm Court charmed Claude: the arching palm fronds in massive marble tubs, the colorful reflections that bounced off the mirrored French doors, even the sounds of clinking china. He chose a table in the corner, partially hidden from the front of the room by a palm tree but allowing a full view of those entering the dining area.

At his table under the pink ceiling, on a piece of paper a waiter had found for him, Claude sketched four empire-style dresses in pastel colors for Valentine's changing figure. He drew beaded capes in lavender, periwinkle blue, coral, peach, dusty yellow.

She entered in a rush, the room's pink lighting settling on her features. She wore a long navy wool coat with cream-colored sheepskin peeking out at sleeves and hem. Claude wished he had designed the outerwear: it was tailored so closely to her shoulders, it looked custom-made. Her boots – how he loved the comforting sight of something so Valentine-familiar – were the beige suede ones. Her face was pale, her eyes bright but watery.

Claude could not help himself; he always noticed every detail about her.

She smiled when she saw him. He took her coat and placed it on an extra chair.

'Valentine,' he said, handing her the envelope of cash.

'Thank you so much, Claude,' she said, reaching down to slip it in her purse. 'I will pay you back as soon as possible. I promise! I'm so grateful.'

Claude looked at the pink embossed menu and peeked at Valentine as she read hers. He was in New York City with his true love. He thought of Anatole and imagined he must feel similarly happy in his church, loving the world and all in it.

'Your turn to order lunch,' she said. When the waiter appeared, he requested the monkfish on *choucroute* fermented with juniper berries for her and the trout with almondine stuffing for him, to be followed by a curly-leafed greens and endive salad.

'As the Americans say, *cheers*.' She lifted her glass of the cranberry juice and soda that Claude had ordered for both of them and looked through it at him.

He echoed her motion. 'To the love of my life and my muse,' he said.

She shook her head at him as if he were joking and smiled and closed her eyes as she took a sip. 'When I was at Drouot, surrounded by art on all sides, with hundreds of pages of catalogs in front of me,' Valentine said, replacing the glass on the table, 'I would think about how wonderful it must be for artists to get out of the pattern the world creates and make their own completely original template! I've always envied people like you, Claude, who know from an early age that they're a species apart from the rest of us, ready to devote themselves to their passion from the start, to sacrifice material life, trusting they won't starve. I can't imagine such faith or confidence.'

He gently placed his hand on hers. 'Actually, at this moment *you're* the ultimate artist.' He hated himself for suggesting this, for reminding them both. 'You, who are creating a child.'

She paused. 'Yes, yes, Claude, that's true – but why do I feel so restless? Why do I feel the need to crack the surfaces of things? You express yourself in colors, in designs. It amazes me what you come up with. But is it something that you physically need to get out, or is it something you just love to do?'

He would say anything to soothe her. 'I work day and night to keep the inner tigers from chasing me. Look!' He produced his cache of napkins covered with designs. 'I try to expel the striped predators at regular intervals. One day, I'm afraid they'll eventually catch and devour me.'

The waiter returned with their order. She picked at her fish with her fork.

'As far as art is concerned, you've painted an amazing likeness of – our apple tree.' It had been said, exposed and accepted.

284

'*Oui*, but I'm not a painter. I do love to paint, like so many of my friends in this business, but I'll never be anything more than mediocre. No, I think collecting art and supporting artists is more my passion, discovering new talents, new attitudes that reflect the mood of our time. Théodore's work – his use of color, for example – sends me over the moon with pleasure.'

She swooped the fork to her mouth; then, out of nowhere, she laughed, covering her mouth, her eyes looking upward.

'It's all so ridiculous,' she said, having finished chewing. 'All these tigers under such a soothing pink ceiling!'

Claude looked up and saw that the pink hue was infectious; everything he noticed seemed rose-colored: the silver urns, the pink-tinged lilies, the tip of Valentine's nose, the innermost part of her eye. Was it possible to *feel* a color seeping through one's skin? Did he smell Valentine's perfume or was the scent wafting his way from the lilies in the nearby urn?

The waiter returned to collect their plates.

'Oh, dear,' she said, looking at her watch. 'I don't want to leave Victor alone for too long. He could decide to go out, and then it's just a matter of hours or days before I get a call from the police or the hospital. Do you think, at home in France,' she said, 'they'd let him out of the hospital like they do here?'

'Valentine, take Victor back to Paris. There you have support: your family, your friends. It's too lonely here, where you know only a handful of people. It would be better for him and for you.'

The waiter arrived with the check.

'Do you think I haven't tried?' She fiddled with the gold bracelet on her wrist. 'I've bought the plane tickets. I've been tempted to go alone and see if he would follow. He won't budge. And as I've told you before, I wouldn't be able to live with myself if I left without him.'

She lifted her eyes to the ceiling, then moved forward in her seat, looking into his eyes. 'Thank you, thank you,' she said. 'For this,' she nodded at the envelope, 'and for the lunch. *Et bien! Alors!* I almost forgot,' she said, as she dropped her head and retrieved another envelope from her purse.

'My friend Irene wants to meet you. Tonight's the opening reception for her show. Don't feel you have to come, though.'

As Valentine rose, Claude detected a thread that had unraveled from the button of her coat's waist-line. He said nothing, but his photographic mind could not help but mentally readjust her measurements, taking in the growing bulge.

'*Merci*, Claude, I should be able to repay you the day after tomorrow.'

Once outside the hotel, she circled her right wrist with her left-hand fingers.

'I've lost my bracelet,' she said, 'the one my grandmother gave me.' She looked down. 'My grandfather gave it to her on the day of their engagement.'

'You had it on at the table.'

'It must have fallen off inside.'

'Let's go back.' Claude took her arm and began to reenter the hotel. She stopped him midway.

'Claude, I've changed my mind. If it's there, let's leave it!' Her eyes brightened.

'Why?'

'I don't want to go back and find out that it's not there. If I lost it there in that beautiful room with you at my side, I'll remember it more than if it were on my arm. As long as I live, I'll remember it as a time when we were together.'

'Valentine, come on; it's your grandmother's bracelet.'

'No. Please, Claude.' She kissed him on both cheeks and ran down the stairs of the hotel. He did not take his eyes off her until she was around the corner and out of sight.

Claude returned to the restaurant. The waiter, seeing him approach, held the bracelet up to him with two hands as if offering a sacred object to a pagan god. Claude thanked him and departed, gripping the golden orb tightly.

Claude sat on a nearby bench and listened to voice messages from his Parisian employer. 'Congratulations, Claude. You've been given another assignment from the prime minister's wife, this time for a suit for her arrival in Greece at the end of January. We must have the design the Monday after you get back. She wants to see the dress by early December.' Next voice mail: 'Please start thinking about the fall ready-to-wear collections to appear in early March.'

Claude had not yet made a reservation for the Thursday red-eye to Paris. He had begun to adjust nicely to the life Lebrais had opened up to him; ideas continued to cascade from his pen to paper. He was once again taking risks in his work, throwing off the knee-length hem, cutting a V-line unevenly, raising the waist.

He had also begun to plot his future with Valentine: Victor's placement in a rehabilitation center, their divorce, her return to Paris with the baby. For a few moments, still under the spell of the Palm Court ceiling, Claude imagined a rosy future.

CHAPTER 24

The gallery on West 28th Street in Chelsea abutted the West Side Highway. The cold November wind funneled down a street lined on each side with shabby gray townhouses. The building that housed the gallery was at the end of the block, a gray box with no windows. A car axle served as the entrance-door handle.

Inside, people murmured as Claude had discovered they did in galleries here. Were they afraid of disturbing the artwork? Or were they criticizing the work behind the artist's back? Immediately, he recognized one laugh. At the far end of the room, Victor towered over a group, the only one talking. Instinctively, Claude felt he should leave. He had arrived toward the end of the show and could see a few people moving around the coat rack. As he quickly scanned the cavernous room for Valentine, a red-haired woman with freckles and light-blue kohl-rimmed eyes opened her arms to him and introduced herself as Irene. Too late.

She wore black pants, too wide for her thick waist, and a drawstring-collared brown lamb's-wool sweater with a large piece of silver and bronze scrap metal in the shape of a wheel around her neck.

'Thank you for coming, Claude,' she bubbled. 'I would know your face anywhere. Let me take your coat. Here, a glass of champagne to warm you up on this windy night. While I've got you, you must come and see one of my favorite pieces. It was just sold. Follow me.'

Irene threw his coat on a sofa with a vigorous toss, her white arms jiggling. Though her face with its blur of light brown freckles was soft, her gestures and voice were fierce. She led him out of the room and into a narrow hall, through an office, and into a small, dimly lit back room. A sculpture hung from the ceiling: a lifesize bronze stallion. It was hanging upside down by its legs, its massive head about three feet from the floor. Claude swallowed.

A symbol of brute strength strung up on a rope. The horse's nostrils flared, the eyes widened in terror, the ears were flattened against the back of the head; veins and muscles protruded in the back and haunches. The artist had captured the horse's attempts to bring himself upright despite the undeniable force of gravity. The horse's genitals, at eye level, dangled miserably, upside down, resting on the side of its underbelly.

Claude smiled to shield himself from the inquiring intensity of the artist. When the phone rang and she answered it, Claude mouthed *thank you* and pointed at the door as if he had an important meeting. He crossed the room in the direction of the sofa at the far edge of the loft. There, coat in hand, turning around to say good-bye to Irene, who had just emerged from the back room of torture, he heard Victor's un-mistakably deep voice.

'Little tailor,' he said, 'have you come to look at art or have you come to feast your eyes on my wife?'

Irene swept up to them, offering Victor the glass of wine in her hand.

'*Non!*' He dismissed her so loudly that the room was silenced. Claude imagined Valentine loving the rich, velvety vibrations in Victor's voice. 'This little tailor is sewing his way into my life, and I don't like it. I know one thing: he did not come to this ugly hole in the highway to look at *this* junk.'

At Irene's side, a slim man with a beard said, 'That's unnecessary. Keep your opinions to yourself.'

'I'm not talking to you.' Victor's eyes had not left Claude. 'I'm talking to this lying little tailor.'

'Everyone has his own ideas,' Irene said. 'Over time, great art stays the course of poor opinions.'

Anger occupied Victor's face in varying shades of red: the portrait come alive. Rohan *was* good. Claude turned in the direction of the stairwell, following those others who had chosen to exit.

Then he saw Valentine, at the top stair, on the verge of entering the gallery room, in her long navy coat, her small bulge barely visible.

Claude shut his eyes, wishing he hadn't seen her. Two departing guests obstructed his view of her momentarily. When she resurfaced under the neon lighting of the stairwell, she looked ghostly, her face pallid, her eyes dark, her lips drained of color.

When she spotted Claude, her eyes brightened. Five seconds later, Claude watched the sparkle die. She pulled her coat tighter around herself.

'Little tailor, don't run away,' Victor mocked. 'Especially now that the apple of your eye has appeared. You're caught in the middle of the web you've woven yourself, aren't you? Here is your lover, and here is her husband.'

Valentine glided slowly past Claude, focusing solely on Victor, as if drawn to him by a magnet.

'Victor,' she said, 'come with me to see the show. I've just—'

He shook her hand from his sleeve. 'Why do you look so shocked? Do you think everyone doesn't know that you've been two-timing your husband?'

Claude took a step toward the couple.

'Who are you, little tailor, vile specimen of low-class trash, that my wife would consider bedding *you*?' Victor slurred his words.

Irene, who had been standing behind Victor, grabbed Valentine by her coat sleeve.

'Valentine, everyone, the show is over. It's time to go.'

Valentine remained glued to Victor.

'Leave, Valentine!' said Claude loudly.

'Come, the show's over. Let's all go,' Irene said, as if she were an impersonal guard at a museum, moving people along.

'Valentine is going nowhere,' Victor said. 'Little tailor, watch me kiss my wife.' He took Valentine's face roughly in both hands and and kissed her lips. Her coat-covered figure sagged inside Victor's embrace. Claude looked away.

Irene gesticulated energetically for Claude to leave.

'No, no,' Victor said, looking up. 'Don't go yet, we've only *begun* the fun.'

'Go!' urged Valentine.

Claude turned and walked down the steps. Once out in the street, he asked a pedestrian how to call the police. When told, he dialed 911 on his cell phone.

'A man, he is mad at a woman,' he told the police dispatcher. He gave the address in his limited English, hung up, tried to reenter the building, but discovered after much pushing that the door had been locked. By whom and when?

Claude questioned his decision to call the police. Had he judged the situation too quickly, incorrectly? Valentine would never want the intrusion of the police. On the other hand, Victor was drunk and angry and potentially dangerous.

Claude knew the best thing for him to do was to stay away; his presence would only aggravate Victor. But he would not leave without knowing that Valentine was safe. He crossed the narrow street lined with parked cars, linked, it seemed, in an endless metal chain. He leaned against a cold lamppost that strangely hosted no lamp and watched, as snow began to fall, like a cat spellbound by a mouse hole, the heavy axle doorknob to the gallery. Nothing. No Irene. He checked his watch. Ten minutes. He walked to the side of the building to check if the lights were still on in the gallery space. They were. He returned to his post. At least Irene was upstairs too. Perhaps the three of them were having a little drink of wine and a nice chat about the opening.

The sound of the sirens arrived before the police cars. Claude remembered sitting as a child on his apple tree counting the moments between thunder and lighting. He started counting now. Two, three, four. Should he show the police the way or stop them in their tracks and rescind the complaint? As he watched snowflakes settle and then disappear on his jacket, it occurred to him that the only thing he had witnessed Victor do was kiss his wife. They were married. 'They are married,' he repeated to himself.

The sirens blasted in closer proximity. Red-and-blue flashing lights arrived, car doors opened and slammed shut. Claude crouched by the lampless lamppost, his heart pounding. He watched two men in uniform push against the now-locked door. They looked at the lit windows above and walked to the rear of the building. A man wearing glasses and a leather jacket passed Claude and noticed him hiding. Before he turned the corner, the stranger glanced back.

Perhaps the stranger would call the police to report a suspicious character by the lamppost. Claude left his hiding spot and walked in the direction of the thudding roar of the highway. He heard another siren whining. The car was heading in his direction. Claude strode faster. From afar, he watched a policeman inspect the cars near the darkened lamppost where he had huddled. What if Victor decided to describe *him* as the madman at the gallery opening? Wasn't *he* the villain in their marriage?

The area where he now found himself was empty of humanity, full of concrete and metal and loud with clunking, honking, and roaring. That something as gentle as floating snowflakes could coexist with the roaring sounds of the nearby highway baffled and yet reassured him.

Turning east, he returned to the street opposite the gallery. No flashing police cars. No sign of life. He hid behind a parked car when he heard voices. Victor and Valentine had emerged from the impenetrable metal door.

'Where is he?' shouted Victor. 'Miserable little tailor. I will make him wish he never touched you with his filthy measuring tape!'

Claude caught Valentine's face in the fading light as the door shut behind them. Her hand lifted to the wave in her hair. Irene was not with them.

The figures receded slowly down the street in the glittering white snowfall.

For an instant, he saw her turn around her face a white moon. Had she sensed his presence? Was she waiting for Claude to rescue her, to jump out from behind and take Victor on? Victor was too big for him. Had it come to that? In this 'civilized' world, did body weight and strength preordain the winner?

He placated himself by thinking Valentine had mastered the art of appeasing Victor. By now she must have become a practiced sorcerer, aware of every spell that could defang a wild animal. Would she tell him to sit still so she could paint him? Had she not told Claude that she loved to paint portraits as a hobby? While she stroked his face onto the canvas, would she murmur into his ear, telling her subject how beautiful he was? He shut his eyes.

When he reopened them, he saw a figure running toward him: Valentine. The shearling hemline of her dark coat flew in different directions, twisting around her body as she ran. He closed the gap between them.

'What is it?' he asked quickly.

'Irene. She's up there. He didn't realize what he was doing! In his drunken state, he's locked Irene in the back studio with no phone! Please take care of it!'

In the faint light, he noticed tears on her cheeks.

She turned to go, but they both heard his voice: the sound of thunder unmuted by snow.

'I knew I'd find you sniffing around, you little tailor, but look, you're so afraid! I can see it in your eyes. Valentine, look into the terrified eyes of your little tailor. He's afraid I will shred him, like shears cutting up cheap fabric.'

'Go away!' she yelled suddenly to Claude.

Victor sprang at him. Claude tried to extricate himself from Victor's grip, but Victor held his body in place with one hand and pummeled his chest with the other. Under Victor's weight Claude fell backward, his head hitting the cold wet cement. Victor was on top of him. Claude struck Victor's cheek. His knuckles ached, his ears rang; he tasted blood.

Valentine was pulling Victor away. He heard her silken voice. He caught a whiff of her lilac perfume. Claude tried to punch Victor in the chest, but missed and sideswept Victor's chin instead. He remembered Irene in the studio.

Mysteriously, the weight was off him. Snowflakes moistened his eyelashes. He heard American voices. He tried to raise his head, but his vision was blurred. He shook his head. Through legs of speaking strangers, he saw them. Victor and Valentine were a couple, promenading happily down the street. Victor's arm encircled her waist. Her head rested on his shoulder, on his shoulder! Her hair was white with snow. No, the snow was a lace veil! She was getting married. Again.

He felt as if he were falling, but he was already down. Despite his swollen lips, his dry mouth, his

297

light head, he said in English, to a man close by, 'A woman, she is locked in the gallery. Second floor.'

The man was a policeman: he wore a badge on his jacket and carried a stick in his belt. 'I'm the intruder,' Claude mumbled in French, touching his lip. In the blur of his throbbing head, he recalled Valentine's words about Victor. 'He didn't realize what he was doing.'

'*C'est moi*,' he confessed to the confused policeman. 'I am the criminal. *He* didn't realize what he was doing. But *I* know what I've been doing. I've been trying to steal Valentine, my Valentine, his Valentine . . . It's my fault.' Valentine would never be his, but she would always, always, be his muse. He would never give that up.

He tried to stand and lift his head but, instead, felt himself fade into a vast darkness, soothingly empty, coated with snow, as sweet a darkness as he had ever known, like the rich chocolate candy he was given as a child at Christmastime. The wetness he felt around his head was like the soft cherry inside.

Despite the incessant pounding in his head, Claude would recognize Lebrais's voice anywhere.

'Where are you?'

With the cell phone to his ear, he looked around him. He lay under covers in his hotel room. The curtains were drawn.

'What time is it? What day?' he asked Lebrais,

finding it difficult to talk with a swollen lip. He touched the cut and tasted blood.

'The day on which you fly back to Paris. I've been trying to reach you for twenty-four hours!' Lebrais was yelling.

Claude removed the phone from his ear. He sighed. 'Yes. I will be on tonight's flight.'

His cell phone beeped, indicating that he had received voice mail. Had Valentine called? He listened to a message from Rose-Marie crooning for another dress. She said the event was too important to discuss over the phone. Her voice seemed to bubble over. Had she caught a wealthy fish-husband on her line?

As he placed the phone on the bedside table, he wondered how he had made it back to the hotel. He spotted his pants hung neatly over the chair, on the bureau he noticed a miniature replica of the disturbing upside-down horse from Irene's show.

He stumbled painfully to the bureau and found a card bearing the name of the gallery. On the back, in loopy handwriting, it said:

Thanks for saving me! I hope you're right side up now. Call me, 874-3399.
Irene.

His head throbbed as he rang the concierge's desk. The concierge informed him that the night attendant on duty and a woman had carried Claude into the elevator and to his room.

Claude hobbled to the mirror to assess the damage. A large bandage covered the area around his left eyebrow, a smaller one hid the skin under his chin near his ear; his lower lip was swollen to double its size. He dressed as quickly as his bruised body permitted. His hand throbbed in pain when he tried to button his shirt.

He slipped his wounded hand into his suit pocket. Valentine's bracelet. Was he purposefully keeping it, a thief again, an interloper proud of his deceit? He would return it to her in person, before he caught the flight that night.

Claude cleaned himself up as best he could, paid for his hotel room, and left an envelope of cash with the concierge for the night attendant. On the street again, his eyes took a moment to adjust to the glare of the newly snow-whitened and sparkling city. As he walked uptown to 68th Street, he clutched the ring of gold in his pocket.

Could it be a mirage? As he approached Valentine's apartment building, he saw her figure under the green canopy! Was she leaving or arriving? Waiting for him? He ran against the wind to catch her.

He felt the bandage above his eyebrow detach a bit, but didn't care. She was just inside the door, heading toward the elevator. Claude careened into the lobby and met the doorman's stare. As Valentine turned around, he caught her looking at the place above his eyebrow. He quickly touched the area and realized the bandage was absent. He covered the wound with his hand.

'Valentine,' he said.

'Your head!' She looked at the doorman, then at him. 'How terrible.' She approached him.

'I'm leaving for Paris tonight,' Claude said.

He saw it. He could not believe it: she had breathed a sigh of relief. Everything about her softened, her brow, her eyes, her mouth.

'Would you step outside with me for a moment?' he asked.

'Of course.' She walked to the door and bowed her head toward the doorman.

'Before I left,' Claude said, now on the bright snow-lit street, 'I wanted to give you this.' He handed her the bracelet. 'Valentine, a part of me wanted to to keep it for myself. Last night, after what happened, I finally realized it was not and would never be mine.'

The wind blew around them, through them. She pulled her coat up under her chin. As usual, her eyes spoke. Her lips proved too confusing to watch; they stirred his desire.

'Claude, you found it! Keep my bracelet! I would be so happy if you had something from me and my grandmother.' Her hands in her pockets, she looked down at her boots. The wind blew her hair around her head. 'I know my grandmother would have liked you—'

'Don't, Valentine. I will not keep this.' He placed it in her pocket and touched her cold hand.

'I think, Claude,' she said, still gazing down, 'it will be better with you out of the country.'

She had said it; she lifted her eyes and squinted against the sun and snow. She took his hand in both of hers.

'Oh, I almost forgot,' she said in a brighter voice. 'I have something for *you*.'

She handed him an envelope. He looked at her hopefully, then shook his head at himself when she answered his upturned eyebrows. 'It's the repayment for your kind loan.' The wind blew her hair up again and into her face.

'Keep it. You might need it. Emergency money.' He tried to act as she did, as if they were no more than friends.

'No, no!' She pushed it into his hands.

'Will you call me if you need help?' he asked.

'Yes, I will – no; no, I won't. Getting help from you is—' she lowered her voice and shivered in the wind – 'too complicated, as we both discovered last night.' She touched the bruised skin above his eyebrow, then moved backward ever so slightly. 'Victor needs all of me now, Claude. He'll come out stronger after all this, I know he will. But, thank you, Claude, for – coming to my rescue. I will always be grateful. I will always—'

She brushed her cheeks against his, her body miles away.

'Say hello to Paris for me.'

He was not prepared for her quick withdrawal, the turn of her head, the sight of the back of her navy coat and beige-booted legs. His head throbbed. He wished he held her bracelet. No glance back from the threshold of the building? No wave of the hand, no smile, no nothing? Yes, there it was. Inside the building. It was no illusion. Just inside the door, out of the wind and snow-glaring sun, she waved. Her broad rosy lips mouthed *au revoir*.

CHAPTER 25

Paris cooed to him, gently cradling and rocking him back to her sweet rhythms. The sweet familiar tonic of the city soothed his sense of emptiness. Despite the gray turban it wore in winter and the cold stamp of the days, the city's narrow meandering streets invited and the cafés beckoned, their small round tables set carefully and efficiently with the predictable cream-colored thick-lipped teacups and plates, awaiting the arrival of a faultlessly crumbling croissant. Despite New York's enviable freedom, Claude would always prefer to live in Paris.

Friday afternoon at 3:30. Papers covered Claude's desktop at the Salon de Silvane like an open field blanketed with fresh snow. Claude could see Lebrais's hand in the design: invitations up front, bills in the middle, and work orders with the company's silver insignia to the left. The one closest to the bottom read URGENT, FINISH BY MONDAY. The accompanying letter was stamped with the government seal, the crest of the eagle. Claude stood back and appreciated the arrangement of his affairs. Lebrais's design left no hint of happenstance.

The office was oddly quiet. Had they started the meeting early? Claude had not checked his voice mail recently. He poked his head out of the doorway, walked down the empty hall, and peeked into Charles's office. Not there. No one in Lebrais's office. Down the hall, Anne the gargoyle informed him, looking at her watch, that all the designers were in the conference room for a 3 P.M. meeting. He must have missed Lebrais's call about the time change.

He slid quietly into the dark room. With a lit pointer in his hand, Lebrais stood next to the projection of a white pantsuit. It looked like an Yves Saint Laurent: the bell-bottom pants pooled on the floor, the huge lapels hung like calla lilies turned upside down, the oversized cuffs. Everything about the suit was outdated and out of proportion.

The shaft of light that entered the room with Claude caught the attention of the ever-alert Lebrais. Claude took a seat in the soothing dark oasis of the back row.

Lebrais paused meaningfully, then continued speaking.

'We're pushing this exaggeration for the fall season,' he said. 'Wider lapels mirroring wider pant legs, earthy colors, rusts and deep maroon reds, scarves using autumnal colors in different shapes, sizes, textures. Furs all over the place – in the hair, around the neck, around the waist, around the shoulder – this is where we're headed.

People want *out* of synthetic, nylon, slinky aerobic wear; this season we're back to nature, hugging the earth in color, texture, and attitude.'

The next visual featured a model with short cropped black hair and thick straight eyebrows, wearing a hip-length scarlet sweater with dark brown fur cuffs, dark brown ribbed corduroy bell-bottoms to the tip of her pointed black leather boots, dark green and olive green wool scarves at her neck. The contrast from the retro white pantsuit was effective. Claude heard the room sigh in relief.

'Think of layering.' On the next slide, Lebrais pointed at the sliver of white T-shirt that could be seen under the model's two-toned camel-and-cream cotton cardigan, itself under a vest with fur trim. The skirt was an orange corduroy A-line. 'We want undressing to be unveiling, like the experience you have when you uncover a Russian *matrioshka* nesting doll to reveal a smaller one underneath, then a smaller and again a smaller. There's surprise at every level.

'Every outfit should have a hat to match. Wool, mohair, and cashmere close-fitting hats will be big this season. *Voilà.* That is all for now.' Lebrais concluded hastily, looking ready to pounce if a question were asked.

'But André.' Charles's voice came from the other side of the room. 'You don't intend for us to bring back exaggerated lapels? They look absurd.'

'Yes, we're oversizing lapels for fall,' Lebrais said.

'They balance the bells on the pants; they refer to the large cuffs. You must know by now, Charles, that you can't have big bells without enlarged lapels.'

'They're too big. I can understand a modified version.'

'We want the lapels to be overstated.'

'You could tone down the lapel with a trim or another texture,' offered Claude.

'I think you all know how I feel about this season's lapels.' Lebrais headed toward the door. 'Please, no more questions for now.'

Claude could see that Lebrais was checking himself, holding back his irritation at Claude's late appearance at the meeting. He knew Lebrais had begun to rely on him as the top couturier in the salon. Small-town tailor, indeed.

Lebrais kept his distance during the rest of the afternoon. Charles asked Claude about his bandage, his trip to New York. The other designers disappeared like bees into their honeycomb compartments.

That night Claude worked until midnight on Madame Lorieux's Greece-inspired evening gown. Despite Lebrais's directive for a stately and regal silk gown, Claude intuited a light and breezy dress. He highlighted her long slender arms with a sleeveless design and covered her slightly large hips with billowing chiffon. The dress would be diaphanous and sparkling, charming and complex. He chose a dark fuchsia crêpe de chine, layered with a paler fuchsia chiffon to offset her light-brown hair. Small black onyx buttons would run from the top of the loose shawl collar down to the tips of her silver-pointed shoes. For jewelry: a black onyx bracelet and black onyx drops on pearl posts for earrings. Her hair would look best in a tightly twisted chignon.

The ideas came easily to Claude. Three hours passed without his notice. He had finished two highly detailed backup designs and in the process had not spent a moment thinking about Valentine. The designs pleased him. He placed the stack of pages on Lebrais's tidy desk.

The day of Didier's birthday party, Claude reached the wet cobblestone streets of Senlis at eight in the morning. He wanted to arrive early enough to watch his hometown rouse from the night's slumber. Its Romanesque square bell tower from the eleventh century at the edge of town, the café on the place Notre-Dame, the winding streets around the town shops, the Hôtel de Ville, the town hall, the linden trees, now without flowers or scent, the tabac, Le Capétien café: all looked like beloved relics of someone else's past. He parked his car on the narrow street outside his studio. What? A new car in the driveway next to his? He walked in the direction of his parents' graveyard off the narrow high-walled rue de Meaux, passing a man in his late twenties walking quickly up the street. A new face? He had not been away that long. He almost bumped into Madame Ruggier, who owned the bakery down the street. She was a bundled-up solid figure, head bent on her way to her shop on the lonely, windy morning.

'Madame Ruggier, do you walk right past me?'

She took a moment. 'Claude, how nice to see you here.' The wind blew a corner of her wool scarf off her shoulder; Claude replaced it. 'Oh, the wind! This winter is as bad as ever, damp and cold.' She took a closer look at him and eyed his bandage. 'Let me treat you to an amandine. They should be fresh out of the oven by now.' Amandines had been a favorite of Claude's since childhood.

'Madame, I would love one.'

They were inside her *boulangerie*, the windows moist with bread-scented heat, the room hot with baking. Madame Ruggier grinned at him, her small eyes alight, then strode purposefully into the back room. She reemerged, proudly holding a small plate carrying an almond tart.

'For you, our famous couturier of Senlis.'

He bowed and thanked her. As he sat at the one table in the shop and watched madame bustle about, preparing to open for business, Claude thought once again of Valentine. She had led him to Paris, away from all he knew and loved. Now he was a traveler, a visitor in his home.

He said good-bye to madame as the shop came to life with children on their way to school, pressing small faces against the glass covering the *pâtisseries* of the day. He continued down the deserted narrow alleyway of the rue de Meaux, which opened onto the charming church of Saint-Vincent, behind which his parents were buried.

Claude met Anatole for lunch at the mustard-colored Le Bourgeois Gentilhomme. Anatole was at the table he always occupied.

'Anatole, Anatole,' said Claude, taking a seat opposite his friend, 'why must you sit at the same table, in the same chair, at the same corner of this café every day of your life? It's boring to others, so it must be boring to you. Perhaps you don't notice?'

'We disagree here,' said Anatole, with a knowing smile. 'When you sit at the same table at the same time of day in the same chair, you never have to commit a single thought about which is the most private table with the best view of the restaurant at the most comfortable temperature. No! You leave your mind free for more significant matters. Once you establish a routine and it's good, why on earth would you change it?'

Claude leaned back in his chair, smiled, and shook his head.

'I like this table and chair,' Anatole continued, 'because you have a view of the entire room and who's arriving. You're close enough to the kitchen to smell what delight is coming out; you're near the bar, so you can catch George's attention and talk with him without getting up. Most importantly, from this window I can see the church. I can see who's coming and going or if anyone needs me. What you take for boring, Monsieur Reynaud, is instead a decision made for thoroughly strategic reasons.'

'Thank you for the clarification,' said Claude. 'I suppose I'm just restless for change.'

'So restless you've been fighting?' Anatole nodded at the bandage on Claude's forehead.

'Yes, it was a fight.'

Anatole nodded again, slowly, everything about him waiting patiently.

'It's all over.'

'Not over by the look on your face.'

Claude glanced out the window at the façade of the church. The cold, impenetrable stone structure soothed him. He would not look at the stained-glass windows. He felt too broken.

George arrived at the table, his large belly covered by a white apron stained yellow in places with what looked like béarnaise sauce. The belly presented itself like the meal to come, at table height.

'Anatole, the regular?' George did not need a pen or pad.

'You see how predictable you are, Anatole! George, wouldn't it be refreshing if our Anatole stepped outside his habits and ordered something totally different – like stewed rabbit, for example?'

'*Non, non, non,* it would not be agreeable at all.'

George vehemently shook his head. 'You see, not only does the cook count on Anatole to order this *blanc de poulet aux salsifis* every Sunday, he looks forward to cooking it.'

'All right, Mr Unpredictable,' retorted Anatole. 'Look at George's menu. Don't tell George or myself your choice for lunch.' He waited until the smiling Claude nodded his head. 'I predict you will order the *ragoût d'agneau* with beets and rice. *Non, non,* don't lie. That was it! Your face says so!'

'What made you guess correctly?'

'It was no guess, my friend. Everyone knows that beets are good for the heart.'

George left their table, laughing.

'Anatole,' said Claude, 'how can you ever say love is a gift from God?'

'I would keep God out of it. I saw photographs of your maternity designs in the paper the other day. Rumor has it that you designed them for your paramour.'

'It's over, my friend! It's over! I'm still smoldering, a fire recently dampened; I'm angry and bitter, but it's no use. She will never have me.'

'I suppose you have come face-to-face with the intense gravitational pull that a baby has on a mother. Only in the most dire circumstances can I imagine a woman leaving the father of her newborn baby.'

'She married the wrong man, just as I married the wrong woman,' Claude responded, too forcefully and defensively.

A long pause was followed by the arrival of the food. Anatole bowed his head and said grace slowly, his words measured as evenly as basting stitches.

Claude looked at the beets and lamb on the large white plate. The cut on his head began to throb. 'Anatole, will you forgive me? I am not hungry and my head hurts. Would you mind if I go home and rest?'

'Of course not, Claude.' His friend looked concerned. 'Were there stitches?'

'Just a cut and a few bruises, but I feel beat up.'

Claude motioned to George, who was serving the next table, and when he arrived, asked him to take his seat and eat his lunch. 'I haven't touched it.'

'I've had my eye on that ragoût from the moment I served it to you. It would be my pleasure. I'll hand this order in, Anatole, and be there in a minute.'

Claude struggled into his coat. Wasn't winter hard enough without coats whose sleeves weren't roomy enough for the clothes underneath? As he lifted his left arm to find the sleeve, he caught a glimpse of Anatole's face in his peripheral vision. Anatole's lips formed an easy smile. Anatole was surely one of God's men on earth. Claude regretted his decision to leave. He sat down with his coat on.

'Anatole, I hope you understand.'

'I won't say more until you ask me. I don't think I've said enough.'

'I disagree: yes, you have *and,* despite your prediction, I really wasn't in the mood for the lamb, nor was I interested in the beets.'

As he was leaving, he saw George, now seated, pick up his fork and knife.

CHAPTER 26

Juliette had a way of making imperfection perfect. Even the brown velvet couch in the living room had the right amount of *wear* versus *tear*. Quiches, mousses, terrines, cheeses, salmon, roasted duck laced with orange slices, baguettes, and butter were laid out on the dining table on different-sized plates of various patterns. The children had raided the baguettes: a trail of crumbs littered the floor from the kitchen. Claude entered through the dog-scratched kitchen door. Chocolat, with his constantly swinging tail, had taken up residence in the Roche household.

A thin, wiry-browed fellow editor at Juliette's publishing company and his wife, for whom Claude had designed a dress suit, welcomed him inside. Why had *they* come to Didier's party?

'*Claude, bienvenue!* Come have a drink,' the editor said. 'Whatever's happened to you? You look like you ran into a truck!'

'I guess you could say I did. Not to worry, just a minor accident.'

'When are we going to publish a book on you and your work?'

'As soon as you wish.' Claude reached down to pet Chocolat, wondering about Pédant, a fine catch for a bird-hunting dog. He had left the parrot with his nephews during his trip to New York.

The kitchen door swung open and Anatole approached, a gently rolling wave without a crest. Anatole in everyday clothes.

Claude introduced the editor to Anatole, then embraced his friend. The now eleven-year-old Didier rushed between the men.

'Uncle Claude,' called Didier, 'what happened to your head?'

'I got in a fight with someone stronger than I.'

'Did he get hurt too?'

'Not really.'

'Uncle Claude, come look at Pédant! Haven't you missed him? He's been saying your name since you left! *Clawd!*, he says, and then he squawks away. He's waking us up at all hours of the night, and he's chewing everything in sight. He chewed my math homework the other night. Now we have to hide everything! Come see him!'

Didier grabbed Claude's wrist and pulled him in the direction of a pack of boys heading into the living room. So many people had gathered in the dining room, more than the normal coterie for a nephew's birthday. Hadn't he seen Madame LaGrange in a suit he had sewn her last year? Why would she travel to the countryside for his sister's son's birthday? When Claude set eyes on his bright parrot companion perched on the back of the couch, he noticed a large white splatter of excrement on the faded blue oriental rug under the bird.

'Pédant! Is that a way to greet your master? Let's clean this up quickly, before someone steps in it,' Claude said. 'Didier, I haven't said *happy birthday* yet!' He hugged Didier, picked him up, and, despite his weight, swung him around. 'Didier, since it's your birthday, you're excused from cleaning up after Pédant. Jean-Hugues, will you please find an old rag and soak it with soap? I'll get some water.'

Pédant ruffled his feathers, shedding several in the process, and flew to his master's shoulder. *Back to work! Clawd! Awk! Back to work! Awk!*

'I'll get the water too,' said Jean-Hugues. 'Henri,' he called to his brother, who had just entered the room, 'go get a rag and soap. Look what Pédant has done.'

'Uncle,' said Didier, reaching up to pet Pédant on his uncle's shoulder, '*Maman* said we should have this party to get you to come home, but I think the real reason is so you will take Pédant!'

Jean-Hugues had returned with the water and looked at his brother, rolling his eyes. 'Didier, you weren't supposed to say that.'

'It's okay,' Claude said, taking the rag and soap from his nephew and scrubbing the rug vigorously. The stain remained.

'Uncle Claude understands. And it worked – not the cleaning – you came back! I knew you would come back. I bet Jean-Hugues a euro.'

317

'Of course you'd come back for Didier's birthday,' said Juliette, swooping in like an owl. How did she know the content of their conversation? She wore a red suit he had sewn for her many years earlier, the color of a healthy McIntosh apple, ripe for picking. It brightened her.

'Uncle, please give us a puppet show! Please!' pleaded Arthur.

'No, he's coming to the stable with me. Right, Uncle?' said Henri. 'We have a new horse in the stable, named Doré, because of his gold tail. Uncle, you've got to see him!'

'Papa told us a story,' said Didier, 'that at first Doré had a very thin tail, almost no tail at all, and that you went to Russia and found, in the closet of a palace, a jacket belonging to Catherine the Great, sewn with thousands of threads of gold; he said you plucked them out of the jacket to sew into this horse's tail so he would be a horse of true splendor. Don't be surprised if Arthur asks you about your trip to Russia. But really, you should see this tail. It really looks gold-spun!'

'Of course,' Claude said. 'Can you imagine how hard it was to slip out of the Russian palace with armed guards at every door? I had to persuade them that I had been appointed as adviser to the government's Department of Cultural Affairs – to count the thousands of golden threads for the history books – and then manage to extract the threads without a trace? Once this poor horse grows back his tail, I promise to return the threads to the jacket and the jacket to the Russian palace and you all can come with me!'

Pédant interrupted. *Get to work, Clawd! Awk!*

'How rude! Pédant has lost his manners since he's been with you,' Claude said, feeling the life flow back into him.

'He's happy you're back, Uncle.'

'Come, let's go to the stable,' Henri said.

'No, no! He's doing a puppet show!' yelled Didier.

'I'd like to admire Doré's tail; however, it *is* Didier's birthday,' Claude said.

'I'm so happy you're here,' said Juliette, circling around him, a bottle of wine in hand, ready to pour.

'*Maman,* let him come with me. He must see Doré.'

'No, the puppet show, for my birthday!'

'Not now, both of you. Uncle Claude is needed in the dining room.'

Clawd back to work! Awk! Back to work! Ribbons to get! Ribbons to get!

Out of the corner of his eye, Claude spotted Pascale. He realized regretfully that he had never designed her dress. She wore a dull brown shift; he could make out a small print. Her cheeks were as rosy as, yes, rosebuds.

Claude caught Juliette winking at Henri. 'Henri, please gather your brothers. Your papa would like to make a toast. Go, go!'

Juliette took Claude's hand and led him into the dining room. As they crossed the threshold, the room burst with song. '*Joyeux anniversaire!* Happy birthday!'

The guests held wineglasses up to *him*! But it was Didier's birthday party. This sizable group was celebrating the wrong person. As he looked around the room, Claude recognized familiar faces, his favorite clients, the laughing Madame le Buisier, Rico. Rico, here from Milan? Even George from the café.

Juliette whispered, 'Happy birthday, brother! It's *your* party! Didn't you suspect anything? We had to use any excuse to get you back.'

Had he forgotten his own birthday? November 17. Was it November 17? But Didier's birthday? Didier's was November 12.

Anatole provided the answer to his questions with a smile and a hug and a wrapped present: from the feel of it, a book. A book of advice for a madman? The foolishness of love? The sancity of marriage? Claude held it, snug in his hand, as his nephews crowded around him, asking if he was really surprised or just acting. Pédant fluttered above him in agitation as Chocolat jumped up on him.

He looked for his sister. He saw Rico approaching. All this for him? On the other side of the table, he spotted his sister Agnes. Agnes traveled from Lyon? He saw his niece, Lisette, with her face so like his mother's. The resemblance was uncanny. Even his mother was represented here. His other niece was not visible behind her mother's legs.

'Happy birthday, brother. Yves couldn't come, but he sends his best.'

'Thank you, Agnes,' he said, hugging her. 'Thank you for coming.'

He thanked his old friends; he explained his bandage with a laugh about tough New York, and described the collections. Juliette reappeared with her famous orange cake, Henri, Jean-Hugues, Didier, and Arthur following with bowls of whipped cream and fruit.

Claude distributed the cake with Juliette at his side. Because Juliette's ear lingered near his lips, because he could not stop himself, he asked in a whisper, 'Did you invite Valentine?'

'Oh, Claude! What *will* we do with you?'

She playfully dropped a dollop of whipped cream on his nose. 'That's what you get for asking such a question!' she said. Claude lifted the bottom of her apron to wipe his face.

'Since you failed to return my voice messages, I did call her. I had to find out if you would be back in time for this. Of course, I invited her *and* her husband. She said her husband was too sick for them to come. For *them* to come, Claude. She said she'd try to help me get you home.'

Rico and Madame Bonnefond laughed nearby.

'But, I do have something, a gift from her, that arrived this morning by overnight mail. I have it in the other room. I'll get it later.'

Claude noticed his brother-in-law, Bernard, looking at him from afar, his glass held high.

'I would like to toast Claude . . .' began Bernard, in his resonant baritone.

Later that night, after the guests had left, Juliette asked Claude to accompany her upstairs. In her bedroom with its soft gray light, she handed him the brown-paper package that was Valentine's birthday gift to him and excused herself to check on the children. How he loved his sister for leaving him alone with Valentine's gift.

Of course he knew what it was. He savored the moments it took to unravel the plastic wrap. Revealed at last was Valentine's small portrait of him. In the dim light, he recognized himself, his wide cheekbones, dark eyes, brown curls of hair under his ears. She painted him with the same recognizable brushstrokes she had used for the apple tree. It was a flattering portrait. But, what was that, on the chest of his black work coat? A bird, a full-throated red-breasted robin. Its wings were uplifted.

No note accompanied the painting. He turned the canvas over. At the very bottom, he deciphered, in her small elegant scrawl:

Cher Claude,
I will not part with Reynaud's apple tree,
but I must return this to its rightful owner.
Valentine.

'She must return myself to me . . .' He leaned the painting against the upright pillows on the bed

and stared at it until the face became a meaningless sea of many colors.

Claude had offered to make his nephews crêpes
for breakfast the next morning before heading to
the train station with Juliette. He smelled coffee
as he entered the unusually quiet house. Juliette
shuffled quickly from the kitchen, her black
sweater falling off her shoulders, a cup in her hand
lifted toward her brother. Bernard had already left.
Claude took a sip of coffee and climbed the stairs
to wake the boys.

Jean-Hugues woke crankily, pulling the covers
high over his head, shutting his eyes tightly against
the light.

'Hi, Uncle,' he croaked.

In Henri's bedroom, Claude squeezed a foot,
sticking out from the covers. 'Wake up, lazy-
bones,' he said. He peeked at the photograph
of Pascale and Henri on the bedside table. The
two held hands and smiled brightly into the
camera.

'You'll have *broken* bones if you keep squeezing
my foot,' Henri threatened groggily.

Arthur's waking was the slowest. He kept his
eyes closed as he spoke, 'Uncle, will you make my
crêpes with apricot jam?'

Claude had never been able to catch the lively
Didier asleep. Didier was the morning bird, the
first up and dressed and now running circles
around his uncle.

Juliette swept the rooms for slow-moving boys. *'Allons-y, les garçons!'*

In the kitchen, alone in last night's morass of dirtied plates, wine-stained glasses, crumpled blue-and-white napkins, and bread crumbs, Claude wondered where to start. If he began to clean up, it would take hours and the boys had to get to school. He found the refrigerator door open; how long? he wondered. The milk? The freshness date had expired. Where was the flour? Didier arrived to help him find the ingredients. No sugar!

'We've been using honey until *Maman* goes grocery shopping,' Didier said, gently taking Pédant from his perch on Claude's shoulder as Claude whipped the eggs and flour.

Didier watched with delight as his uncle flipped the thin pancakes expertly and filled them with homemade plum and apricot jam. The boys gobbled them within minutes. Henri had to leave quickly and with his good-bye kiss brushed his uncle's cheek with sticky jam. Didier could not find his belt. Arthur was asking for more crêpes, and Jean-Hugues was tipping his few remaining scraps into Chocolat's open mouth. The boys left two by two, dragging parts of themselves along the way: schoolbags, belts, jackets, and books.

'I have to catch the next train,' Juliette said. 'Come, Claude. We'll leave the dishes for when I get back. Do you have everything?' She was halfway out the door, key in hand.

★   ★   ★

As soon as he was inside his office, Claude hung Valentine's portrait of himself next to his desk. The nose was too long and thin. He did not care. He loved every brushstroke.

He sat down at his desk to sift through the Lebrais-arranged invitations. He immediately recognized the thick government-embossed card and crest: an invitation from the prime minister to be a guest, along with 'an elite group of designers,' at a formal dinner at the Élysée Palace. Claude closed his eyes.

He worked feverishly through the day, designing a Christmas dress for Pascale, a pale-blue taffeta with twelve red velvet ribbons zigzagging back and forth at the waist. The red would pick up the color in her cheeks. He also sketched a square-necked blue-green boiled wool dress for his sister and a sprightly bustled chemisier dress with a slimming waist for his ex-wife that he felt confident would wrap up any deal she was arranging with her most recent suitor. He was about to pencil a maternity gown for Valentine, a crinkle-pleated, high-waisted Empire gown with handfuls of rosettes and yards of ribbon along the hem – but he caught himself and stopped his pencil.

The next day at work, Henri stopped by after a school trip to the *musée Rodin*.

'Uncle Claude . . .'

Claude raised his eyes. 'Henri! *Bonjour!* Your mother mentioned that you might come in for a visit. If so, I decided that today I would teach you how to draw an A-line skirt, the most essential line in our business. You're at just the right age to understand cutting on the bias. But first, let's not forget your hot chocolate . . . How's Pascale?' he asked casually, on the way down the hall to the office kitchen.

'She's been exercising another new horse in our stable for someone from Paris, who comes only on the weekends. The horse is a Thoroughbred and raced at Deauville for the last three years. His name is Araman. We thought Doré was perfect. Araman is beyond amazing! He's seventeen hands, a chestnut with a long black mane. Pascale told the owner she would exercise and groom him, but she would never trim the mane. It's so long and shiny. Araman's smart: he can tell when we're coming, half a mile away. Riding him is like riding the longest wave in the ocean. I think Pascale should show him in a jumpers' exhibition. But it's when she lets him go free that they're unbelievable.'

Henri also told his uncle about the broken bell in the church and how some parishioners, angry about the annual cost of its upkeep, were pressuring Anatole to replace it with a recording.

'I've never seen Anatole get so mad,' said Henri. 'He said as long as he lived, he would make it his business to keep church bells as church bells.'

The two took their cups of hot chocolate back to Claude's office and, using the dress form of

Madame Lorieux, Claude taught Henri how to hang fabric on it. He also showed him the taffeta dress he had designed for Pascale.

'Won't she be exquisite in this?' Claude asked proudly.

Henri nodded, smiling. 'She says this will be her first dance.'

'A first dance. Then it will be your job to make it her best.'

Henri nodded again.

'Pascale seems so quiet,' Claude said.

'She's shy sometimes, but when she's with me she talks a lot. She said her father doesn't like a lot of noise for the horses' sake, so that's why she's always whispering in the stables. But we know the horses love it when we talk out loud.'

'Who wouldn't love to hear your voices?'

'We talk a lot about our future, how she wants to be a world-class jumper and how every inch of her room will be covered in blue ribbons. She said I can be her manager and design the horses' and her show clothes, and we'll travel the world together, entering and winning show after show.'

'Has she had many riding lessons?'

Henri squinted his eyes. 'I don't think she's had one. She's watched hundreds, so she learned that way. But anyway, to show she'd need her own horse.'

'Sounds like she could use a few lessons.'

'Next year, she's planning to work in the café in town after school to save some money.'

Claude opened his desk drawer, found his checkbook, and wrote a check for 100 euros. 'This is for Pascale's first lessons. An early Christmas present. It's such a waste to put dreams on hold . . . Now, let's address the lines and curves on riding pants.'

Until the last hours of sunlight, Claude sketched uninterrupted beside his attentive nephew, showing him how to draw patterns for skirts, dresses, and pants and – most important – how to hold a measuring tape. As he held the tired old yellowed tape measure, he tried to erase from his mind the memory of his hands, gliding slowly along Valentine's waist on her first visit to his studio.

That night, Claude accompanied Henri home to Senlis, picked up his parrot, and slept in his studio home. Somewhere in his sleep, a bell was broken: *Ding, dong, di, di, di, di, di, ding, dong.* The next day, he would give Anatole the funds necessary to repair the bells of the Cathedral of Notre-Dame de Senlis.

CHAPTER 27

Bells, bells, more bells, but no. Where was he? It was his phone. He was in Senlis, the old familiar wooden post bed, curtainless window, dawn rising in the form of a speck of sunlight that squirmed through the crack between two distant hills. The ringing continued. He scrambled to his cell phone, which rested on his bureau, but the sound belonged to the shiny black phone on his desk.

Juliette's voice. 'Claude. Please come to the hospital. It's Pascale. She was out riding late last night with Henri and took a jump, an impossible jump. She fell. We rushed her to the hospital and everyone thought she'd be fine, but now . . . it's different. Internal bleeding . . . It's so awful. She's . . . Come, now, please. Henri wants you. Come right away.'

'I'm coming,' he said.

Seven A.M. 'Hospital,' he repeated to himself, looking in his closet for something to wear, feeling as if he were stealing clothes from a stranger. The pants he grabbed were loose around the waist. He threw on a cotton T-shirt and a dark green

329

cashmere sweater Juliette had given him one Christmas. He had patched the elbow with suede.

'Hospital,' he said to himself again. Juliette's voice had been so strained . . .

The building's fluorescent light hit him like a bad memory. He hadn't been inside these antiseptic tiled walls since his mother's death, seemingly a lifetime ago but only last spring. His mother. What would she think of him now?

Claude did not know Pascale's last name. How ridiculous that he'd never asked. 'I'd like to visit Pascale's room,' he said.

The nurse's face dissolved into a sadness he had not expected. Nurses were not supposed to do that.

'Room Three-oh-one. I'm so sorry.'

He headed to the elevator with renewed urgency. Hushed voices emanated from one unmistakable room. How bad could this be?

As he rounded the corner, he caught sight of his seated nephew, gazing blankly at his hands. Claude noticed the hands were wet.

Juliette, in her white terry bathrobe, her eyes red, rose from her chair and hugged Claude.

'Neck injury,' Juliette whispered to him. Claude felt his eyes fill. 'There was nothing anyone could do. She has just left us.'

Claude took in the mournful room. A man Claude recognized as Pascale's father, Jacques, who ran the stable, Bernard, Henri, and Anatole sat in metal chairs around an unoccupied, unmade bed. Could there be anything sadder than these recently emptied gray-white hospital sheets? Sheets from such cheap synthetic material were not substantial enough to fold: they were rolled midway up the bed. The pillow held the imprint of a small head.

Juliette guided Claude out of the room into the hallway. She began to cry, a slow-to-come plaintive cry. Bernard joined them in the hallway.

'When we called you, she was still hanging on. For Henri, I think. You should have seen them,' Bernard whispered hoarsely and looked down. He wiped his eyes. 'They said good-bye as if they believed they would see each other again. We watched her go, so gently, so quietly. We watched her go.'

They returned to the room. Jacques stood and approached Juliette, his face wet with tears, his voice cracking, '*Why*, madame? Why did they take my only child?' Juliette hugged his shaking frame.

Claude looked at Henri. His hands, side by side, worked like shutters, covering the window of his still, small face.

Back at Juliette's, the stillness was unbearable. Henri had left the room; the younger children were at school. There was no explaining, no justification, no *what ifs*. When his cup of black coffee was empty, Jacques left the group wordlessly.

'All he had was his daughter,' Bernard said. 'She was all he lived for.'

Anatole joined them from the other room,

shaking his head. 'Henri and Pascale, they had planned their life together,' he said.

'Henri told you that?' asked Claude, red-eyed.

'In so many words. He asked me once how much money it cost to get married. I told him it was free.'

Claude walked across the lawn to the stables. It was raining again. Raindrops pelted the tin of the stable roof. He walked up to Araman's stall but stopped short when he heard a voice.

'It's okay, Araman. It's okay. She's okay.'

Henri's deepening voice. Claude looked into the stall. Henri, with his brown hair and brown sweater, was camouflaged by the horse's chestnut coloring. He leaned against the horse's neck. His hand moved back and forth through Araman's mane, his voice quietly repeating the words: 'It's okay. It's okay.'

'Henri,' Claude called gently.

Henri looked up calmly. With his red face and red eyes, did he smile? Was a smile possible?

'Uncle.' He went back to petting the animal.

'Henri, I'm so sorry.'

'Isn't he the most beautiful stallion you've ever seen, Uncle? Look at this mane. Look at these strong, fast legs.' He touched the legs from top to anklebone.

'Yes,' said Claude.

'Pascale loved this horse. She told me she'd dreamed her whole life for a horse like this. You should have felt how good it was to ride him. I think it's the closest you can get to flying – I mean, without a plane. It was like being an eagle, so high up. Look at these nostrils. The wind flies in and out of them.'

Henri put his arms around Araman's girth, rested his head on the animal's shoulder, and began to cry quietly. He wiped his eyes roughly with the bottom of his shirt, a childhood reflex, the napkin he had used all his life.

Claude looked out the stall door for Anatole but saw no one. Quiet except for the *ping* of the rain-drops on the tin roof and, in between, the small sounds of a crying fourteen-year-old.

'I wish I could ride you one more time with Pascale,' said Henri, addressing the horse. 'We could sail up to the clouds and puff them up as pillows for Pascale's head.'

He continued to stroke the animal's thick black mane. He had stopped crying. He turned his head to the side, wiped his nose on his shirt, and murmured as if to no one, 'I don't get it. Why did she do it?'

Claude did not answer. Henri's eyes grew focused on the horse's eyes.

'She knew Araman would do whatever she wanted. How *could* she have done it? How stupid. It's so stupid! I think I hate her for doing this. She's ruined everything!'

Araman stamped his foot and slowly closed his huge black eyes.

'She was always pushing for more risk, more

danger. "Let's get a bigger jump. Let's jump over the fence, over that six-foot-tall tree trunk; let's jump over the house!" she'd say.' He wiped his nose and eyes again angrily with the back of his hand. '"Let's jump over the moon together." It's almost like she wanted to jump *too* high. It's almost like she *wanted* to kill herself. How could she have? She knew! How could she want to take risks like that?

'Do you know what she tried to jump?' Henri's eyes were unnaturally bright. 'Remember that huge pine tree that fell down behind our house? It must have been two hundred years old. I told her over and over again, the trunk with its branches on either side was too wide to jump, even for Araman. She jumped it anyway. I prayed harder than I've ever prayed that Araman would take her over, and Araman did. But that wasn't enough. She wanted to jump the fallen tree where the branches were standing up – what, ten feet? – and stuck out on three sides like spokes. I told her, 'No way, don't ever do that; you'll kill the horse and yourself!' She did it anyway. Without warning me, there she was, jumping it, with me watching. The horse *made* it. Amazing horse. No horse could make that jump. Pascale would have been fine, but she tried to avoid a high branch on her right side, and when she moved to the left she fell.'

The tears poured like the rain outside. Henri sat down on a bale of hay, his head in his hands.

'It's like she wanted Araman to make it, even if she fell off. It makes me think she did it on purpose.' He looked up. 'But *why*, Uncle?'

Claude placed his hand on the boy's shoulder, rested it on his growing bones. 'Let's go back inside and warm up a little.'

Claude walked behind Henri up the path into the house, through the living room – they could hear the other children home from school and the dog barking in the kitchen. In his bedroom, Henri threw himself facedown on his bed. 'We had promised each other that nothing would separate us, nothing!'

Claude sat on the bed's edge. The room had darkened. With one hand pressing Henri's heaving back, he imagined them, Henri and Pascale, in the open land bordering the grand forest of Senlis, galloping side by side, their horses' flanks brushing, rich horse smells, small hands lightly manipulating the reins, the wind in their upturned faces, every hair on their bodies alert and moving.

He heard the soft, regular breathing of the boy-man finally sleeping. The storm over, the body was restoring, refreshing itself, washing away the previous day.

CHAPTER 28

Lebrais's voice was in his ear before the light of dawn.

'*Oui, oui, je viens ce matin.* I'm coming to Paris this morning,' responded Claude.

'The meeting is at nine. Everyone will be present for assignments for our fall collections.' What day was it? Rain fell heavily from his rooftop onto the cobblestones outside his bedroom window. Six A.M.

'I will be there.'

Claude lay in his simple bed. Four days since he had left New York. Four hundred years. Pascale. This afternoon was the funeral. He planned to go in to the office and return to Senlis by two.

Again, Claude peered into his closet. Working for Lebrais had sharpened his eye toward his own wardrobe. Half a year ago, the suit in his hand would have been perfectly acceptable. The jacket had the soft texture of a finely woven Scottish wool and beautiful lines that echoed each other from lapel to jacket pocket. This was no longer enough. Working in Paris with the designers at the Salon de Silvane, Claude had become conscious of something he had never before considered important: fashion trends.

Claude called Juliette to see how she and Henri were faring. Juliette told him Henri would not get out of bed.

Claude drove into Paris, watching the city awaken. Little quivering strokes of life grew stronger. Storeowners and residents unshuttered their windows onto the quickening avenues. Big and little dogs pranced out of hiding on leashes; the sun finally broke through and christened the glistening Seine.

Claude parked his car and walked to the salon. He found Lebrais in his customary position in Claude's office (was he ever in his *own* office?), standing behind his desk, sifting through the papers on top of it. When he saw Claude, he looked up and then returned to his paper shuffling.

'I've assembled the fall collection lines and colors for you to look at before our meeting,' he said, continuing to arrange the white rectangles on the deep wood surface. 'We're insisting on muted colors, blanched yellows, lime greens, tangerines, pale blues. We're keeping our conservative hem lengths to below the knee. Stick to it.

'And I have some exciting news for you,' Lebrais added. 'This came in yesterday. The prime minister's daughter has asked that *you* design her wedding gown for March. Congratulations, Claude! She's given you full authority over the design.'

Claude paused.

'I'm sorry, André, let Charles or one of the other designers take it.'

Lebrais looked shocked, then recovered. 'The

last wedding dress got you into trouble, didn't it?' Lebrais laughed. 'Claude, I'd never have suspected so much – shall we call it complexity? – from a poor tailor from the country! Refusing to design the prime minister's daughter's wedding gown!'

Claude looked at Lebrais's face but suddenly felt too tired to return the quip. He took a few papers from his desk and looked at them. They could have been hieroglyphics.

'How *is* the beautiful Valentine?'

Again, Claude did not respond but continued to stare blindly at the papers.

'Don't be a fool, Claude. It is an honor and privilege to receive this commission.'

'I won't do it,' Claude said, raising his grim face to Lebrais.

Lebrais's secretary, dressed in her predictable steel-gray suit, arrived at the door. 'André, the meeting.'

Whether Claude's face revealed the previous day's sorrow or whether Lebrais had finally realized his designer was a man to be respected, Lebrais nodded his head to his secretary and said gently, 'Let's go, Claude.'

At that moment, with the speaking of those two words, Claude felt their relationship change. Lebrais opened the door for Claude, and they entered the screening room together.

Black crows were silhouetted against the gray sky. Stone slabs stuck up from the rain-soaked ground randomly like blackened crooked teeth in an old man's mouth. On his way to Pascale's burial place, Claude stopped at his parents' grave sites.

'Did passion reside anywhere in those old decaying bones of yours?' He addressed his father's tombstone. 'Perhaps you had a mistress. Perhaps she's still alive! Father, why didn't you prepare me for the ripping of the heart? When you were teaching me how to stitch a basted hem, why didn't you tell me how you can die while you live?' Claude shook his head sadly. 'So much you didn't tell me, Father.'

Casting his eye around him, Claude observed that there would be room enough in this grave-yard plot for him. He loosened the scarf about his neck as he walked toward his family.

The young girl was to be buried on the western side of the hill. Claude took his place next to the downcast faces. Anatole spoke, but Claude only half listened. He caught something about 'Death as the great uniter.'

'Pascale has reunited those of us here. She has taken a part of each one of us up with her to God, so that God can be revealed to us in a new way. Every death we experience brings us closer to His kingdom. Belonging to God is only truly complete when we die from this earth. Ashes to ashes, dust to dust.'

A clump of soil had landed on top of the wood box. The disturbing thud roused Claude. He wished he had not looked into his nephew's young face. Innocent shock had been replaced with a hardened acceptance. A flock of geese flew overhead.

Henri lifted the next handful of dirt. His fist clenched, he seemed poised to throw it. Instead, he stepped down onto the coffin. Juliette gasped. They watched openmouthed as he knelt on the box and emptied his hand, spreading the dirt about. Then he lay face down on top of the wooden lid, his arms hugging the sides of the small coffin.

In minutes, Bernard was beside his son. They climbed out together. Henri covered his face with his soiled black hands, walked to where Jacques was standing, and put his arms around him. Then Bernard led the boy to a car on the edge of the cemetery.

The crows scattered at the movement. *Caw, caw, caaawwwwww!*

Low murmurs and subdued visits from some twenty townspeople to Juliette's home occupied the rest of the day. Jacques, who had been brought up as a stable hand in a small town near Deauville, had no known living relatives.

Claude's shoes were soaked through when he reached the door to his studio.

His cell phone rang from his pocket. Lebrais.

'I would like to call Nathalie Lorieux today to tell her you will design her dress.'

'André, I need to call you later about this,'

Claude said, standing at the window, viewing the water-blackened branches of the old apple tree. How had Valentine captured in oils, after only two visits, the trunk he knew so well?

'How about tomorrow?' Lebrais asked. His voice was gentle, not acrid. Had Lebrais read or heard about the tragedy in Senlis?

'I will call you tomorrow.' Claude could barely say goodbye. He switched off his phone. His raincoat was dripping on the floor and he didn't care. He changed into dry shoes and socks. He could not sit still. He left his studio. Senlis's shopkeepers were pulling down their shutters on the day. He walked past Madame Ruggier's bakery. The door to the bakery was open, but he smelled nothing. He continued out of town on the ancient cobbled rue Vieille de Paris toward the river. A single ray of sunlight pushed its way through the leaden end-of-day sky. Except for this momentary glimpse, this had been a day of little sun. He found himself walking toward Juliette's house.

Despite the chill, the front door had been left open. Henri sat silently at the kitchen table. Claude watched him for a moment before announcing himself. His nephew's face looked blankly ahead; his hands rested in his lap. He did not move when he noticed his uncle. Claude placed two pencils and pads of sketch paper that he found in the kitchen drawer in front of his nephew and sat in the chair next to him. Henri slowly picked up the pencil and then dropped it.

Claude began sketching on one pad. He started with a face, a long face with no features. He drew long hair and then a thin body, jodhpurs on. Wordlessly and slowly, Henri picked up his pencil. He looked at the blank pad for a moment and then began drawing, methodically at first, then faster and faster. He sketched a figure on horseback. Her hair flew behind her. The proportions were excellent, the lines flamboyant and confident. He sketched the young woman's jacket with lapels and pockets. Expressionless, the boy continued, drawing the background, the fields, and the distant steeple of the Senlis cathedral of Notre-Dame.

As Claude watched Henri's purposeful hand, it occurred to him. He would accept the wedding assignment and, together, he and Henri would design the bridal gown. The dress would celebrate springtime, white apple blossoms, and new beginnings. It would be dedicated to the memory of Pascale. As it was, the season of wedding dresses was fast approaching.

ACKNOWLEDGMENTS

I thank my husband, my boys, and Grandma Smiles. I will be ever grateful to Wendy Weil, my friend and agent, whose enthusiasm for the first fifty pages made my heart leap and who found my novel a happy home. Thank you also to Sally Arteseros for her early support; to Colleen Bushby for keeping me on track; to Pascale Luse for correcting my French throughout; to Benoit Jamar, Pierre Fay, and Patricia Bataille, who helped me discover Senlis; to Anthony Nahas, my Parisian guide; and last, I thank Jennifer Barth, who had the faith to take *The Dressmaker* into the world.